Books by S. F. X. Dean

NANTUCKET
Soap Opera

NANTUCKET
Soap Opera

S. F. X. Dean

New York • ATHENEUM • 1987

This novel is a work of fiction. Names, characters, places, and incidents are either the product of the author's imagination or are used fictitiously. Any resemblance to actual events or persons, living or dead, is entirely coincidental.

Library of Congress Cataloging-in-Publication Data
Dean, S. F. X.
Nantucket soap opera.
I. Title.
PS3554.E1734N3   1987   813'.54   86-22296
ISBN 0-689-11875-9

Published simultaneously in Canada by Collier Macmillan Canada, Inc.
Composition by Maryland Linotype Composition Co., Inc.
Manufactured by Fairfield Graphics, Fairfield, Pennsylvania
Designed by Laura Rohrer
First Edition

For *NINA, NORTON,* and *EARL*

The great American philosopher James Durante used to close his act with a song called "Shipwreck." It ended with a line worthy of Santayana:

Pull for da horizon, it's better dan nuttin'.

You three always knew that.

"There is no such thing to be found in the writings of the ancients . . . "   *Lord Shaftesbury*

"Now, what Caricatura is in painting, Burlesque is in writing . . . the Monstrous is much easier to paint than describe, and the ridiculous to describe than paint . . . the only source of the Ridiculous is affectation . . . affectation arises from vanity or hypocrisy. Great vices are the proper objects of our detestation, smaller faults, of our pity, but affectation appears to me the only true source of the Ridiculous . . . "
Henry Fielding

"Let us fly, let us fly! Old Nick take me if it is not Leviathan described by the noble prophet Moses in the life of the patient Job."   *Rabelais*

"Very like a whale."   *Hamlet*

"If you should write a fable for little fishes, . . . make them speak like great whales."   *Goldsmith to Johnson*

"The Spermacetti Whale found by the Nantuckois, is an active, fierce animal, and requires vast address and boldness in the fishermen."   *Thomas Jefferson*

" . . . the horrid transactions we are about to relate, belonged to the Island of Nantucket."   *Narrative of a mutiny*

"Days of Our Lives"; "As the World Turns"; "All My Children"; "CBS Evening News" . . .
Names of soap operas

Those who know Nantucket will realize as they read that I have, for fictional purposes, made some modest changes in the island. Acting in the spirit of those Starbucks, Coffins, and Folgers who built, tore down, and named the town pretty much as they chose, I have where I needed to built a small church, laid out a convenient nearby cemetery, razed a sweet shop on Main Street and built a fine new bank in its place. I even added a little deck onto Mrs. Lowell's house down on Madaket Road. For these and any other improvements I charge the town nothing. The police there, and the librarians at the Atheneum, and scores of others were so hospitable to my many questions that I feel it was the least I could do in return.

S. F. X. DEAN
Nantucket
Spring 1986

NANTUCKET SOAP OPERA

cast

The Hollywood People
William Olds, producer
Panda Olds, director, his daughter
Barbara Gold, actress
John Finn, actor
Milo Milano, cinematographer
Jake Jones, driver, sometimes actor, sailor

The Young Artists of the "Faces" Co-op
Liam O'Farrell, poet, comedian
Wendy Foster, weaver
Jon Van Veler, musician
Guy Furey, designer, entrepreneur
Nell Vizer, jewelry maker, bookkeeper, and
mother of C.J. (Caroline Jensen)

Others
Neil Kelly, scholar
Dorothy Allen, editor
Jack Darling, fisherman
Eddie Dallen, sailing instructor
and several policemen, lawyers, and reporters

NANTUCKET
Soap Opera

1

The White Dory on India Street in Nantucket is a good place to be at six-thirty in the morning for hot muffins and for hearing the fishermen's gossip. Neil Kelly, as was expected of an outsider, took a seat down the far end of the counter and ordered his usual. The counterman, who had been serving him for almost a month now, accepted him as something just slightly better than a tourist, an out-of-season writer. Neil accepted the neutral status granted to visitors to the island who knew enough to dress in sensible working clothes and keep quiet, and he knew that it would take some rather spectacular event, as measured by local standards, to make him either more or less welcome.

"Artie, you still going out?" A lanky, balding man on his way out stopped to talk with the burly fisherman two stools away.

"Oh, sure. Still plenty out there, why quit now?"

"Blues?"

"Blues, you name it. Pretty good yesterday."

The departing one hit his friend on the back. "Maybe I quit too soon. Marcia said we better start putting up the boat, patch the bugger . . ." He shrugged and left.

A fat man in two checked shirts down at the other end asked Artie if he had seen Phil. "Wait till you hear what he says."

The counterman turned from stacking doughnuts to get into it. "He swears, Duff. Claims he saw a whole school of spinning sharks off Tom Nevers Head."

"I thought Mitch said off Sconset there," another eater chimed in. "Gimme some more coffee, Jay, will you? Denny says he saw them, too. You ever see any of those bastards?"

Two Shirts said, "Jimmy says he saw that big bunch that came in way back—the ones that got written up in the *New York Times*, *National Enquirer* . . . you remember that?"

Several of them laughed and made scoffing noises at that one.

"*Enquirer* says giant shark found to contain whole bodies of entire Nantucket family still alive." Duff waved such nonsense away. "That was a school of hammerheads, real monsters, but they didn't have no whole families in them. One of them had about fifty big blues in him, though. We had to read that in tenth grade, remember, Donnie?"

The counterman was not going to relinquish his role of anchorman for the local morning news. "Jimmy says he saw real spinners. He was out with his father then, just a little kid about ten, and they saw them cruising out there for a week, just hanging around scaring the shit out of the blues and the bass. He says the buggers would jump right up out of the water and spin like a top, like those trained dolphins they got down at Marineland. You ever see those?"

"How big?"

"Phil says these are up to eight foot."

"Those kind man-eaters?" another man asked, putting money on the counter as he got up to leave.

"Shit, man, mosquitoes are man-eaters. Anything likes blood is a man-eater if it's hungry."

"Channel Three is supposed to be sending a camera crew out."

4

"Maybe I'll wait and see them on TV. I don't want those fuckers jumping in my boat, but I'd like to see that spinning thing, show my kids."

The counterman poured Neil a fresh coffee and grudgingly but fairly included him in the general conversation. "You ever heard of spinning sharks?"

Neil swallowed a bit of buttery muffin. "First time I've heard of them this far north. I saw a school of them off the South Carolina coast once. Down there they call them requiem sharks."

"Requiem sharks? You hear that, Duff? Requiem, like a requiem mass for the dead. Jesus, that sounds too scary."

"It will be a fucking requiem for somebody, be like the demolition derby out there if all the boats go out at once, people trying to take pictures. The paper said they'll pay fifty for a good shot of them . . . "

A sudden, total hush swept down the line and stilled the busy little restaurant, as if the wind had suddenly dropped after a squall. Barbara Gold, the movie actress whose picture had been featured in last week's paper in a story about the film company visiting the island, had entered. She stood for a long moment looking down the line of men, posing from lifelong habit, knowing full well that her clinging T-shirt over nothing at all but thirty-eight inches of marvelous chest was being carefully studied. She hadn't dressed appropriately for the weather since she was eleven.

"I've got goosebumps," she said breathily.

No one contradicted her. Every eye in the counter mirror followed her splendid progress as she walked down toward Neil, peering at each seated figure as though fascinated by them all. She was severely myopic, but men generally assumed her peering interest in them was a flattering personal assessment. When she arrived at the empty seat next to

5

Neil Kelly, she slid her admirable bottom, shrink-wrapped in white jeans, onto the stool and said, "Hi, Professor."

There was an audible groan of pleasure or perhaps pain from someone down the line. She looked quickly over her shoulder at them all and made her eyes bigger, the sex goddess accepting her orisons, and turned back to Neil.

Up close the starlet was vibrant with that sensuality only animals in the wild and a few dangerous humans possess and which cannot be learned or faked, a physical presence resonant with raw sex. Her skin was clear and fine, without a trace of makeup, and her green eyes had hazel edges to the iris, although there were deep half-circles of violet fatigue beneath them. Her hair was thick and black with red lights in it. Neil could no more help staring at her features than anyone else. The dreamt-of body was perfect lushness just under discipline.

"Mind if Goldie joins you?" she asked innocently. "What's good?"

"Everything," Neil said, embarrassed as a boy. He heard a muffled "You can say that again" from down the row.

"Can I have a coffee, love?" She smiled at the counterman, entirely at home with male admiration. "Black, no sugar," then the hoped-for, inevitable . . . "I have to watch my rear end."

And the clockwork rejoinder from down the line, just loud enough to be heard, "Don't you bother, honey, I'll do that."

"Gawd," another voice said in a stage whisper, "and my wife signed that petition to keep them from making that movie here."

"Divorce her."

Goldie just opened her eyes wider at Neil, then winked. She obviously gloried in the cheap bawdry. The girlhood Carolina twang returned to her voice when she scolded them

6

all. "Now all you good ol' boys just hush up, will you? Don't you all have things you want to do?"

She fed them lines from some medley of B-movies running in her brain, then flounced a shoulder at them and turned to Neil again. "My public. I guess you don't approve."

He wasn't about to play straight man to her coffee-shop coquette. He said nothing and drank his refill of coffee. He was suddenly getting more attentive service. He realized that it was impossible to make the slightest gesture near Goldie—Artie was dunking his doughnut with elaborate lewdness—without being aware that someone would probably translate it into a salacious metaphor.

Boy, how would yew lak to dunk your doughnut in that? Keep yer eye on the doughnut, boy, not on the hole . . .

She sipped her coffee gingerly. "Why are you so hard on Billy O., Neil? You are, you know."

"Your boss and I are beginning to understand each other at last, I think, Miss Gold. I just don't want to get involved in any way in this project he's planning." Neil had already dealt with her boss and his proposed movie project for Nantucket.

"Aw, goodness, call me Goldie. I don't mind my name, but Panda says I should. Mind. She thinks because I was an exotic dancer once in LA and that was my stage name, I should've changed it when I started acting, but gee . . . Would you?"

"Would I change my name if it were Goldie and I had been an exotic dancer?" Neil pondered the problem solemnly and decided that he would. "Yes."

"Really?" She looked thoughtful. "Not me. I had like a real following, guys who'd come to see me every night practically. So I thought, gee, they deserve to recognize me when I'm like dressed, too, in the movies . . . You probably don't go to strip joints much, so you probably never saw me . . . "

"I'm sure I'd remember if I had."

"Panda says you'd really be perfect for the judge. In the film. Are you really a college professor?"

"Yes."

"Jesus, you must be smart. What's it like, being that smart? I mean, knowing all the stuff you must know, y'know?"

Neil thought about that and answered her. "It's fine."

"Gee. Panda went to college for a while, but that was just to study film and she already knew more than those guys. I mean, UCLA isn't like Harvard or anything, is it? Did you go to Harvard?"

"Yes, in graduate school."

"Graduate school!" She said it as if he had said he'd died and returned to earth. "After college? Jesus, you must have degrees up the wahoozie!"

Was anyone on earth as dumb as this woman had decided to appear? Her final observation seemed rhetorical and he left it unanswered, although her colorful way of putting it did suggest the essential worth of most graduate degrees. He paid for his breakfast and excused himself to Goldie.

"Where you going now?" she asked. "Just walking like up the street or are you going someplace special or anything . . . ? Because I wanted to ask you something if you'll let me, that is."

"I was simply going to walk down to the harbor for the exercise and just watch the boats. Sometimes I watch the early boats going out. No one seems to mind; they don't pay me much attention."

She stood up and lifted her hair with both hands, shaking it out. There were four distinct bruises on the underside of her arms. "They will if you're with me," she said

8

cheerfully. "Can we walk out that little street there by the beach sort of? I parked my moped there before the damn cobblestones start. I tried riding over them once and almost busted my ass." She left the shop without paying her bill, rubbing the afflicted area. Neil wondered if she had ever paid for breakfast in her life.

The reinvigorated talk behind them increased in volume as Neil held the door for her.

"Duff, I think I know what's attracting those spinning sharks, buddy."

"Wouldn't you just love to take a bite out of that you was a shark?"

"Hey, Artie, you suppose she's a man-eater . . . ?"

Goldie had given them all a final floradora flirt of her fanny as she left, but kept right on talking in her little-girl, breathy voice to Neil.

"You know, Billy is tear-ass about the cops coming down the boat. You know? This thing with the kid that got raped or something by whoever did it? The little girl?"

"The Jensen girl, yes. I met her with her foster mother once."

"Well, Billy is sore at everyone. The town cops came around the boat and the house and he gives them the big hello, but he'd like to shoot them all, you can tell . . . They think we're making porn flicks, chicken stuff, y'know . . . ? With little kids? Out on the coast that's a big business, but Billy wouldn't do that . . . They were asking me and Milo and everyone all these questions . . . This kid said something to her shrink or the cops or someone about Jake doing it to her . . . That's what, y'know, they practically said . . . abusing her? And one of them told me the state cops would probably be around, too . . . "

Neil wondered if her employer, whom he'd detested from the moment they met, had sent this sensual angel to

9

deliver some message. Where the infamous William Olds was concerned, he knew that anything was possible. All that Neil wanted was to be left alone by these Hollywood sharks, yet he had felt for the past two weeks that he was being drawn into their circling orbit.

"But why would she—the child . . . " Neil was annoyed at himself for picking up her scatty syntax. " . . . Why would the child say that if it weren't true?"

"I dunno, for Chrissakes," Goldie said, as if astonished that anyone had solicited her opinion on anything. "You asking *me*? Kids! I'd rather work with ducks or some fucking farm animals like kangaroos than kids. I did a commercial once for cheese with two kids. The final footage was all those two little bastards. All you could see of me was this frilly apron they made me wear. Anyways, Jake has disappeared, and Billy's wild. Milo says—and even crazy little John says, hey, if he didn't do diddly-squat, you know, like raping this kid, why's he hiding? Did you know somebody threw a big rock through one of the windows on our boat? You don't think anybody killed Jake because they think he did bad stuff to this kid, do you?"

Neil hadn't realized that the scandal surrounding the Jensen child had gone that far, but he wasn't surprised. Everything this unholy gang of California yahoos touched seemed to tarnish immediately.

"Why should I know anything about your friend Jake?"

"Well, you know, maybe . . . " Goldie shrugged expressively, an exertion that might very well be illegal in public. "Jake and Billy and even Panda, Christ, even that little prick John Finn—they're all kind of obsessed—is that the word I mean?—with you. They talk about you up at the house all the time. Billy is real mad that you won't write this script for him. He says who does this sonofabitch hick professor think he is telling *me* off, and like that, you know?

10

I guess we all thought that Jake might have gone over to your place to like hide out?" She trailed the unasked question off without appearing to know what to say next. "No one would kill him, would they, like one of these good ol' boys?"

Neil was thoroughly exasperated. Someone had sent this disingenuous interrogator to him to ask if he knew anything about their friend Jake. If the man had molested the Jensen child and then taken off when the police found out, he would do well to hide. There were a lot of men on the island who wouldn't bother with legal niceties if they thought some Hollywood freak had hurt one of their own children.

"What is it exactly that you want to ask me, Goldie? Do you really believe that I'm hiding Jake at my house? Or that I know where his body is hidden?" He bit the question off sarcastically.

Tears actually welled up in the enormous green eyes. Goldie wiped them away savagely with the backs of her hands, then the hem of her T-shirt. Neil could scarcely believe what she revealed so casually, nor could the two men unloading vegetables onto a stand at the corner of Federal Street. One of them dropped a crate of lettuce on the other's foot. Goldie had another blue bruise beneath her right breast.

"I hate it when I cry. It makes me completely blind," the actress said bitterly. Was she actually offended by his sarcasm? The temptation to comfort her must have moved many men; it moved Neil now.

"Not me, for crying out loud. Panda." She paused and looked in a shopwindow at her reflection. "She said you always came downtown and got like coffee in the morning, and would I ask you about this like conspiracy . . . that's her word for it . . . like did some people put this little

11

kid up to it, you know, telling the cops she got screwed by Jake or us making chicken flicks? Like to get public opinion against us so we couldn't do the show . . . ?" She let her question trail off in splendid disarray, but, having got it out, she seemed relieved of a burden. "She says if anyone would know, you would, because that Liam told her you know all those people, like artists, down at Faces . . . that kid's mother or whatever . . . "

Neil glanced at her sharply. "Has Liam been talking with Panda?" Liam O'Farrell was the boy who had got Neil entangled with these Hollywood people against his will, a friend of a friend who needed help.

"Oh, yeah. About maybe a part. She thinks he's a gas and a half. I think he's crazier than John Belushi was, if you ask me." She stopped and showed Neil her chest, at which, he realized, he had been strenuously not looking since she had bared it briefly. "I got this T-shirt down there at that Faces from the guy who designs them, the cute one. See—" she pointed unnecessarily, causing a construction truck to swerve onto the sidewalk—"he put 'Goldie' right there below the beach umbrella. Cute?"

Indeed he had. The "o" targeted her left nipple admirably. Neil turned to look out over the North Wharf inlet at the dozen boats bobbing in the early breeze, white, blue, red, and black.

"You can tell Miss Pamela Olds, for whatever she thinks it's worth, that I think the Jensen child is telling the truth, but that she could very well be confused about the facts."

"Huh? Come again?"

"I'm sure that someone did abuse her, probably raped her. Someone she knew and trusted. God knows it happens often enough in this country, in day-care centers, in schools,

12

and I suppose even on boats. And I'm sure that there are more than a few men on Nantucket who wouldn't hesitate to take the law into their own hands if they were convinced that one of your film crew was guilty. If Jake has disappeared, then it could well be because someone with vengeance in mind found him walking at night on a deserted dock or because he suddenly decided to go on a fishing trip to avoid that sort of event."

"He better not've. Billy has to okay any of us going even to the john, for Chrissakes, let alone away. Anyways, the boat's still here, so figure it out. He's not a bad guy, you know. Like he's a Jew and all, but he can be really sweet sometimes. He has these wild stories, like he claims he was a hero in the Israeli navy."

Neil knew that story, which, predictably, Goldie had screwed up. "If the child is confused in her own mind about exactly who it was that hurt her, or if she is mixed up because she is trying to protect one person and at the same time trying to hurt another one—whatever her motives, I don't believe that she is being used by any faction to block your show. I'm sure of that."

"Gee, Panda will be relieved. No shit. I can see why you're so smart. I mean, the way you figured out that maybe she was just confused or trying to slam one guy while she protects this other one. I done that plenty of times. I guess even little kids learn how to do that, huh? Boy . . . "

"I've got to go back to work, Goldie. But if it's any consolation to you, I don't think there's enough opposition on the island to block your group from filming here. So your starring role is safe."

She gave him a foxy look, then grimaced. "Aw, you probably already figured out, Billy isn't going to give me no big part. That's just his way of bullshitting me to keep

13

me happy. The thing is, I could really act if he'd let me. I'm not kidding. I studied at Pasadena Playhouse and I had a supporting role there that they said I was wonderful in . . . real critics, not just guys I was dating or anything . . . Can I tell you a whopper—I mean, you know, a big secret? Panda is the one who thinks I can really act. Everyone knows I look great on camera, but, Jesus, like the Dallas Cowgirls, you know, all T and A. Panda says not to say anything to Billy, but she thinks there really will be a part for me in it. Isn't that something?"

Neil agreed that it undoubtedly was. He watched her unlock her moped and ride off with a wave. An ignorant doll. A live, exciting, do-it-yourself bubblehead almost happy to be coddled and conned by her Hollywood dream bosses.

Fair breeze, the sun just high enough to color the shallow harbor water blue. Neil watched a boat being loaded from a tippy skiff by a young boy and turned away to return to the old square and get his morning paper. Down by the Pacific Club, to test the notion apparently that if he saw it he was entitled to kill it, a barefoot kid winged a rock at a bird, but missed by plenty. Neil could have sworn the rockee, a starling, cocked a quick eye and then took off out of there. The kid scooped up another rock and trotted off hunting for something else to do with it. Was the kid working out a problem in ballistics, which you could say makes it science, or working off a grudge against life, which is just plain meanness? Am I really watching myself, Neil wondered, trying to see if that kid and that whole scene, that nearly murdered bird, has anything to do with me?

Nantucket might be one of the last clean places left on the inhabited earth, but that didn't make it any safer for innocence than a city slum. Sleaze and violence just go wherever people go, but it certainly seemed as if some carried more of the old pestilence of original sin with them

14

than others, like this accursed Hollywood crowd who had invaded Nantucket.

Neil stood at the cobblestoned head of the square by the steps of the old bank and recalled the first morning, just two weeks ago, that he had seen and recognized William Olds, Hollywood producer, superstar, and cultural cutthroat.

2

The instantly recognizable movie star was enjoying commercial intercourse with the exterior street-level orifice of the Nantucket Bank. The blazing blue eyes were not visible, but one had seen them photographed so often, heard them described by dazzled reviewers so nauseatingly often, that they seemed included in any view of Olds, even with his back turned, a hyper-real illusion. Even the chiseled profile was actually only one-quarter on view, but even to an infrequent moviegoer the *gestalt* was instantly the famous man. Had Neil ever read that the star had a long white scar down the side of his neck? One showed briefly when a gust of salty sea wind off the harbor blew up Main Street and filled the man's low-buttoned silk shirt like a spinnaker.

Neil digested his small dose of celebrity with one thin-lipped gesture of annoyance and decided that he could ignore it and had no doubt Nantucket could, too. Hollywood's imperious Billy O., star director, star actor, star despoiler of starlets, and captain of a notorious entourage of jet-set sybarites, was not likely to shake up old Nantucket any more than the thousand other pirates who had visited there.

But it was the man's saintly if not entirely fatheaded good will that required Neil to watch him as the star chatted unselfconsciously with the machine he confronted, inputting identification and outtaking cash, just a simple tourist a few bucks short like the rest of us. Yet it takes special qualities of spirit, not all of them lofty, to stand facing a brick wall with an armored window in it exchanging pleasantries and coded passwords with electronic voices. Someday someone— in one of those California drive-in churches, most likely— will be canonized as the patron saint of electronic fund transfer. They will say at his beatification ceremonies he never swore at a machine and he was always a perfect gentleman while doing his business. And what could any Devil's Advocate say except that the Devil himself preferred machines to persons?

Billy O. did politely chat away at the window as he might to the large-bosomed lady inside the bank, the actual teller, chanting his number as he punched her keys, answering her greenly printed GOOD MORNING with his own cheery spoken reply, then awaited her pleasure with the famous head tilted as if listening for her subtle inner harmonies to reach their climax. When, this achieved, she released his money with an automatic injunction that he have a good day—even then he took what came in generous spirit and did not fail to return his partner's wish in kind.

He turned from his sordid transaction unashamed, caught Neil's astonished eye, and grinned, not concerned about being admired. "Wonderful machines. I love to give them my business."

Neil gave him that sort of smile one gives to uninvited confidences from drunks and loonies, and, trying not to seem superior, continued with his original intention and entered the actual bank.

A yellow sports car driven by a scatty girl jounced and jammed to the curb of the cobblestoned street in front of the movie star. Olds seemed as glad to see the car as he had

17

been to interface with the bank's wall; he patted it and spoke to it, told it that it was looking good, even before he spoke to the driver and got in.

Neil was frozen for just one fraction of a second in surprise which turned itself to outrage to hear the scatty one say plainly to the star, "Never mind I'm late, that's him right there. The old geezer going into the money store."

Appalled, but with immense dignity, Neil Kelly brought into play that aplomb he had learned to reserve for the sort of occasions when teenage clerks asked him if he was a senior citizen ("because there's this discount if you have your card, sir"). He entered the bank with his liveliest step, being careful not to overdo it; he didn't want to appear to be an elderly jogger.

Standing surrounded by the comforting tangle of red ropes swagged from brass stanchions, a fifty-eight-year-old man of substance who was allowed into banks everywhere, a college professor who, even if no film idol, had nevertheless written a well-known book on seventeenth-century poetry, he breathed slowly until he had dismissed from its hold on his energies the overheard fragment of inane conversation referring to his alleged geezerhood.

In its place there dawned an awareness that, never mind the libel, William Olds' young driver had referred to him, Neil Kelly, as *him*. Who was he to that squirt or she to him?

The simmer of resentment crept back in. There probably *were* no fifty-eight-year-old functioning humans in Hollywood. Fifteen-year-old millionaire singers, thirty-year-old millionaire drug addicts, and producers who would be seventy except for daily injections of monkey-gonad pheromones which made them smell forty to women of certain sensibilities.

18

Why *had* that brat pointed him out to William Olds?

Irene Sullivan was, as a partner in commercial—well, fiscal—joy, far preferable to any machine. The Nantucket Bank's chief cashier enjoyed exchanging guesses about tomorrow's weather, was an old-fashioned, unashamed Red Sox fan, and had a Victorian bosom. It was her pleasure to wear plunging necklines with a shield of lace spanning the great divide; she knew that her embonpoint was a local joke and enjoyed it, nothing gave her more pleasure except her own girlish witticisms at the expense of all off-islanders, especially New Yorkers. "New Yorkers" was to Irene Sullivan a term of infinite comic variations—like "Polack" or "WASP" to others.

Neil was learning from her to look out for fog if the wind shifted before noon, to understand that as Dewey Evans went, so went the Red Sox, and to see the inner logic of her views concerning New Yorkers. What electronic hussy with her recorded, bosomless GOOD DAY gave as much value?

Since he had arrived on Nantucket two weeks earlier, after the close of the high summer season, there had been sufficient time in the slower pace of island affairs to make his face and name known to the professionals who would service his public needs for the next five months. He had come here to work on his Ben Jonson book (which was not revealing itself with much grace so far), a task which provided him with the time and excuse to hang around coffee shops and bars, become familiar, and be accepted as harmless.

Nantucket in summer would have been no place to write. Nantucket in summer is the Republican's Hyannis, and no one in his right mind goes there for any reason. The twenty-year-old BU sophomore girls who go there to get laid by yachtsmen and the twenty-one-year-old boys from

BC who lie to them and accommodate them cannot be said to fall within the limits given; in their right minds they may be, but they are so young and ignorant it doesn't matter.

From October to May the island town returns to the possession of its rightful inhabitants, who simply sweep and scour away the tracks of tourists. Off-season renters like Neil, who came for honorable purposes (all books about Nantucket are welcome, she poses like a siren for them), were fairly rare birds, tolerable if they wiped their feet and wore reasonably old clothes while they wrote their books.

Irene Sullivan, wearing her plunging bottle-green jersey today, greeted him, asked him in the syntax that permits no reply how about them Red Sox how about those four home runs in two nights for Dewey Evans against Toronto, hand-stamped his check, and counted out his seventy-five dollars. Then, first things first accomplished, she leaned forward the inch secrets required and her prow permitted.

"You're not connected with this bank robbery, are you, Professor?" She flapped her tiny white hand at the air and giggled madly.

Neil had no rejoinder, witty or witless, but he didn't want to appear senile, geezerish, out of it. He tried "Was the bank robbed?"

Irene Sullivan was very proud of her small white hands. A suitor from Woods Hole had once told her that they were like lilies (his actual words, uttered in an understandable excess of poetic feeling engendered by just having hefted her left breast, were "like l'il teeny lily flowers") and she had used them ever since as a flamenco dancer uses her eye-lashes—to comment, to instruct, to seduce, and to lament.

Now she extended her palms toward Neil, pushed at the air, and ogled him humorously between her fingers. "You pretending you haven't heard?" she cried merrily. Her amusement made her more confidential still. She placed one hand on her bosom—a gesture roughly equivalent to laying a single lily on a rolling hillside, perhaps a well-loved battle site in Virginia—and looked to heaven for appreciation. "Apparently this bunch of New Yorkers and Californians and God knows what are going to make a movie out of it." She gestured majestically to the mural on the wall behind him. "With William Olds? Be still, my beating heart. Isn't that the limit?" Both hands flew up.

It seemed only reasonable to Neil to agree that it was. The young man behind Neil in line, who had sold him a Ross Eurotour (used) bicycle from a garage near the dock for forty dollars last week, edged past him with a nod, slapped down his deposit slip, and eagerly took up the trailing edge of Irene Sullivan's ecstasy as Neil navigated through the proper velvet-roped channel into the broad hall of the bank. He paused to look for the first time closely at the inept mural above officers' desks to the right. It showed only the original Nantucket Bank, founded the same year that the town had changed its name from Sherburne to Nantucket. The penny still hadn't dropped, and he studied the thing. The original bank, he knew, had stood down Main Street from this present one, approximately where Buttner's Drygoods now stood. Then he recalled the piece of history that had slipped his mind and suddenly understood what must be happening.

His heart sank a bit as he regained the street and headed across to the Hub to get his paper. Off-season bustle might be a boon to a lot of merchants, but he had come to the island this academic term through winter for the quiet of the place, to walk the empty beaches, perhaps think about Dolly Allen a little, and write the Jonson book, for which he had already been advanced a sizable chunk by his publisher.

21

Reflecting for a moment on his stalled hopes for "rare Ben," whose ghost had refused to haunt Neil's study lately, and realizing he was spending what he wasn't yet earning, Neil winced. The book had seemed like such a good idea when he wrote the prospectus, and his publisher, starry-eyed at the idea of another commercial success like Neil's John Donne, which had made a profitable TV mini-series, had not balked at a $20,000 advance.

Neil was, if no Renaissance man, an example of that rare academic species, the commercially successful scholar-author. His American editor was positive that there was more TV gold in the seventeenth century (contemplated, Neil knew for a fact, an eventual Shakespeare series from Neil) and Neil was getting biweekly phone calls about his progress.

Neil knew that if he ever did finish the Jonson book it would be good, but he wasn't entirely sure that it was finishable. He was willing to admit to himself if to no one else that this sojourn on Nantucket was as much to get away from his college, Old Hampton, in western Massachusetts, where he had taught perhaps too long, as to write. And his London editor wanted him to return to England and settle there. With her. She was Dorothy Allen, Dolly to everyone in her trade, the best, most sensitive, toughest editor he had ever had. And his lady love. She could make arguments that were economically convincing, but he distrusted their logic, because he knew that where she was concerned illogic ruled his judgments. If he were not haunted by the fear that he would lose whatever creative edge he had gained by honing his writing skills *within* his teaching, he would quit Old Hampton tomorrow and be on the next jet to Dolly and Camberwell. He felt the pull of her sweet memory and her place. She lived in a sumptuously crumbling vicarage just two blocks from where John Donne had once served as a parish priest, and along with a lively ambiance that reminded Neil of Brooklyn Heights, Camberwell, South London, gave him a marvelous sense of being in the right place always.

He had just this past week, after a struggle, begun to sense the same rightness, the same fit, about this handsome, tidy island off the Cape coast. Now he was suddenly beset by feelings other than the simple temptation to chuck it and go to Dolly. If some meretricious movie-making sprawl was going to take over whatever parts of the island suited their stupid purposes, erecting fake eighteenth-century façades on the Main Street shops and conning otherwise sensible townspeople into making idiots of themselves as extras in sunbonnets and linsey-woolsey britches, Nantucket might as well be Burbank.

He picked his way slowly, as the old cobbles required, across the sixty-foot-wide street, which, like all of central Nantucket, had been redesigned and improved after the great fire of 1846 that had leveled the whole center of town.

The *Inquirer and Mirror* amplified, not by much, the cashier's breathless speculation. Under a characteristically no-nonsense headline: WILLIAM OLDS CONSIDERS FILMING HERE, it reported that the famous actor-turned-director and his newly formed Oldsun Film Company were visiting the island to study the possibility of making a film based on the historic Great Nantucket Bank Robbery of 1795.

Neil wished that somehow he could go back inside his little cottage on Madaket Road and shut the door, then come out again and rerun this morning to discover that the newspaper story was a dream or a hoax. That or leave at once for London and Dolly Allen. Ah, but would he get Ben Jonson down on paper if Dolly were there to distract him? No, he would not. Here the Devil, there the deep blue sea. Here a rock, there a hard place. Here a rub, there a rub, everywhere a dilemma. Old Neil Kelly had a frown.

Neil went slowly back to his cottage at the end of Main Street, walking the familiar route without looking up from reading his paper except to dodge the two loonies on mopeds who came careening out of Gardner Street. He sat on his tiny deck, protected from road noise by his fenced, uncut hedge, and sipped a warm Heineken and thought about it and read the rest of the unpalatable newspaper account.

William Olds, who was duly identified as the star of stage, screen, and TV for the past twenty years, was shown admiring the quaquaversal sign downtown, beloved of tourist photographers, which showed the distance to twenty places on the globe and their approximate direction from Nantucket. Reverent words were expended on *Remember Love*, the god-awful film that had amassed forty million dollars for its star (Olds) and director (Olds) and screenwriter (Olds) and chief investor (Olds) in exchange for ninety minutes of joyless vulgarity about a moronic but sexually abandoned student who had taught her virginal Literature professor (Olds) the Real Meaning of Life, which apparently was a mélange of break dancing, bum grammar, and sex in the bathtub. Neil, who had gone only because his old Harvard tutor had a joke bit part as a waiter in it, remembered only the enormous compulsion he had felt and obeyed to walk out after the opening credits, which displayed a background of Harvard University buildings, identified for the exiguous purposes of the film as Leverett University, with Lowell House cunningly labeled Cabot Lodge.

The perpetrator of that inanity was now here on Nantucket with an entourage of epigones and lackeys from his film-and-TV company to see what they could debase.

Neil was once again strongly moved to leave after the opening credits. The only hope was that this gaggle of California geese would take one air-conditioned ride in their

24

Mercedes pickup around this unspectacular, cleanly beautiful island and recognize instantly its total unsuitability for a film about Nantucket. Surely their vestigial minds and indoor imaginations would grasp instantly the elementary wisdom of shooting the whole film in Las Vegas, updating the eighteenth-century village tempest to a war between rival computer terminals in the vaults of rival Mafia gambling houses.

But if they were serious about staying and using the island as their location, if the only possible months of Neil's writing vacation were to be invaded by this inflated charade in which dollar-starved off-season islanders were persuaded to prostitute themselves for the glamorous William Olds and thirty seconds of plastic glory in a polyester epic of Olde Nantuckette, was there any decent alternative to flight and relocation?

He wondered what Olds would do to the facts of the old, famous story. Neil knew as much as any student of American history about the original robbery and a bit more. As a graduate student he had flirted with American Studies and written a casebook study of the event in a high-school series called *Contentious Americans*. Later, in collaboration with a friend from the American Studies program at Chapel Hill (who had also needed the money), he had co-authored a ninety-minute TV play for the lamented "Playhouse 90" which had been seen, then passed into oblivion unremembered except by its authors. They had split the $1500 they got for the script and dissolved their playwrights' collaborative on the spot.

The so-called Great Nantucket Bank Robbery was one of those historical events, small in themselves, which forever after they happen serve as benchmarks. It had been judicial farce, civic tragedy, and preposterous Quaker burlesque all in one.

25

It was always capitalized in the minds of old island families: The Great . . . etc. The actual sum stolen was—even for the end of the eighteenth century—not great: $20,000. There was no initial violence. It was a burglary, strictly speaking, and not a robbery. Three men entered the bank at night, unlocked the vault with a homemade key, took the money, and fled. The immediate and long-range consequences were to split the town into two feuding camps, as witch-hunting had split Salem, and as slavery had split Virginia.

Three hoodlums, Seth Johnson, John Clark, and Zeb Weathers, on a Saturday night in June 1795 took the money from the first institution of banking ever established on the island, almost the first week it was open. The bank was a wildly unpopular venture to most islanders. Half of them suspected the very idea of a bank, never having seen one before. Few in Nantucket had ever seen a check or taken one in retail trade. Banking, like whoring, was something you went to Boston for if you really needed it.

The founders of this shaky new venture in commercial capitalism were so flummoxed when they opened their vault early that following Monday and found it bare that they couldn't decide what to do, so did nothing—a technique later refined by greater malefactors and given the designation "stonewalling." It did not enhance the bank's reputation when, after a week, the town inevitably discovered that the bank had no cash funds.

Democrats (who were then called Republicans) blamed the Federalists. The first group, who had been abused rebels during Nantucket's very Tory Revolutionary War history, had always known the Tories were thieves. Quakers, who had shrewdly always worked to keep the island neutral because England was their best customer for oil, accused non-believers, who themselves generally suspected that all

Quakers were pious crooks. Non-Masons, who were by and large Democrats, lost no time in sniffing out a Masonic conspiracy.

Three local Federalists who were also Masons were arrested and charged. Eyewitnesses to their leaving the bank in the early Sunday hours carrying full sacks were found and sworn. One was the town moron, Libbeus Coffin. One was the town drunk, William Worth, until that hour the worthless nephew of the bank president. Walter Folger, a Harvard man who had studied the Science of Physiognomy as well as being very rich, had no difficulty at all in "fingering" (a technical term in the science of head-reading) his oldest enemy, Randall Rice, the bank cashier, as the chief culprit. It is, naturally, just possible that what Folger felt and identified as a bump of burglarious intent was in fact merely the proud swelling of Federalist patriotism or even the benign hematoma of Masonism, but scientific evidence was taken as seriously then as now, and it went badly for Rice. Two further henchmen, Joseph Nichols, a court clerk unloved by Folgers and Coffins, and his son Billy were bound over with Rice when another persuasive coincidence of cranial abnormality and addlepated witnesses made their skulduggery clear.

Never mind that a Grand Jury convened in Boston dissolved in hilarity and threw the whole case out. Or that everyone from Charleston, South Carolina, to Boston had heard the actual crooks bragging to all listeners about their feat and their new wealth. Ignore the detail that Jack Clark, one of the felons, confessed, and then Zeb Weathers was captured and confessed also (was captured and escaped four times, confessing the Nantucket job freely on each occasion). The townwide tempest boiled on, neighbor accusing neighbor, shipowners lining up against shopkeepers, islanders against off-islanders, in a prolonged orgy of soul-satisfying,

27

hateful parvanimity. Many were imprisoned, noses were bloodied on Main Street, lawsuits and countersuits enriched the ordinarily thin soup of island gossip for years. Witnesses were bribed and jurors suborned. Men lied under oath (Quakers lied under affirmation, lying under oath being counter to their strict moral principles), and the introduction of banking as a popular pastime on Nantucket was somewhat retarded.

Thinking back over those old griefs, the now nearly forgotten enmities splitting the island into factions for more than two decades, Neil Kelly had for the first time a keen personal sense of how it must feel to be a party to a community feud. If anyone came up to him right at that moment and asked him to sign a petition to encourage the town to let Olds make his damn movie there, Neil would have instantly punched him in the nose.

The white Rolls that rocketed past the house, then braked with a scream of tires, then backed at top speed to screech to a stop in front of Neil's cottage, first enraged him on top of the simmering resentment in his mind, then disgorged a hearty, bounding William Olds shouting, "Kelly, you're coming to work for me!"

The first thought that registered in Neil Kelly's mind was: *The hell you say.* The immediate second was: *Over my dead body.* Before it all ended and an exhausted island could run the bitter credits, there were to be three dead bodies, and as much of hell as ordinary lives could bear.

3

When William Olds won his first Academy Award, he had made a tearful speech thanking his immigrant parents, Chaim and Frieda Olzelewski, for the gift of life. They were both dead by then and past embarrassing him anymore, so he figured it was worth a shot, with his new immigrant picture, *Steerage*, in the works.

Chaim Olzelewski had arrived in Boston in 1908 along with three hundred other Polish Jews but essentially alone.

Chaim was no scholar. In his home village they were not even sure that Chaim had all his buttons. He made his Bar Mitzvah, but his Hebrew never got beyond what he had to memorize or get thumped by the rabbi. He couldn't play a musical instrument, he had failed his apprenticeship as a tailor, and the one time he had been entrusted to drive a cartload of vegetables to market, he had run into a ditch and broken an axle.

What he did have, and the village had no need of it, no way of utilizing it, was a gift for imagining the impossible. And so when no doting relative in America seemed willing on the basis of the family's accounts of him to send the necessary thirty-five dollars American to buy passage and entrance to the new country, Chaim figured out how to steal his way.

He had listened to plenty of whispered family plans

for slipping across the border into Germany to escape the necessity of a government permit from the Russians, who then owned the village. He knew by heart the place at the border where for a few crowns guards would let through refugees from Russia, and a barn where a *landsman* hid them until they could be put onto a train to Danzig. He knew that the steamship companies were competing for the Jews' business by sending agents through the villages with prepaid ship passes to be sold at marked-up prices, their cagey argument being that if you arrived at Danzig with a ship pass already in your hand, you were guaranteed immediate passage while the others might have to wait weeks for the next ship, months even. When such an agent came through his village, Chaim met him outside the district afterward with a bottle of vodka he had stolen six months earlier.

The clever agent given a ride in the two-wheeled cart by the stupid peasant boy did not find it difficult to impress him with his tales of travel or his ability to outdrink him. He did, subsequently, find it difficult to explain to his employers later how come he had been entrusted with forty ship passes but could account for only thirty-seven.

The successful young thief never said goodbye to anyone. He found it simple to sell his two ship passes in Danzig for fifteen dollars each, even though the steerage fare was in fact only ten.

Without any help from the educational institutions of his village, without reading a word of modern philosophy, and without ever thinking twice about anything, Chaim Olzelewski had managed to become a nihilist, an atheist, a materialist, and an emigrant. No one on the S.S. *Dorman* arrived in America better equipped to prosper.

In Boston he turned away instinctively from the Hebrew Immigrant Association lady organizing the newcomers into groups for resettlement in the neighborhoods of Chelsea, where, they were assured, the shops sold kosher and the rabbi would teach the children. Not for Chaim the new shtetl under the old iron hand of the rabbis.

He was seventeen, he was in America, he was rich, but, most heady of all, he knew that he was totally unafraid, totally unwilling to put himself under anyone's control or protection. Chaim was that rarest and most dangerous of human beings, a true loner. And something told him he had arrived at a place where the dangerous loners were the winners, he could smell it, taste it. He had discovered his vocation and it made him strong.

He became a junkman, and with a horse and cart he drove through the streets of Malden and Everett and Revere and collected rags and papers and metal and took them to the long avenue of junkyards in Chelsea and sold them for twice what he had paid. By 1912 he owned his own small junkyard. He had discovered from a banker named Kennedy in East Boston that nothing actually ever had to be paid for if you bought something big enough. Twenty-three pounds of scrap from a dismantled school furnace, you paid the janitor three cents a pound cash. But a whole business with an employee—he, Chaim Olzelewski, had an employee now—you could buy through the bank, which would lend you the money. The second-generation Kennedy, in his early twenties the youngest bank president in America and later the father of two senators and a President, knew a kindred spirit when he met one, and was, in fact, becoming famous for spotting and financing commercial talent among the young immigrants around Boston.

Five years of free night school later, Chaim was lending money himself, through a storefront in Chelsea that was a combination burial society and credit union, but which he called with native shrewdness a Lending Bank. When the

31

city finally decoded the Yiddish on the front window and discovered he was not running a kosher meat market as they supposed, they told him he couldn't run a bank without a charter. He shrugged and apologized for the mistake and changed the name to the Benevolent Society.

He married a homely girl who could do bookkeeping, bought a house in Winthrop with tenants on the two lower floors, and produced from his loins three sons and four daughters, all of whom grew up with his new name, Olds, and of whom the third son was William. No Chaims, no Abes, no Jacobs—Charles, Michael, and William. About the girls he cared less, let his wife name them. Rachel, Charlene, Cynthia, and Tiffany marked Frieda Olds' personal progress toward cultural neutrality.

William alone inherited his father's genius for imagining the impossible and instantly daring it.

Nobody had to tell Billy Olds that life was unfair, not even his grouchy father whose foreign accent embarrassed him. The Irish kids waylaid him on the way home from school, and the Italians who ran the variety store cheated the Jews on prices. The religious Jews they knew shunned them and the Protestants who lived up on the hill wouldn't spit on them. Billy Olds was red-headed and freckled and had small bones and a pretty, little, girlish face. In the schoolyard, boys were always giving him wedgies by the seat of his pants and girls looked at him out of the sides of their eyes and he believed they knew he had dirty thoughts.

Wanda Berkman, the seventh-grade slut, whose mother allowed men to visit their house all hours of the day and night, asked him one day if he was circumcised. He was shocked.

"Course. You know anybody who ain't?"

"Jews are the only ones who *are*, stupid."

32

"Yeah, sure."

"Haven't you ever seen any of them?"

Billy was reeling. What was going on here? "You?" How could she?

"Only about a million times. You wanna see one?"

"What, you got one on you?" His first made-up joke. Hilarious. It broke both of them up.

"I'll kill you if you ever tell, but I know where we can see some guys. Did you ever see people do it?"

We. Holy cow. "Do what?" The sweat was running down from his armpits. He was having the most amazing conversation of his life. His penis was jumping around in his pants like a wild thing. Unimaginable dirty things were possible if a girl could talk like this, even slut Wanda.

"Stick it in each other, stupido. You know, sex." Wanda put her hands on her hips like Miss Hamish waiting for the answer in Geography, tapping her foot. Finally she said the dread, impossible word. "Fucking."

In 1946 the word was not in wide use. In fact, in Billy Olds' neighborhood, only Hot Dog Peroni, who owned a Caddy and was said to be a big crook in dog racing, ever used it in public. Billy's epileptic member became rigid with terror and hope.

"I seen it, sure," he improvised wildly, not wishing for this incredible, filthy girl to abandon him. "But, you know, they was all Jews. Like."

Wanda was not deceived. She had escorted more than one schoolyard virgin to the back hall closet in her mother's upstairs, from which vantage to watch the goings-on in their star boarder's bedroom, and she knew the signs, the need to lie wildly.

"Okay, but if you ever tell on me, I'll kill you and I'll tell Hot Dog Peroni and he'll cut your schwanz off."

A Jewish girl who knew Hot Dog Peroni personally

33

enough to ask him that kind of favor? More and more incredible. While he digested her threat, Billy saw that Wanda's nipples were beginning to show through her dress. Why had no one ever mentioned this phenomenon? Was she the only one? Did girls get hard up there? "You know Hot Dog Peroni?" he blurted.

"Who do you think's our landlord?" the lordly girl asked him disgustedly. "Don't you know anything? Listen, first I have to sneak us into my house through the cellar."

The adventure that followed, cutting through the Slomovitzes' backyard around their barrel shed, sneaking into Wanda's bulkhead and up the inside cellar stairs to the kitchen, then listening until the coast was clear and racing up the back-hall stairs to dive into the hall closet, was at least the spiritual equivalent in terror and education for Billy of his father's dash across the German border thirty-odd years before. A whole new world was opening up for him.

First, in the stifling closet, lit only by leaving the door open a crack, smothering in woolen coats and wading in overshoes, they located the crack between the laths in Rosie's closet wall that enabled them to spy into her room between her dresses. It wasn't much more than a slice of frowsy bed and part of an end table, but Billy stared at it as though it were the promised land, waiting for God knows what dirty thing to happen.

The pile of rumpled bedclothes moved and revealed Rosie herself dressed in a slip. Wanda whispered in his ear, "We have to wait for her to get a customer." Then she kissed his cheek and reached over and grabbed him through his pants. His astonishment froze him. Were these people not Jews at all, but actually Jew-killers? After all, they were in with Hot Dog Peroni. Did they get young boys up and then cut their schlongs off? He wanted to be anywhere else.

He could just hear his father if he came home with his dick cut off.

Wanda put her mouth to his ear again. "I ain't got any pants on, feel."

Feel? How could that be a plot? God. He'd better feel, there was no telling what she might get her landlord to do if he didn't. He felt. He had his hand right on it. It was moist.

"I knew that would make you get a stiff one again," the smug seducer whispered. Her slightly hairy (!)—why had no one ever mentioned that? Was Wanda some kind of freak?—pussy was rotating madly, inviting his finger to explore. He moved closer to her, stepped into a gigantic man's rubber, and almost fell over.

She steadied him with a glare he could feel even though he couldn't see. She unbuttoned him and let his aching member out of its prison. She was whispering again, but the roaring in his ears was louder than a train. He thought he was dying of his feelings, was that possible? Only when Wanda nudged him hard in the ribs did he realize that Rosie had admitted a customer to her room.

Hands on each other's private parts, Billy still standing in her father's rubber, they peered together through the wall and watched Rosie whip back the bedclothes, pull off her slip, exposing what looked to Billy like the biggest ass in the world, and then a beefy guy who worked in Sloan's Furniture on Broadway letting Rosie pull his pants off, and then two mountains of flesh, one of them almost entirely covered with black hair, joining and convulsing on the shuddering bed. Wanda the slut kneaded his swollen dick frantically during this last episode while artfully wiggling herself onto his aching finger, suddenly producing from him with a force he never could have managed alone a gigantic jet of come.

35

They stared at each other point blank in the dim closet light, she smirking, he nearly insane with fear that this would force her to notify Hot Dog Peroni that jerkoff Billy Olds had just come all over her mother's wool coat with the fur trim.

"Pretty good, huh?" she hissed cheerfully. She produced a wool sock from a bag on the floor. "Here, don't get your stuff all over Ma's coat. Boy, you really shot a hugie, didden you?"

He was considerably encouraged to grasp that what he had just done had elements of manly achievement in it. He wiped up proudly by feel, wondering what to do with the wet sock, finally stuffing it into the pocket of the coat.

" 'ja see?" his companion in crime asked him as they skinned back out through the bulkhead. "His hairy one wasn't circumcised."

Billy was too ashamed to admit that in the drama of his sexual initiation he had neglected to note this detail of the main event in Rosie's room.

"Yeah, I seen it. But I heard circumcised guys have bigger comes," he said cockily.

Billy Olds' sexual education nearly ended the day it began. At supper on the day he had sampled the delights of Wanda the slut, his father exploded in some unfathomable rage at his oldest brother, Charlie, who was married and sold siding. Charlie had somehow acquired what their father referred to screaming as "the clep."

To Billy it sounded like something they had studied in Music. With G clep upon the staff, the first note is F. Or C or some stupid thing. But it soon became clear through the tirade their father was pouring over all of them that Charlie had contracted that Black Death of schoolyard conversations, The Clap. Charlie's stupid wife had told Ma.

"Em I supposed to hev deformed grandchildren?" their father howled, hitting himself on the head.

"Syphilis." "Gonorrhea." The terrible names piled up like the titles of destroying furies out to get Jews. "Clep!" his father moaned over and over while their mother wept silently. "For this I walked halfway across Germany in wintertime? For this I put my neck on the block—" he hacked at his own neck with the edge of his hand—"for the Czar's soldiers to cut it off if they felt like it? For this I carried junk in a horse cart from Ferryway Green to Everett Avenue, that my oldest son should get the clep from a hoor?"

It was the last word that struck terror in Billy's heart. If he understood what he had been trying to work out all afternoon, that word meant exactly what Rosie did. It probably also included exactly what Wanda had done to him in the closet. He probably had The Clap! He felt sick.

"Look, look, you made your brother sick to his stomach," their mother wailed.

" . . . and when your putz falls off and you go around with softening of the brain like Hymie Lipshitz . . . " their father was shouting at Charlie.

The world was suddenly a darker and more frightening place.

It was his brother Mickey who took Billy aside later and calmed him down. "Jesus, kid, don't take it so hard. Dad is full of shit, you know that. Let it be a lesson to you, though. If you're going to do it with any of your little girlfriends, for Christ's sake wear a rubber."

Billy was stunned. How did Mickey know that? Was this some joke? Had Wanda told on him? "I did, honest," he blurted.

Mickey punched his arm. "You little bastard. Already

37

you done it? Jesus, I was in tenth grade. Hey, are you the one who took the rubber out of my bureau drawer, you little prick? I blamed Charlie. I'll be damned."

Once again Billy unexpectedly basked in the glow of someone's misinformed admiration for his sexual know-how. He made a mental note that there were two kinds of rubbers and that he could steal the right kind from his brother's drawer.

"I catch you taking another one, I'll paste you, buddy," Mickey said, as if reading his mind. "Buy your own. They're a nickel at Galotti's. Go down by the phone in back and tell Ziggie you want a Trojan and he'll take care of you, but for Christ's sake don't let old man Cronin hear you."

First he stole the exotic, rolled-up white balloon from his brother's drawer along with a dirty magazine of Maggie and Jiggs that really killed him. He carried both in his pocket for a week, burning holes, before he thought of how to use either to maximum advantage. He bought four more condoms in the dark end of the drugstore and then, with a minimum of salesmanship, he talked Artie Rosen, Joey Fanelli, Paul O'Leary, and Jason Guberman into paying him a quarter each to have him get Wanda the slut to watch them all jerk off in his cellar. That settled, he suavely persuaded Wanda that he knew where a bunch of guys were going to have a circle jerk and she could watch for a quarter. He showed her the porno comic book he was going to lend them. He was impressed by the speed and force of her agreement. If it got worldly Wanda that excited, what would it do to Artie and Guberman and those guys?

The event, his first piece of business as an impresario, was a financial and artistic success. The high point of the proceedings was surely when he produced his own white rubber and skillfully rolled it on. He assured his companions with a solemnity he copied from his brother Charlie talking

38

on the phone about aluminum siding that it was possible to get the clap or syph or both from jerking off with dirty hands. They all happily forked over a dime each for rubbers.

The Maggie and Jiggs had Guberman practically falling on the floor, staring at Wanda with his moronic pale eyes and drooling. Wanda offered to give anyone a hand job who would pay her a quarter, but Fanelli was the only one with any dough left, so they all went nuts watching her do him. Everyone pretty much agreed it was the best afternoon of their life.

Somewhere between Wanda's mother's upstairs hall closet and Hollywood, California, William Olds was to become so confused about sex and his own sexual connection with the world that he became different from most men.

In junior high, girls worshipped him because, without acne or embarrassment, he suddenly became beautiful. Some other boys in the locker room touched him sometimes and he found it not all that weird. His Chemistry teacher, Mrs. Dolan, kept him after school to write out the table of elements, and they ended, as he had guessed they would, in her bed. He was sixteen and she was thirty-two, but she was married to the gym teacher, whom he disliked intensely. He wouldn't do the same for the French teacher, Mademoiselle Friend, who was unmarried and too obviously pleading for it.

By the time he was a college senior he knew that he could use sex for any purpose he wanted except to make love. The idea that anyone used it that way he was convinced was the biggest con of all. Movies were movies and life was life; only the boobs confused them.

And when he realized that he enjoyed any fantasy more than every reality, he knew that he belonged in the movies. If he lacked a resonant voice and an impressive physique, he had in abundance whatever that indefinable

39

quality is that the camera loves. Better yet, he loved the camera. More, the critics said, than any male star since Valentino, as only Marilyn Monroe had among the girls. Like Marilyn, whose picture he kept above his bed, he could make love to the lens without shame, open himself up to it, move into it and through it by the force of his giving, and emerge as the fantasy male of millions of women. And apparently of millions of men, too, another Valentino gift.

For twenty years he was one of the three most bankable stars in Hollywood. His marriage to Tara Teluva, the cover girl who later became a crummy actress in a soap opera and then a new rage as the leading lady of a series about the modeling life, did not even put a ripple in his popularity. Life is life; fantasy is where lots of people prefer to live. His photographs with their tiny, golden daughter, Panda, his tight-lipped, wan bravery while picking up the pieces after he and Tara crashed in his famous gold Ferrari, killing her and nearly severing his head from his body, his long recovery from what the press called miraculous surgery, only seemed to endear him more to his fans.

When he decided, announcing the decision on a TV talk show late at night to what the trade papers counted as a larger audience than the fifth game of the World Series, that he had decided to forgo acting for directing, his enemies in the industry licked their lips and waited for the crash off the pedestal. The picture was one of those in which the special effects are the real stars, and Olds won his first Director's Oscar. He knew what no one else in Dreamland had yet quite grasped: that America was a land in love with magic machines, that it had always been his picture they loved, not him; their fantasy was grounded in an ultimate acceptance of the tough reality that what is human is a lot less attractive than what is manufactured, and creation matters less than production.

He adored all machines that could translate what he imagined into something sellable. He loved the camera best. An Italian actress said that being directed by William Olds was like being caressed. What she actually said was that it was like being fucked by the camera, but the PR office fixed that.

He prospered, his fame grew monstrous, he triumphed over every enemy in the business. His films became the new wave everyone else copied. William Olds succeeded at everything except growing up.

4

Neil watched him bound up the short path, a picture of self-confident narcissism. He had taught many students like Olds over the years—so full of a sense of their own utter likability that it admitted no doubts of possible unworthiness. An astonishingly high percentage of them committed suicide before twenty-five; many of the survivors had to go to a drunk tank or a tranq farm before fifty.

Behind Olds came two of his group. A fourth stayed behind the wheel of the Rolls, a Greek sailor's cap over his eyes, eating an ice-cream cone.

The star was easy enough to recognize at any angle. The famous white smile still perfect, and now the red hair turned snowy, crisp white made the smile seem somehow even more sincere. The face of a man just battered enough by life to be interesting; the eyes sea blue and candid. The message was: Trust me; I love you.

He greeted Neil as if this meeting were the high point of his day, even though the man he was greeting didn't say a word.

"We need you. My research people told me all about you. I bet you thought that play you did for Dan Buckle on the old 'Playhouse 90' was dead and buried, right? Wrong. Dan works for me now in R and D. Told me what you gave them, beautiful. Hey, these are my colleagues."

He turned with infinite generosity and shared the lawn with his followers, whom he introduced as Sidney Milano, who wanted to be called Milo, and John Finn, who didn't care what you called him, right?

If William Olds looked like the archetypal playboy tycoon, Sidney Milano looked just the opposite. "Everybody calls me Milo." He flapped his hand loosely at Neil. His mustache was ragged and uneven, his balding head was sweaty, and his hairy belly stuck out through the gap between his yellow shorts and a gray T-shirt with "Property of LA Rams" printed on it.

"Milo's my cameraman. Cinematographer, actually. *Numero uno* in the world, but don't tell the guy in the car that. He thinks *he's* my cinematographer." They all laughed hugely at the inside joke.

Milo shuffled in his dollar-fifty green flip-flops over to the rail and sat on it. "Yeah, yeah, yeah. You're fulla shit, Bill, you know that, don't you?"

Olds' second companion was a withered homunculus of a man with a leprechaun's sharp face and a leprechaun's meanness about him.

"Meet John Finn. John is my good-luck charm. My trademark, really. You remember how the late, unlamented Alfred Hitchcock, just possibly the worst director who ever lived, used to make a cameo appearance in each of his own films? Fat man's chutzpah. John is my Hitchcock alternative—been in every picture I've made. Once for twenty lines, John?" A nod, a glare. "Once for a single frame. And everything in between. Here I'm going to give him a major supporting role, absolutely guaranteed Oscar stuff, right, John?"

The wee man glowered at both of them, sat in the unoccupied lawn chair, put his head back, closed his eyes, and feigned sleep. Olds rubbed his head with gleeful, savage

43

affection. "John's nuts. Totally, absolutely bananas, but I love him. Couldn't make a picture without him. He's my Cabbage Patch doll."

Neil didn't try to make conversation. It was apparent that it wasn't necessary ever if Olds was always this manic.

The star turned his back, took in the view over the moors, and spread his feet and cocked his head, as if he were getting ready to make an offer for it. When he spoke, he was still in profile to Neil, making it hard to know whom he was addressing until Neil realized that he expected everyone to listen. Two's company, three's an audience.

"I have to admit, the first time I saw this island, looked around it, all I could think was, what a great place to hide a body! I mean, it's this little tiny island, but it's still three-quarters wilderness."

In the student-published *Confidential Guide to Faculty at Old Hampton College* it said of Neil Kelly: "Warning. He does not suffer fools gladly."

"And it hasn't occurred to you yet," he said evenly to his intruder, "that what you thought was a stupid, barren, frightful idea?"

John Finn opened one eye for one moment, then shut it.

Olds was unruffled. He grunted thoughtfully. "Hell, Kelly, you've just described the collective mentality of my profession. Except for 'barren,' maybe. Am I right, Milo? Think of it as 'fertile' in a new, frightful way, *voilà*—Hollywood. And besides, isn't it? What I said. Imagine yourself committing a murder tomorrow. Today." Neil thought about it. "Now, you're on this little island. You don't have a private plane. They can search all the outgoing boats, ferries, and so on. What do you do with your corpse? Am I right? Moral: look for a hiding place or don't do the crime, Kelly. Now that I've taken that load off your mind, let's talk about you going to work for me."

Neil had never seen anything like the performer Olds was up close. His eyes shone, he radiated good will, he grinned and chuckled like a shy college boy—Neil supposed it was the good ol' Ron Reagan style that had persuaded so many Americans to part with their votes in exchange for some vague sense that this fellow would see to everything.

"There may be a lot of people on this island who would think it a privilege to have this chat with you, Mr. Olds, but I'm not one of them. Please just get back into your Rolls Royce and go away, because I don't want to work for you in any capacity."

"So think you now," the laughing superstar said. "But wait a darn minute, Kelly. Gimme a break. Boy, you're cold, Kelly, do you know that? Man, you. Are. Cold. I'll bet you saw my daughter, Panda, and I outside the bank this morning. And heard her. Most people do. Big, big mouth, Panda."

"I saw you and yes, I heard her."

"I'll tell you something funny. You heard her say something like, 'There's the old buzzard right there,' right? Am I right? And you thought, 'Who the hell does that squirt think she's calling an old et cetera, et cetera?' Am I right? But listen, listen, this is, as they say at Radcliffe, the beauty part." He put his arm on Neil's shoulder so that they stood beside each other and the oh-so-famous face was just inches from his, as if saying: Look, no flaws, even at this distance. "She wanted you for one thing, and I want you for something entirely different. Great? Ironic? You're a professor of literature, right? You're into irony. Listen, Panda is my assistant director here; that means she's my casting director. So we've been talking about the judge in this goddam film. Panda sees him as an uptight, self-righteous, tight-assed Boston Puritan. So, naturally, when she saw you giving her the big sour-apple stare for jamming her MG on Main

45

Street—you know, mussing up the cobblestones—she immediately said to me, 'That's him.' "

Neil disengaged himself from the million-dollar embrace and sat on the edge of his deck, waiting for the man to run down.

Olds showed no sign of affront. "At almost the same exact time, my R-and-D people are telling me by phone in a conference call with New York that you are the bird who wrote the old 'Playhouse 90' script that Dan was so meshugena about. Coincidence? Fate, baby. Karma. Destiny. Kismet. You name it. I'll pay you one thousand a week to come work for me, help me organize this project on paper, historical, dramatic stuff. Do we go? Are we ready to fly?" He opened his eyes wide and lifted his hands in a gesture of helplessness, a gesture that said if you won't do this little thing for me, you'll destroy me, a plea. "Hey, if you want to play the judge, too, why the hell not? I mean, Panda has final authority there, but—" he winced pleasingly, aw shucks—"I think she's right and I'll put in the good word."

"Save her the trip, Mr. Olds. And save any more words, assuming you have any left. I'm not accepting any film roles this season, and I'm not about to work for you on your film. I have work to do and you're interrupting it."

"Beautiful. Panda was right. That's exactly what she wants, that way you say, 'I'm not accepting any blah blah blah' in that terrific Brahmin accent. Perfect. What are you working on now that can't wait?"

The little man in the lawn chair answered for him. "William, you're being obtuse. Thick. Dumb like an Oirish peasant plowing the sidewalk to plant potatoes. The man wants us to go away."

Neil looked at him almost gratefully. He didn't know what John Finn knew: that the way to make Olds double his efforts, which where they came from meant doubling either the price or the charm or both, was to frustrate him, deny him what he wanted.

Neil looked at his watch.

Olds professed amazement. "Jesus, Milo, when was the last time you saw a pocket watch? I had a watch like that when I was eleven years old. What is it, an antique? Can I see it?" He was genuinely excited.

Neil handed him the watch. "You can buy one exactly like it in any drugstore for eleven ninety-eight. It is a Westclox Bull's Eye and it's what I always carry."

"John, get me one. Look at that. I'll give you twenty for it right now, Kelly—no, wait. I'll give you one hundred thousand for it, but. You've got to come with it and work for me for one year." He brushed the air, sweeping the time aside as not an interruption worth discussing. "Then if you still want to do your research or whatever back here, you can buy this little house here and do it. What are you, renting? What do you pay them, five hundred? Eight hundred? What do I know?"

Neil reached for his watch and took it back. "No thanks."

"God, Milo, look at this guy. I offer him more for his watch than he makes in a year being a professor—am I right?—and he says stick it. What is this, the famous New England integrity or are you putting me on, Neil?"

"You're a little hard to get through to, Olds. Maybe you swarm all over people like this back in California and they go gaga, but you are boring me and you're starting to offend me."

"That's it exactly, am I right, Milo? John? That stern, unbending 'Don't give me any of that West Coast shit, Olds . . . '" He drawled nasally in a genuinely funny imitation of Neil's accent. "God, this is thirsty work. John,

47

get me a popsicle from the car. Green. You want one, Kelly? You see my Rolls? See old Jake in there gobbling the ice creams faster than you can say 'No, no, William Olds, I don't want to buy your rotten bananas'? You know where they come from? Watch John."

The little actor had jogged the ten steps to the car and opened the back door to look in the freezer behind the front seat. "We ain't got no green. Orange or red is all."

Olds clapped his hands in disappointment. "Damn, who ate the green?" He cupped his hands around his mouth to shout at the man sitting in the car. "I'll fire you, Jake, if you eat the green popsicles again, you greedy bastard!" He turned to Neil, laughing at his own humor. "Get it? I had the bar taken out and an ice-cream thing put in. No booze. As the whole damn world I guess knows, Billy O. was a drunk. Hallelujah—" he slapped himself on the chest and threw up his hands to heaven—"thank you, Jesus . . . " in an outrageous black accent. Then he strutted across the lawn four paces and back, hands on hips, Rod Steiger playing Mussolini. "I'm a born-again tee-fucking-totaler. I swear. No booze, no pills . . . that's all yesterday's candy." He took the unwrapped popsicle from John Finn, inhaled its bouquet, and bit into it with gusto. "I'm in the best shape of my life. Brought my whole rowing machine, Nautilus, you name it, I've got more gym equipment than the Olympic team, brought it all with me on the plane. Every morning I'm working out before these slobs are even awake."

Neil was honestly curious about the mentality of people who hired equipment to do outdoor things indoors for their health. He had watched a four-year-old boy climb with fear and delight around the huge bole and roots of an ancient tree that grew right up through the Main Street sidewalk, splitting the brickwork with its slow brute strength. The

48

child's mother, impeccable in beautiful togs, waited angelically for him to finish his exploration of this foreign thing. The little boy looked up at her with his face shining after he had circumnavigated the tree and said, "Oh, Mummy, can we buy one of these?" The woman had grinned a hard smile at Neil and shrugged.

"Why don't you just rent a rowboat for four bucks an hour and get into it and row around the harbor?"

Maybe there was something Olds considered a reason. If there was, he chose to miss the point of the question.

"Hey, I've got a boat. Have you seen that big sucker? Fifty-foot fly-bridge cruiser, all fiberglass. Twin Cummins VT 903 diesels. Delta hull, prettier than any girl's ass you ever saw. Well . . . " He chuckled appreciatively at his own hesitation. "Single-level layout, sleeps six. God, I love that stateroom. You can walk all around the bed—the berth, excuse me. Completely around. Room. Bought it from a guy in Woods Hole. Jake is my skipper. He used to be a sailor in the Israeli navy or some goddam crazy thing. *Lucky Oldsun Three. One* and *Two* I gave to the Merchant Marine when they got dirty. All that polishing. Did you know you can get the whole market value off your taxes if you give a used yacht to them? And I'll bet you're one of those bleeding-heart liberals who want to close the tax loopholes."

Neil grasped for the first time that Olds was desperate. He was a seducer, an immensely successful, a champion seducer, and he was standing here in Neil's yard charming his heart out for the attention and agreement of someone who was telling him in front of his courtiers that he wasn't having any.

John Finn, all antennae despite his apparent somnolence Neil was sure, promptly popped up and started to gabble about something to do with their schedule. At that exact moment Milo jumped down off the fence and started talking urgently to Olds about letting Panda do it. It, Neil supposed, was a reference to breaking down Kelly.

" . . . won't wait all week, William," piped Finn.

" . . . then the hell with it. Is it worth all this bull-shitting around?" Milo asked his master.

Olds seemed frozen in his determination. He glanced at each of them, deliberately put the end of his popsicle stick into the ground, drove it slowly out of sight with his foot, and looked at Neil again. "You're afraid of us, aren't you? Am I right? You're a kind of historian . . . I know, literature and all that, not politics and all that, but you deal in historical stuff, okay? And you're afraid this motley crew from the godforsaken West Coast is going to take this little historical anecdote of yours and turn it into chopped liver."

Neil was willing to engage him on these terms, close to truth. "Isn't that what you people always do? Take simple, human truth and hype it into any crap mixture that will sell?"

"You think my long-range aim is to make a movie like Ralph Waldo Emerson the Secret Pornographer? Emily Dickinson and Her Hot-Potato Diary? X-rated stuff that will neglect the true greatness of the subject and substitute some genital mindwash? And what do *you* want when you go to the movies, Neil? That's what we poor slobs from Hollywood are asking, you know. Tell us what you want, you people, so we can give it to you. What should I make for my next film if not this? Quo Vadis, Pequod? A Jungian voyage through Herman Melville's lower intestine? A lecture by you on Transcendentalism with subtitles for the part of Immanuel Kant? Name a movie you liked last year. Just one."

"The Dresser."

50

Olds crowed and lifted his arms in triumph. "*Of course* you liked *The Dresser*. Wasn't it a play first? Wasn't it foreign? Wasn't it just jam-packed with the juiciest Shakespearean allusions? And wasn't the final minute drawn out long enough for a low-budget feature to be fitted in? Right up your goddam static, pathetic, literary alley. Cold oatmeal. Dogshit, British canine coprolites. And you and your *New York Review of Books* chums ate it up. But you East Coast cerebral mafia ain't America."

"It was a movie that assumed I had a mind, an ear for the felicities of my own native language properly spoken, emotions higher than an irritated lust complicated only by the spiritual insights of rock lyrics, and a tolerance for fine acting."

"Okay. If I give *you* a free hand—I swear, an absolutely free hand—to write me a screenplay with all the felicities of your mother tongue preserved intact, and with the loftiest goddam emotions you can get on paper, will you work for me on this project?" Olds almost said, "Checkmate."

The expression "hoist on one's own petard" came to Neil's mind. Olds was shining-eyed, gleeful.

"Wait. Before you answer that. You better know something about this project. John, Milo, I'm gonna tell him. Should I tell him? I'm gonna tell him. Professor Kelly, this is not just a one-shot deal we are discussing. Yeah, yeah, I know all the bullshit we gave the papers to keep them happy. But the part about filming the bank robbery is just the beginning. Part one—a pilot for a soap opera." He beamed with an intensity Neil wouldn't have believed could be faked—he really was stirred by what he was saying. "Get it? We—" gesturing around at his crew—"are going to develop a soap opera for evening viewing, called simply 'Nantucket.' Complete reversal of the 'Dallas,' 'Dynasty' thing. Real history, drama wound around a core of real events. You remember that play by Arthur Miller—what's it's name . . . "

He was drowned out by the hourly tourist bus that went by the cottage on its way to Madaket. Sometimes a yellow boxy schoolbus, sometimes a dusty gray van, but always the same wisecracking driver, who, just at this point, always said over his loudspeaker, "Now listen up, you people, because there's going to be a quiz on all this stuff at the end of the trip and anyone who fails it has to ride with me all over the island again."

"I'd put it on one of those buses," Milo said disgustedly. Olds looked at him.

"My dead body that I murdered," he added thoughtfully. "I'd prop it up in one of the seats and the damn thing would just go round and round for a week or two before anyone noticed he was dead. You see those people? Glazed." He passed his hand in front of his eyes, staring blindly ahead.

"*The Crucible*," John Finn said in a basso voice. "I appeared in *The Crucible* in Williamstown in the summer of '62. Or was it '72? '52?" He professed astonishment. "I didn't know we were going to do a remake of *The Crucible*, William."

"My pals," Olds groaned. "They're trying to tell me I'm telling you more than I should. What's he going to do," he asked them rhetorically, still looking at Neil, "run down and tell them at Channel Three?" Olds had that boasting, half-rueful look of the man who cannot resist confessing his own cleverness. "Hey, you guys on the bus, come back and hear it from the great Billy O. himself. I saw you ogling my Rolls, you dumb bastards. Did you see that broad almost falling out the window trying to get her camera set?" He made a megaphone of his hands and roared down the street after the bus. "We're going to make a soap!" He lowered his voice to normal conversational level again. "Actually—and this is the bit the media would like to know most—that daughter of mine in the yellow peril you saw this morning is going to direct it. Big Daddy is going to be the producer. Her first big independent shot."

"Har har har," Finn brayed rudely.

"You think I'm going to get in her way, don't you, you little fart? Watch me, just make sure you watch me. Hands off. No interference . . . "

Neil asked the obvious question. "Did she send you here, then?"

"Smart. See that, Milo? This man earns his bread with his brain. Major premise: Pamela Olds is in charge, not William Olds. Minor premise: William Olds is trying to get the professor to work on the project. Conclusion: *She* sent *me*. Well, essentially, Kelly, we're going to collaborate on the concept."

"That's something Californians apparently find possible; I've never attempted it and I see no reason to start now."

Olds blinked and shook his head, pretending to have missed something, gazed around in bewilderment. "Did I miss something?"

"No, *I* did. I've never collaborated on a concept. I suppose it's like angels dancing on the head of a pin—you really have to see it to comprehend it."

Olds laughed, put a finger to his head, and pulled an imaginary trigger. "Get it, John? You're always pretending to be an intellectual locked in the body of a dwarf. I lead with my only Aristotle quote I remember from college and Kelly raises the ante with Thomas Aquinas. I gotta remember that one. I'll use it with Jack Parker the next time we conference . . . " He was winging it, Neil could see, shifting and juking emotionally and intellectually, running up trial balloons like an over-eager stud trying to pick up the best-looking girl at the singles bar. He knew he couldn't score with questions about her birth sign, so he was racing through his entire repertoire of lines. Now it was college man to college man. Neil almost, but not quite, felt sorry for him. That would be fatal, as every good-looking girl in every singles bar knows.

Olds was back on track, serious and didactic. "All kidding aside. We're talking about the only real American popular dramatic form. You know what movies have become. Hell, I ought to know, I helped make them that—giant arcade games, special-effects thrill packages, a tourist bus through the galaxies. I'm through with that. I pioneered it, but I'm abandoning it. Listen, you must've read about that professor from Amherst College, the literary critic, who appeared on the soap opera, got all that publicity by saying he watches the soaps all the time . . . ?"

"Nothing meretricious is alien to Amherst, as Pliny the Elder is said to have said to Pliny the Younger when they were going over his college acceptances."

"Doesn't this guy kill you, Milo? Well, the guy is right, Kell. Listen up, Neilo, as the bus driver says to the passengers: We are going to produce the biggest, best, longest-running, most successful continuing drama—soap—get this, based on the life of this town, starting at the end of the eighteenth century. How long did 'M.A.S.H.' run? Eleven years? And it was about a little war that lasted three years. I want 'Nantucket' to run for two hundred years, minimum. We start with the robbery, yes . . . " He was starry-eyed with his own inventions, reeling off notions as fast as he could talk. "Through the robbery we begin to see the lives, the passions, the loves and hatreds of these Quakers and sea captains . . . The whole point is, they're just like *us*

. . . Sure, they're Federalists and blacksmiths and all kinds of crazy shit, but they eat and drink and scratch and screw and cheat on their wives and cut each other up just like the people in any other small town . . . The glitter-people thing is all worked out . . . We're after something almost literary . . . Wait, wait, don't interrupt me until I finish . . . Think of Shakespeare . . . Listen for the lives, the heartbeats of ordinary people. Remember the movie *Ordinary People*? Remember *Terms of Endearment*? The wave of the future is the ordinary . . . we're into a cultural paradox here, Neil . . . nothing you ever did will be as much fun . . . trust me. What do they pay you at that college you teach at?"

Neil knew they were back to the point where the blue-eyed college boy rang his doorbell and introduced himself and told about how many points he was earning toward his scholarship if you, sir, would just subscribe to any or all of these magazines.

"It's not discussable."

"Money's always discussable. I'll get you an agent. Without an agent you're naked, I'll cream you on points if you don't negotiate with me through an agent. I'll call Danny Bann and tell him to take you on. Great agent. I love to fight with Danny . . . " He rummaged in his shirt pocket for a scrap of paper and scribbled a number on it. "C'mon, take it, for Christ's sake . . . he'll get you double what I offer you. It's a big game, Neilo . . . For God's sake, play, play . . . "

"I'd rent a cottage for mine, and then prop him up in the window sitting at a typewriter so the tourists could take his picture every day as they went by in the bus. It would be months before anyone knew he was dead. *And*—" the actor looked up from under his pointed brows at Neil— "he might in the meantime write a new masterpiece of

55

seventeenth-century scholarship." He thought about it and added, "But that might not be entirely watertight. You academic mavens do go out the odd night, do you not? Didn't I see you in the Ocean House last night, possibly even enjoying yourself, laughing even, Professor?"

"I was there," Neil said. "I don't remember laughing. Sick humor is not my favorite intellectual exercise."

"Our Panda thinks that comedian there has something, wants to rent him for her show here if she can only think how to use him." He looked inquiringly at Olds, then back at Neil. "Don't you think he has something?"

"It might be called a rhetorical synathroesmus syndrome—a tendency to beat his subject repeatedly with a verbal cudgel. The gentle critic John Ruskin even had a touch of it. He called a play he didn't like 'a clumsy, blundering, boggling, baboon-blooded, affected, sapless, soulless, beginningless, endless, topless, bottomless, tuneless doggerel of sounds.' "

"By God, I think he's the bastard who reviewed my performance in *Dark of the Moon* off-Broadway. No, no, that was John Simon."

"Topless and bottomless?" Milo asked, giving his eyebrows the Groucho workout.

"It meant something different then, Milo, relax," his boss told him. They were all scuffling, loose now. They, at least, thought some barrier had been breached, some checkpoint passed in their approach to Neil. Had it? He checked his emotions and found he was weary, but still angry at their presumption.

"That young man," Neil said, "struck me as someone mad at the world who might be better off working on a lobster boat or taking a meditative sabbatical in a Carthusian monastery."

"Mort Sahl? Lenny Bruce? Don Rickles? Joan Rivers,

for God's sake? Are you telling me all the tough-mouthed comics should be put away in a jacket somewhere?"

"In the seventeenth century, in the most enlightened nation in Europe, witty people used to be driven out into the country to laugh at the mentally ill confined there. I suppose it's a kind of progress that now we pay them and put them on TV."

They all laughed at his retort and started naming all the best comics they had seen—Eddie Murphy, Richard Pryor . . . While it went on, one topping the others, Neil clamped his jaw hard on what he knew. The young comic who had dismayed him so much was someone he was supposed to visit and talk with, the son of a friend who thought the boy, Liam, might be about to do something more drastic than usual.

"Then it's all set, Neil, right?" Olds twinkled at him suddenly. Half joking? "I mean, you'll think about it, right?"

"You'd better believe me, Mr. Olds, I have no interest. Zero. Zilch. Nada."

"Hey, I get it, I get it." The star laughed and covered his head with his arms in mock fright. "What can I say to change your mind? Remember, I'm just saying think about it." He went over and started kicking Milo on the soles of his feet. "Wake up."

John Finn looked at Neil with one eye, making him appear to be winking. "Are you a student of the great Brian O'Nolan, by any chance, Mr. Kelly, sor?"

Neil recognized and relished the allusion to his favorite Irish writer, a man with two aliases. Finn was telling him something. The little actor was a master of timing and just possibly the brightest one there, more dangerous perhaps than his master knew.

"The great Flann, is it?"

"The same. Or Myles, of course, before we sleep." He

57

put out a restraining hand. "Go back to sleep, Milo, not you. An Irishman of multiple names and talents."

Neil had been reading Brian O'Nolan, aka Flann O'Brien, aka Myles naGopaleen, ever since he had first discovered him in a bookstore in Cambridge, a mad book called *At Swim Two Birds* in which the author, who was the hero, was taken prisoner by his characters and made to be a character in the book they were writing. Dolly called him a writer's writer's writer.

"If you were himself," Finn said, jerking a rude mouth at Olds, "you'd be in John Furriskey's state, prisoner of your own prisoners." He roared phlegmily and spat into the hedges. Neil looked at him closely for the first time. The man's short legs stretched before him in faded green jeans, child-sized, with an assortment of flower patches all over them. His face was pinched and yellowish and not much bigger than an ordinary cantaloupe. He had a monkey's eyes, bright and endlessly shifting, brown and blinky. He was on the dangerous side of mischievous, like a precocious infant everyone makes the mistake of trusting because he is miniature. Only the voice he could produce when he wished was large, a rolling, resonant baritone that Neil was to learn was his musical instrument, his credit card, his chief tool of trade, and his sinful pride. With it he could produce an Irish brogue honey-thick, a docker's bray that would frighten an angry dog, a lounge lizard's lisp that could make listeners start edging away vaguely muttering excuses, or a patently working-class matter-of-fact, nasal Long Island Knights of Columbus bleat that would charm a Queens cop into accepting his alibi for anything. An actor's voice. And with it now he was telling Neil something he obviously wanted him to know about Olds. But what was it? That Olds was not to be taken seriously? That he was to be taken very seriously? That he was Galatea who imagined himself

Pygmalion? That all this talk of a soap opera was some pipe dream? That the great William Olds was just nuts? Curiouser and curiouser, as another literary character on the other side of the looking glass might have said.

"We're going back," Olds announced promptly. He flicked a pair of gold-framed sunglasses from his shirt and clapped his hands once, the sort of thing a sultan might do to signal a slave. But his imperious gesture seemed to conjure up something else. The yellow MG Neil had seen him petting in front of the bank earlier arrived in a storm of road dust and complaining brakes. Olds' daughter had a voice only marginally more pleasant than her brakes.

"Did he say okay?" she yelled at her father before she was halfway out of the car.

Olds laughed and made a megaphone of his hands. "Come ask him yourself. The old geezer is a tough cookie."

He turned to Neil with a gesture of helplessness, Dad to Dad. What am I going to do with her? "Brace yourself."

Neil was already too weary of this whole troupe of cultural acrobats to do any more bracing. He distinctly heard her one-syllable epithet as she slammed the car door behind her, while another woman got out the other side and closed her door gently, hanging behind. Panda didn't just arrive at the deck where they were gathered, she invaded it, a thin, bleached bristle of energy in beaded tennis shoes, shorts, and an embroidered chambray shirt open halfway to her belt. She threw a pair of aviator sunglasses back over her shoulder in the general direction of the car. The woman behind her could have caught them, but neatly stepped aside and let them bounce on the grass. Neil guessed her age at twenty-five, but she had so many cosmetic tricks and tanning sessions and costume touches altering her here and there that she could have been twenty or thirty.

"What is this crap? Are you kidding? I told Bill he was

59

a shitty salesman . . . Leave it to me, I told him . . . But not old Superstar . . . he's screwed up my beautiful idea, hasn't he? Did he tell you *I* was the one who found out about you writing that great 'Playhouse 90' script? What, you don't like the idea of me sitting in judgment on you?" Olds colored, caught lying. *Why?*

She had an ugly mouth because she used it as a weapon. Neil didn't bother to listen to her, but he looked at her carefully. He had taught students with the same undirected fury in them if you threatened their egos. No matter how he looked at her, Panda Olds had no focus as a person, was blurred. She had no center in her, no place in herself where she was ever simply at repose, at peace.

William Olds was trying to whisper something to John Finn. She pulled him away and yelled at both of them. "Hey, am I being ignored? John, shut it. Hey, Mr. Kelly, sir, I asked you my humble question, where's my answer? Are you one of those sexist old bastards who won't talk to a woman director? You think all women in the movies should be Alice Faye?"

There had been tantrums not unlike this in Neil's office more than once in thirty years. He looked at her steadily until her mouth stopped operating. "I am ignoring you because you are an unmannerly brat. If you were a woman, you'd know how to act in decent society. You stormed onto my property and asked me nine questions embodying three implied insults. You are offensive and unwelcome."

"I'll be damned," she breathed, and turned to her father insouciantly. "You said he was a prick." She turned to the woman who had come up behind her, a far more attractive human being, with a voluptuous body and the face of a professional model. "I'm not staying here, Goldie, let's go." Her father's tone to the echo.

"I don't think Neil has met Barbara Gold, Pammy. Neil

this is my friend Goldie. We all call her that. She's going to be in 'Nantucket'." Olds winked. More Dad to Dad. "And do forgive my daughter's manners and vocabulary. She went to Dana Hall."

The actress smiled. She really was beautiful, in the way that one can be with enough cultivation over a natural base of healthy good looks. She smiled once at Olds, then once, like a tired athlete posing, at Neil, and waved her fingers at shoulder level.

"Hey, Goldie," John Finn called to her impishly, "what would you do with your body if you had one?"

"You know me, John," she caroled at the little actor. "Take it to bed."

"I'm talking about a dead one," he called after her.

"Mine's half dead. God, I've never had so much fresh air in my life."

"It wouldn't do any harm, Goldie darling," Olds said, patting her gorgeous fanny as she passed him at the gate, "if you took it on a nice ten-mile hike with full field pack."

"Then you'd really have a corpse on your hands, Billy," she whispered throatily to him and kissed his cheek as she passed.

"My woman," he explained to Neil. "She mauls me every chance she gets. I try to give her what chances I can fit in."

"Har har har," Milo recited tonelessly. "You have nice light here," he said seriously to Neil as they filed out.

"Now see what a foin mess you've got us into, Olly me lad," Finn said foolishly over his shoulder, crowding into the back of the MG. "I'm going to rough it with the girls," he called to Olds, who simply shrugged and got back into his Rolls, shaking the driver awake when Milo was safely in the back seat. Both cars roared off in a vicious U-turn, back toward town. One thing at least was clear:

William Olds wasn't running anything in his relationship with his daughter, Pamela, whom he had from infancy called Panda as though she were his toy. It was apparent that quite the contrary was true; no matter what the world thought, Neil knew that she was the superstar in that unhappy family, and that her famous father was scared to death of her. Neil watched a bird hopping in the Lowells' driveway, which always seemed to be crammed with cars. Innocent of bestiaries, invested with horses, the shortbodied, spotted bird a child might have drawn with a brown crayon hopped on bare twigs of feet between a white Mustang and a green Pinto. Why was it so hard for some people to grow up? Billy and Panda indeed!

5

Neil had spent the entire next morning trying to find the rhythm of his work again and failing. The Hollywood people had left a stain on the day after their departure, and Neil had spent almost twenty-four hours trying to put them out of his mind and either think creatively about Ben Jonson or get a sensible letter off to Dolly.

He assembled a lunch for himself of cheese and bread and tea. He knew, glancing with an ironic reflex at his own solemn image in the chrome of the kettle, that many of his colleagues back at Old Hampton College mocked his monkish habits, but his habits were ingrained now.

Had he fallen into a dull rut in his middle age? Was that what was getting between him and Dolly? Too bad you couldn't go to a clinic in Boston and get a major personality change, the way you could get a nose job or a healthy kidney these days. He knew that the stasis in his work was caused by his being divided against himself, and he couldn't see any way out of that internal civil war. She had goaded him once in a letter, saying his life was half over and he'd better decide what he wanted to do with the second half, or did he just want to let the waning energies of the first half run down slowly.

As he munched smoked Gouda and dark rye bread, inhaling the perfume of the loaf he'd got fresh-baked that morning from the bakery on Orange Street, he scribbled a poem to her on a strip of brown paper bag. She was used to such enclosures by now.

To D

Love, it's *me* that's half over,
My life refuses to grow at all,
Keeps dancing around like a damn kid.
Every early,
whether there's work
worth doing gladly
or drudge feet deep
drifting to my sills,
Damn life gets up crowing,
elbows aside covers, dignity—
naked as your open eye
all for getting at it,
the invisible, inevitable future.

He stuck the lyric in his back pocket, brushed D out of his mind, and let life tell him to get back to thinking about the chapter he was writing. The book was going badly. He had sat at his little wicker work table enough mornings now looking out over the wildflower garden to the moors, the yellow poppies and scarlet hawthorn berries distracting him from the blank page, to know he had all the symptoms of total writer's block. In normal good spirits he was a fluent writer. A lifetime of study and writing and talking about his subject moved the work unconsciously. When it moved. Now his hands felt heavy as iron, thick, and the words clogged in his mind.

Dolly Allen again unceremoniously bumped Ben Jonson from his head and refused to be ignored.

Middle-aged lovers are a great embarrassment to

64

younger ones, almost unimaginable. When one is twenty and the air is golden around your love, and you are experiencing it all for the first time—the nimble-be-quick tricks hearts do when we actually play in the fields of the Lord, making even dull spirits smile—the idea that people the age of one's parents are abandoning themselves to the same lovely lunacies is at best improbable, at worst obscene.

Neil and Dolly had been brought together in London by the simple chance of professional meeting. She had been his British editor long before they met. To her he was simply another American academic whose seventeenth-century studies commanded a respectable audience. But when Neil had gone to London to be present for the publication of his enormously successful book on Donne (and to prepare the British market for the American TV mini-series based on it), the English editor and the American author had discovered in themselves an English hunger and an American thirst that were not sated by dinner dates, a dozen lovely lunches at out-of-the-way places, picnics in Regent's Park, or even finally a breakfast in bed in Birmingham's belle-époque Grand Hotel that stretched into a twenty-four-hour hilarious, erotic marathon and lifted the hearts of the entire staff. The idea that they could ever be really happy apart was difficult to accept after that.

But now they were apart. Thirty-six hundred miles and four months apart, and it was taking its toll on Neil's writing. The mad letters, the insanely expensive transatlantic phone calls, the stream of small surprises in the mail (the last had been a crushed rose she had stolen at great peril from the Queen Mother's garden in Regent's Park, where he had recited Herrick to her)—all these engorged rather than relieved his loneliness.

He read the sheet in his typewriter about medieval courtly love poetry, ripped it from the machine, and popped it across the room through the small basketball hoop affixed to his wastebasket. Two.

He started a letter to her instead.

D:

> *I am slowly going nuts. Make that quickly going nuts. Sitting on one of the most beautiful islands in the world on a day God designed for joy I am moping like a schoolboy with a term paper due and the book unread. Oh dread, oh boredom, oh D, darling D, where the hell are you instead of here with me?*

He stared at the page. D. He hated her nickname, Dolly, and she hated her real name, Dorothy. Once in Ireland he had composed an entire alphabet for her of the letter D only. All the things D could stand for—darling, dearest, dopey, delicious, demon-woman (they had argued about accepting hyphenated meanings, but she had finally accepted them if nucklehead could be on her list for him)—had become his private names for her. This week he had added the wonderful epithet "dizzard," a distant cousin etymologically of "dizzy," and it was scheduled to be included in today's letter.

He stopped typing and looked out the window. He remembered her frank sensuality in bed, so sharply contrasted with her professional reserve. He remembered the precision of her diction, her unwillingness to waste words in any discussion of work, and her wholly unpredictable, uninhibited blather when they were alone. Their nonsense talk before, during, and after sex. The sort of babble all lovers play at and would die of mortification to hear played back to them.

He remembered that he had, one long breath's moment after they had made love for the first time, burped sonorously. An appalling, protracted belch whose vulgarity had chilled him. There is a point early in any romance, known in the manuals of technique as Too Soon, in which the sudden announcement of any non-sexual natural function can bring the whole edifice tumbling down. In the fractional pause while he was wondering how to apologize without magnifying the faux pas, Dolly had recited in plummy Royal Shakespeare tones from her pillow, "And he burbled as he came."

They had started giggling. He said from his pillow, relief at the happy silliness of it flooding through him, "Hit was the Jabberwock wot myde me do it, m'lydy."

"The Jabberwock?" she asked, shocked. "But where was your vorpal blade, my good man? I distinctly heard it go snicker snack."

"Ah, m'lydy, ma vorpal blade ain't wot it uster be."

"There, there," she said, patting it nicely, "I'm sure it will be its old self again soon. Let us hope so."

They had hugged and laughed and thumped their pillows and whooped and hugged each other again until they slept. And when they awoke, sure enough, it was.

The memories tumbled over each other in his mind. In Waterford in the rain one evening they had eaten fish and chips from a folded newspaper, then ducked into a dreadful Italian western movie set in Spain with American actors, but with the spoken dialogue still mysteriously dubbed in Italian, with incredible English subtitles bearing no apparent relation to what any lipreader could see the actors were saying. The villain—or his horse, it was impossible to tell—was called El Duro.

Their lodging that night, arranged by a cheerful tourist guide down at the Viking tower by the harbor, was an unbelievably clean stone room in one end of a brewery where a widow kept living quarters and rented one room. She had fussed over them and let them know she took them for late newlyweds, not that uncommon a thing in Ireland. She had a pot of tea hot for them at bedtime when they came in drenched. Unwilling to disabuse her of her interpretation of their truly unsacramental state, they had sat with her in the parlor and drunk the dark-red wonderful tea and talked about her cousin in Brockton, Massachusetts, and agreed with her that it was indeed an amazing thing not to have met, him being from Massachusetts himself.

In the big double bed, the flannel sheets warmed somehow by their shy, busy hostess, they had grabbed one another and begun a fierce bout of Spanish lovemaking as it might happen only in an Italian film.

"Hold me, Juan. I fear the coming of El Duro."

"Ha ha, you foolish female, Maria Mariachi, do you not yet know the terrible troot?"

She covered her lips with her kunckles. "You mean . . . ?"

"Of course I mean, you poor leetle fool. I, Juan Candelaria del Canaria del Nosotro Nostrillos, John Canary Nose, am truly him whom you fear. I. Am. El. Duro."

She ripped the nightgown from her bosom passionately. "Eef it is for my country, or my ceety, or my leetle town, or my willage, or my seester's honor, or the honor of my sainted mother, then take me, El Duro, but spare everywan else. I weel be your leeving sacrifice."

"Not so fast, Maria Mariachi, fairest of the fair. You have a seester? Is she young? Would I like her better than you?"

"Take me, El Duro, take me. I am ready to do anything you command me of."

"First tell me about your seester."

She bit his ear. "She is old, werry werry old. Seventy-five at least. My mother had her when she was only seven. Oh, are you truly the terrible El Duro, thee hard one?"

68

"Here, wench, see for yourself."

She gasped and put her knuckles to her lips again. "Eet is true. What shall I do? I guess there ees no hope. Take me, El Duro."

The stone walls were wonderful for keeping the noise in. Mrs. Doherty brought them a breakfast of eggs and bacon and soda bread and the red dark tea and never batted an eye, wishing them the top of a very fine morning. They were unwilling to believe that she could have overheard any of their adventure in her guestroom and still beamed so sweetly on them. As it happened, they were wrong, but it was unimportant.

Neil knew that it had been his trip to the post office two days ago that had cemented him in at the bottom of his slough of despond. That trip was part of each day's easy early routine. Neil's house-sitter back in Oldhampton had strict orders to forward only first-class mail, and he wasn't expecting any. His publisher knew his address here was General Delivery, Nantucket, and so did D. The fact that there hadn't been a letter from her for over a week had him as fractious as hell. "Words is one way," he had once written her, "we touch." And it was a palpable touch when he saw her handwriting, it could affect his breathing and pulse.

The two overseas airmail letters were easy to spot and he grabbed them hungrily, ripped open the earlier-dated one, and read it as he stood on the sidewalk on Federal Street. By the time he finished, strolling in a daze down South Water to the coffee shop, he was clenching his teeth hard, not smiling.

It was annoying enough that she apparently knew someone here on Nantucket and asked Neil to drop in on him. It was doubly damned annoying that she mentioned some psychiatrist named David Humbles three times in three pages. Once to say that she had met him at Sybil's end-of-season party, once to mention rather more off-handedly than Neil thought natural that she had met him for lunch at a new little Vietnamese place in Chelsea, and once to say—a bit coyly, he thought, for an experienced editor—that David had asked her judgment on a paper he was to read in Paris. God, the nerve of some people. Why the hell didn't she ask him to cure her allergy to tree pollen and see how *he* liked being used professionally for nothing an hour.

The second letter, savaged through while he tore several doughnuts limb from limb, was not unlike the first. She repeated her request that Neil visit her friend, who needed cheering up, apparently (Ha!), and she tacked on a gleeful footnote to say that David believed all allergies were rooted in self-doubt, and had suggested she try a combination of bee pollen and biofeedback for her tree allergy. *And, it was working wonders!!* What had happened to his tough-minded editor who would kill without pity any writer who employed such *Cosmo* punctuation? She'd be dotting her i's with little circles next and putting a little smiling face under her signature.

Self-doubt and bee pollen. What an awful quack this Humbles must be. What a goofy name, to be frank. Probably haughty as a goddam peacock in full plumage. He knew the type, *Quackus Britannicus*, hacking jacket cut with just a bit too much flare, foulard silk handkerchief piled up in the breast pocket, wore formal clothes with tremendous distinction, brushed his gleaming hair back over his ears in rich arabesques, like a goddam aftershave ad for something called Heather and Leather.

Together. That's what it seemed D and this Humbles were increasingly. And apart was what she and Neil had obviously been too long. He stuffed her mail into the side pocket of his windbreaker and pounded over the bricks up the length of Main Street muttering at anyone who dared speak to him.

It wasn't enough to walk the mile home. He went right past his house and kept pounding along the roadside halfway to Madaket before he turned back. The Commons on both sides of him were a splendor of purple and green and islands of gold wildflowers, but he ignored it all.

It was not until he had slammed into the house and drained three fingers of Jack Daniel's in two swallows and hurled himself into the deep chair and sat for twenty minutes staring at the wall that he was able to reorganize his emotions and take a deep breath.

He had spread the crumpled pages of the two letters out and forced himself to read them through again, just trying to read the words as written and refrain from projecting his own enraged suspicions into them. She didn't actually say anywhere that she was fond of this Humbles. She did refer to him in the first letter as "rather conceited" and later as "smug." Good, okay. She did indeed devote a paragraph in each letter to an expression of her own sense of loss at their separation. Fine. And she did plead with rather more than ordinary social urgency that he look in on this stepson of her old chum Marjorie Lilly, this Liam, who was alleged to be a budding poet of great merit, but apparently very close to suicide. She reminded him that they had actually seen the boy acting-up at some garden party they had attended in Kent, an occasion when wine had permitted him to tell her what he had never told anyone else ever: that the boy struck him rather poignantly as desperately trying to decode himself in public and it had reminded him of himself and what he had always expected to see in a son if he had had one.

Neil could not know then what a later letter would

convey, the rather sensitive fact that Marjorie was the first wife of David Humbles. By the time he got to know that he was actually performing an errand of mercy in a round-about way for David Humbles, Neil had already tracked Liam down working in a nightclub on South Water Street and decided to talk with him. It was Liam that John Finn had been referring to yesterday, the bitter young comedian at the Ocean House.

And now William Olds and his horrible daughter and his asinine notion of an historical soap opera. He felt like a character in a low melodrama thinking it, but he thought it nonetheless: Dear God, what next?

What makes soap opera such a powerful cultural force—and the critic from Amherst is right about this—is precisely its predictability while pretending to keep us in suspense. If Neil had thought about it for just a bit more, he could easily have answered his own weary question. The answer was: three murders, several betrayals, a double infidelity, and an ugly, brutal scandal involving the obscene abuse of a child. Just like soap opera.

6

Neil rustled and slumped around the house, the letter to D abandoned, the book abandoned. He took the last chunk of smoked Gouda from the refrigerator and wrapped it in a torn triangle of pita he'd unearthed, munching without tasting, staring out at the garden. It was spitting rain. He picked some moldy bits off the bread and lined them up on the windowsill. He picked up for the third time the new murder mystery Updike had written and found his place; he had only managed to reach page sixty. Some woman had done away with her husband and had him pressed into a set of place mats, and she and her nutty friends, who apparently were all witches, were eating off him. Neil suspected there was some joke he wasn't getting—was it ghost-written by Updike's *anima?*—as tasteless as the stale bread and cheese.

He tossed aside the book without even dogearing the page and rummaged under the cupboard for a beer. One left, cool but not cold, perfect. At last then something, as Robert Frost said to Emily Dickinson. Fifteen or twenty bottles awaiting return to the store took up most of his storage space. He shut them in guiltily.

He drank beer and sat down and typed half a page. Reading what he wrote made him wince. Lively Ben Jonson turned to wood. Sell it by the cord, writing like that. He supposed he should read Francis Steegmuller's unscholarly, vivid biography again to get back his feel for the times and the man from someone whose heart had obviously been in the work.

Poor Ben, imprisoned again, this time in Kelly's dank prose. He was almost surprised there weren't patches of mold on the paper. He ripped it out and canned it without another look.

A writer with nothing to say, confined by circumstance to indefinite solitary confinement in his own dull spirit and experiencing that emptiness of soul that feels like brain death, is bad company for himself and might as well go for a walk in the rain.

Like most sane men, Neil would rather walk along a beach on a wet, windy, cloudy day with one foaming breaker after another combing the scree from the sand ahead of him than work. Writers have the grand alibi that they are really working, or at least getting ready to work by meditating, or at least doing the preparation for meditation by getting some exercise—even an inexperienced writer can extend this litany of justifications the length of any beach. And the writer on an island has the sweet surety that, no matter how far he strays from his typewriter, geography will bring him back to it eventually.

Sense will always infer, if we are patient, Neil thought, what nature implies. If we get it right. We are the world's habitat, not the other way around, and the seventeenth century knew that cold. Cape of Good Hope was someone's hope once. Death Valley someone's doing-in. Bitter Creek a human disappointment, and this Nantucket, the Indians' "faraway island," someone else's remote retreat a thousand times before.

Henry James has described one of his favorite English

74

cities as "a feast of crookedness for Americans"; Nantucket is a feast of simplicity. Still open, still scoured by wind and lit by sealight everywhere. Every other crowded American place has slowly committed suicide, if a place can destroy itself, after calling into being a crushed underclass to pull the trigger, but this small island still has a chance to survive, honest, bony, barefoot, and clean. Though he remembered as he walked its gray-and-white streets and bare beaches that Eden was the site of the first lie, the first murder, and the first family soap opera. Indian summer seemed to be dwindling down to a last pinch of late light and softness; the air had a vagrant chill.

An hour later Neil found the Faces store where he'd been told to locate Liam daytimes. The misty rain had turned into a drenching downpour. When he entered the big, white and wood store with its three display counters and racks of track lighting, the end-of-season sale stuff piled carelessly on display, a young woman with a long, thick plait, wearing an indigo shirt, was sketching and another, in a threadbare cotton sweater, was using the antique adding machine. He introduced himself, and saw the brief flareup of hope that he might be a customer fade out when he asked for Liam. The young comic was apparently still sleeping after performing till one a.m., then partying until four.

"If you're from the film company and it's about a job, I can get him up," the bookkeeper volunteered. "I'm Nell. That's Wendy over there."

"Sorry," Neil assured her hastily, "I'm just a friend of the family."

"Oh."

Nell went back to totaling her paper strip of figures, but added, "Wendy's our weaver. She did those shawls."

He nodded to each of them, not sure if he should wait or leave. Neither of the young women seemed to care one way or the other.

A slim, dark young man came in from the street with a clipboard that he threw on the counter with a noisy clatter, then snatched up again when he saw Neil, wiping the rain from its plastic cover.

"Fresh blood. Sign my petition? You look like a friend of civility; we're going to prevent them making a movie on Nantucket."

Neil smiled, but shook his read. "As I just told a colleague of yours up on Federal Street, I share your opinion but I'm not a registered voter here."

"Great, all the better. Listen, tourists carry more weight around here than the islanders. The selectmen know who pays for their damn budget. They want to turn this place into Hyannis, for Christ sake."

"Before you sign it, though, if you're a friend of Liam's you might want to talk to him first," Wendy said. She was sharpening a pencil with a single-edged razor blade. "He thinks he's going to get a part in it. At least, he thought so last night."

"Shut up, Wendy," the petitioner said. "We've heard enough from the radical right. Let the man follow his conscience and sign." He was still urging the clipboard and pen on Neil. "Are you going to sign, or are you one of those professional neutrals who decide by not deciding?"

"Jesus," Wendy hissed at him, "you are your own worst enemy. Let the man alone. He's a friend of Liam's."

"And it wouldn't exactly hurt this co-op if one of us could get a winter job," Nell said. "Our cash flow is about to dry up and start acting like a deficit." She shook the long tape at him, glaring, then turned abruptly to Neil and asked him if he'd like a cup of instant coffee. The rain outside was making itself heard louder than ever just then and he accepted with gratitude. He sat down in a sagging canvas chair to drink it after making sure it was all right for him to wait there for Liam to get up.

"As I said—" He was trying to get the young man's attention by catching his eye, since no one had bothered to give him a name. Both women seemed fed up with him or afraid they'd set him off if they spoke. Neil caught his glance and continued. "—I share your view that these Hollywood people should pack up and go and leave Nantucket alone. But it's been a long time since I did anything—signing a petition or anything else—simply because some well-intentioned person with a chip on his shoulder tried to force me to."

Wendy began to hum sunnily at her work.

"Sorry," the boy said coldly. "I wasn't trying to make a big thing of it. I'm kind of pissed off. I only got fourteen signatures." He left the clipboard and pen on the counter next to Neil and walked out the door.

Nell seemed to feel obliged to explain them all and calm any troubled waters. "That's our Jon. He's kind of down right now, you know?" She paused and seemed to be asking herself her question before she voiced it. "Maybe this sounds stupid, but I was thinking this morning that people our age have moods—you know, ups and downs, happy one day, then depressed the next day—a lot more than, well, people your age. Do you think that's true, or does everyone at every age think that? About themselves, you know."

"I'm sure you're right," Neil said with a laugh. "I wouldn't be twenty again for anything. Up one day and down the next is just what I remember about that strange time. One of the relatively few advantages of getting older is that one also gets calmer; the mood swings generally take longer, just like everything else, so life seems a steadier trip."

"God, I'll be glad to reach thirty, then," Wendy said with unfeigned sincerity.

Liam sauntered in bleary-eyed and pronounced a magnanimous absolution over all in the room. "Careful, Wends. When Jesus reached thirty, his mother threw him out of the house. Told him to stop hanging around playing God and get a job. And you have to admit he was original about it—modeling a line of crosses isn't my idea of a career, but they say he made it really big. Dangerous age, the thirties. Mozart, Alexander the Great . . . " He stopped his impromptu nightclub routine to open his eyes fully with some apparent effort and look at Neil.

Nell rushed to provide an introduction, probably fearing that Liam would manage to insult the visitor before he even knew who it was.

"I know your stepmother," Neil said. "A friend of hers in London asked me to say hello if I saw you."

The boy put a finger to his cheek and pretended to think deeply. "My stepmother? The inimitable Marjoram?" He raised both eyebrows rapidly twice. "She didn't mention sums of money by any chance?"

Neil recognized him fully only then. He was the beautiful boy who had disrupted the party at Marjorie's by dressing up as a girl and flirting outrageously with a fat lord who then made the awful faux pas of caressing Liam's bottom in the garden. The boy/girl promptly began to urinate against a tree, saying hoarsely over his shoulder, "Be with yer in a second then, Guv."

In his club act he had been wearing chalk-white makeup and blued eyelids. Now he was beginning to wake up and show wary interest that Neil might be the long-awaited emissary from home, possibly bearing gifts. He asked after

Marjorie, kept turning every observation into a one-liner, and finally said to Neil, "I remember you now. You solved some awful murder down in Devon. 'The Donnish Detective,' I believe my favorite paper called you."

Neil winced and changed the subject. He told Liam that he had enjoyed his act, even though he hadn't understood most of it. In fact, the evening had been almost wholly unendurable. First a trio of electric-guitar players dressed like motorcycle thugs and called Lobster, Liquor, and Lust had screamed and twanged for twenty minutes. Then a talentless, skinny girl with stringy hair had drawled a breathy ballad while laying her hands randomly across a zither. The song appeared to be about the death in battle of a Scottish earl who had promised his true love that he would die with her name on his lips. Had that been part of their generation's ups and downs? The stoned audience had listened to the incomprehensible ballad with the same reverence their parents had probably given to "The Battle Hymn of the Republic." Then Liam had come on and done his weirdly Weimar-vintage act of poisonous humor and decadent effects. His major themes seemed to be butchery and death, his minor concerns pain and punishment. For the first five minutes Neil had been convinced that the young Irishman was dangerously sick in the head. Then he realized that everyone else in the room was having a wonderful time laughing at Liam's jokes, and he grasped in some inchoate way that if Liam was sick, they all were—that he was acting out their inner fantasies, which they greeted with hoots of laughter and screams of recognition. In the low room choking with sweet smoke, with the amplified boom of electronic music still making his head hum, Neil had watched himself watching all of them and had known that he was the odd man out. No outsider so far out as the generational outsider. Old fart. Dad. Was the problem saving a graceful island

79

and a life of possible grace from being poisoned or was it adapting, learning to live with ecological and commercial disaster? Did the expression "selling one's soul to the Devil" still make any sense at all? If Liam represented everyone in that reeking room but Neil himself, how could anyone even say he was eccentric, let alone sick?

"I shall tell you my life story," Liam announced promptly. "Then Wends and Nell and Jon can tell you theirs, then anyone who comes in from the rain can tell theirs—hey, listen, everyone, this is what the immortal Biff Loman would call *a feasible idea!* We'll all tell this learned writer our several stories and he will put us in a book and we'll only charge him half the profits. Me first." He assumed the third ballet position, clapped his hands, and began to tell them about growing up in County Waterford.

LIAM

Liam O'Neil O'Farrell was a milk-skinned Irishman from Dungarvan with a thatch of wild black hair above a handsome, cadaverous face. He had gained a reputation even in grade school as a wit simply because, no matter what he said, he looked funny saying it, cocking one eye, drawing his thin mouth into a knot, pulling on his long, narrow nose. That whole style of performing the easiest recitation, which he could no more help than Joe Fallon in the next seat could help blinking, got Liam into trouble with the nuns and eventually with the priest, because, being stuck with it, he mastered its use. He tried it one morning while serving Father Dooley as an altar boy during the funeral mass for Francis X. Murphy, deceased bigwig of the parish, and got the seven Murphy children in the front row giggling uncontrollably, an eruption of mirth they tried vainly to disguise as unmanageable sorrow, but Father Dooley was

80

neither fooled nor forgiving. A gentle man with women parishioners but hell on wheels with the boys, he smacked Liam across the face in the vestry afterward. He took it on himself later to explain the incident to Liam's mother, pointing out that Liam's "mobility of features" could take him a long way in either direction, depending. Mrs. O'Farrell took his meaning. In Dungarvan there were only two directions in spiritual matters, up and down. And when the pastor said "depending," he always meant depending on whether or not he got a Catholic education. The poor woman convinced herself that he had said "nobility of features" and, wholly unable to afford it, started working at another job to pay for the right training, letting herself assuage her weariness with delusions of sanctity or at least a priestly vocation for her harum-scarum boy. As she remarked to Mrs. Doyle, who worked next to her at the drygoods store, weren't many of the greatest saints little buggers when they were small? God was good to her, she died that year.

Liam arrived at the seminary at age fifteen, to be trained up by an order so impoverished for volunteers that they took anyone who could complete a sentence. Apart from a reputation gained instantly as the wittiest speaker in the school and the winning composer of the First Year Class hymn ("O Jesus, Are You Here Again"—a song ostensibly about the second coming, which his classmates delighted to decode into a commentary on Brother Benjamin, who did the bedchecks in the junior dorm), he made no great strides. It was his second-year book report on the life and works of a saint no one else ever heard of (St. Upgard of Bohemia, who, he reported with wincing mournfulness to his enrapt peers and poor dumb Father Billis, had been subjected by Diocletian to the terrible torture of having a live coal inserted into her from the beneath side, and who immediately rose into the air and praised God, to the consternation of the Roman authorities) that occasioned Liam's divorce from the religious life. "They were hardened men, these Romans," Liam assured the breathless class, "but even they were moved to tears by the sight of the saint moving effortlessly across the courtyard with fire streaming from her fundament." Further, he assured them, on the authority of what he called "original sources printed only in Latin," "whenever the saint answered a call of nature after that, a small pile of glowing coals would be found on the spot." During the severe winter of 69 A.D. when fuel was scarce all over Bohemia, she was said, he reported, to have saved her village from death by freezing simply by dropping in for a visit and a dump in every house.

Father Billis awoke from the nap he availed himself of during all book reports to roaring applause and knew that O'Farrell had been up to something, but gave him a B-plus anyway; the boy had unmistakable talent. It was Father Superior, standing out in the hall listening with his hair on end, who took the occasion to sack the incorrigible. Liam left the seminary, and if he left without a live coal up his kazoo, it was not because Father Superior was squeamish about fighting fire with fire, but because of his deference to the penalties of civil law.

The day Liam was bounced from the seminary was also the day his father, Dermot, a gambler and freestyle rogue, and his stepmother, whom Dermot had met and married in England, had a notable row in the Savoy dining room that broke many things including the marriage bond between them. After a brief bout of notoriety in the pages of the more vivid dailies, Marjorie went home to Sussex and her own stepmother. There was little for it but that Liam and Dad, two jokers from the same deck, must hie themselves to America.

Liam was stuck into a public high school in Miami while Dermot took up residence at Hialeah. The Irish boy's now well-evolved mobility of face, mouth, feet, and wit easily guaranteed him the editorship of the school newspaper and yearbook. His one terror, girls, of whom he had seen only monstrous projections in his mind while learning of matters sexual at the hands of senior boys at the sem, finally yielded to the unmatched directness of Mary Dunne. He had, with what he imagined to be infinite guile, lured that outstanding sophomore cheerleader into the back of his Econoline van and there began chatting her up in a stream of hysterical improvisation. But it was too dark for her to see his funny face, and all Mary Dunne knew was that nothing was coming off except that this boy seemed to be going nuts on her. She finally cut short his babble by unbuttoning her shirt and saying, "Here, Liam, would it make you feel better to feel these?"

He moaned wordlessly in his first direct heterosexual pleasure. It seemed that there were some situations indeed too much for words. Feeling *those* had been precisely the guiding principle of his past two months' fantasies. He grasped them with tender, even holy awe, realizing for the first time what it was Jimbo Corcoran had probably been experiencing when he had laid hold of Liam's own manly adornment in the dorm and growled like a dog.

"Ah, the silver apples of the sun, the golden apples of the moon," he crooned in approximate poetic salutation to the two dear things.

Mary Dunne squirmed. No one had ever called them apples before, but she decided she liked it. "Talk some more poetry to them, Liam," she sighed. "Call them something from Shakespeare."

And dull men who have never known them continue

to deny the sensual delights of a sound literary education. Liam, not unlike his patron saint, Upgard of Bohemia, rose majestically and soon streamed sweet fire.

By the time Liam was eighteen, Dermot had disappeared into the American West. Santa Anita, actually, but who was to guess that? The witty boy threw himself on the rich, rich mercies of his onetime stepmother's family. They provided fare back to England, and arranged for him to matriculate at the University of Kent in Canterbury. If the authorities there had been more sensitive to his literary potential, he often thought, and more willing to overlook his fondness for the odd undergraduate drunken prank (such as the one that found him lying in state, costumed and be-sworded, atop a knight's tomb in Canterbury Cathedral, from which perch he had scared hell out of a batch of American tourists by leaping down at them with blood-curdling cries that he had come back to avenge the death of St. Thomas à Becket), that seat of learning might eventually have accounted a major English poet amongst their alumni.

His stepmother's exiguous charity expired after Liam smashed up one of her cars driving drunk on the American side of the road. When the judge called him a suicidally stupid child, Liam leered happily and agreed with him. There seemed no alternative to returning to America, where judges had much less leeway in what they were allowed to say to defendants. He earned a series of precarious livings—as a clerk in a Greenwich Village bookstore, an occasional stand-up comic in a tiny cellar club in NoHo catering to sado-masochistic homosexuals, a guard in a museum, and a counterman at a natural-foods restaurant.

He eventually went to Nantucket simply because another entertainer from the NoHo cellar had a job singing and telling jokes at a club there and he invited Liam to come along for a few laughs, hoping to seduce him.

The not so seductive comedian faded away and Liam took his place. Jonathan Van Veler was a standby musician and waiter at the club, the Ocean House, and he and Liam became friends. The Irishman accepted the offer to join the new co-op group Jonathan belonged to. They called themselves Fishlots Arts & Crafts Experimental Studio, but their acronym, FACES, was the way everyone referred to them.

He wanted to write poetry, but he did the group's lettering and display cards for the windows. Instead of thanking the Irish nun who had made him learn the italic hand, he cursed her.

His comedy now cast long shadows, became darker, went to black. He drank more than he could handle or pay for. He caused rows in the co-op, and finally he and Jon had a set-to and Jon got the group's support, telling the scowling Irishman that he'd have to shape up or ship out. It had only been half in jest that he had written his bleakest letter of all to Marjorie, cadging funds and announcing that he intended to clear all his debts and then empty the world of his presence, which he knew was accomplishing nothing creative.

Jon re-entered the shop drenched from the downpour. He crossed the room without speaking and proceeded to strip to his underpants.

"This is still a store the goddam public is supposed to come into, you know, Jon," Nell said disgustedly.

"Let me know if any of them do and I'll put on a tux. Who the hell's going to shop in this typhoon? We might as well close up."

Liam performed an introduction, ringmaster style. He

lifted an imaginary top hat, bowed deeply, and presented his wet colleague with a complicated flourish of the hand.

"May I present Jonathan Van Veler. Singer, musician of many instruments not excluding the razz-a-ma-tazz, rambunctious, reproductive piccolo, and a wounded veteran of the great San Ysidro hamburger massacre! No kidding, folks, this man survived McDonald's last stand in southern California. Show the man your adorable left buttock, Jon." His gleeful, manic style gave him a kind of wizard's authority over them all.

The dark, slim youth took a mock bow, turned, and presented his rear, lifting his jockey shorts to display a puckered red scar. "Ta da!" He seemed suddenly embarrassed by his own extravagant gesture. "Liam is ineradicably amused by the fact that I was a fast-food clerk at a hamburger store in California where some nut shot the place up with a machine gun, including a small, valuable piece of my ass as I dove out the door. I told him it's a rite of passage any red-blooded American boy expects to enjoy before he settles down, but he thinks it makes me unique. I apologize for getting pissed off at you before."

Neil looked at him carefully. He could remember seeing on the news the event they were bantering about. A man with a machine gun had actually shot more than seventy people in an insane rampage apparently triggered by some vague feelings of anger against the world. More American hyper-reality quickly forgotten, like the sordid nightclub act. Yesterday's news. Just a few more American childhoods ended in bloody trauma.

Egged on by Liam and with hilarious and sometimes ribald interjections from the women, who were giving themselves wholeheartedly to Liam's proposed group confession, Jonathan was persuaded to tell about how he had come to Nantucket.

Neil had the odd thought pass through his mind that the actor John Finn would appreciate this better than anyone, the writer being held prisoner by his characters inside their own stories.

JONATHAN

Jonathan Van Veler had been voted the outstanding boy in his Arenia, New York, senior high-school class. He had won the all-school talent show with his magic act, organized a five-piece band for which he was also lead singer, and managed to get elected to the National Honor Society while also earning a letter in cross-country. And although his testicles had ached for three years from being confined to the same English class as Kathy Werner's amazing breasts, he had no time for girls.

Thomas Van Veler was so proud of his talented son that he permitted a temporary truce to be negotiated by his attorney with the former Miriam Van Veler, then Mrs. Ambrose Butterfield of Greenwich, Connecticut, so that she could attend Jon's graduation. A dinner with wine for Jon, his first under his parents' eyes, was arranged at the Four Pillars. Sadly, the family effort at celebration and temporary reconciliation was doomed, because Jon chose that evening to pack his clothes and skis into the new Saab his father had given him for graduation and drive off to California. Kathy Werner, into whose admiration and private innermost parts he had managed to insert himself during the senior picnic at Tanglewood, had convinced him that the oldest American dream was still attainable, in Hollywood, but only if he had the balls to break with his father. She had touched him in a sensitive place.

Kathy had an intelligence quotient only marginally larger than her upper body measurements, but to her thrillingly insipid arguments in favor of living together in a sleeping bag on Malibu Beach the cleverest boy in Arenia had been able to offer no more than a few feeble rhetorical questions. To his "Do you mean it?" and "Holy shit, Kathy, do you really think I'm good enough now?" she had only to stretch her palpable self full length in a kittenish yawn while entirely unclothed. Jon, who for all his feigned worldliness had never seen actual blond, curly pubic hair before, understood her "Are you kidding?" as logic irrefutable and command irresistible, almost edible.

Their westward odyssey was not vastly different from that undertaken by ten thousand other couples that June. In Tulsa they quarreled for the first time when Kathy disappeared for four hours with a tall young man in a cowboy hat who had pumped their gas at the Exxon station. She explained tearfully that the cowboy had lied to her, telling her that his uncle knew some big shots in Los Angeles who helped young musicians get started in the recording industry, and that she had practically had to fight her way out of his house when she discovered no uncle lived there, just two other men in cowboy hats. She showed him the tear in her painter's overalls, which were her sole traveling costume. Only by crying when he said he didn't care about what the local cops did to him, he was going to go over there and let them know what he thought, did she dissuade him from defending her honor. Since Jon was, to his deep inward shame, terrified by the thought of what the three cowboys would do to him if he actually confronted them, he let her kiss him and make him drive on.

They quarreled again in Las Vegas, where Kathy received an offer from a fat man in a white suit who slid into their booth at the Burger King to work as a hostess at his club, with even greater show-business opportunities in the offing. Kathy loved Vegas and wanted to stay a few months and see all the casinos. She lost four dollars in the slots, then won seventeen and was hooked for life. Jon said either they left together or he left alone. Kathy had had her period while they drove through Arizona, and it had begun to dawn on Arenia's pride that for at least one week a month his classmate was not only unendearing but actively poisonous in body and spirit.

They yelled at each other until the motel manager schlepped over in curlers and flip-flops to tell them to shut up or get out. Jon packed, starting to be embarrassed by the skis, gave Kathy one last chance to change her mind, and took off again westward. They never met again.

His arrival and brief stay in Los Angeles were unheralded except by the used-car dealer who treated him like an obvious new star and relieved him of the Saab for $1800 under book value. Jon slept for one night on the grass of the USC campus, then answered an ad in the "Apartments to Share" section to join two other guys who described themselves as communal, humanistic, non-smokers, and actors. They were also as gay as parakeets, and one of them, Sidney, was a casual thief. They conned Jon out of a $500 security deposit, then left him and the apartment one day with two months' rent due, lifted his wallet with $400 in travelers' checks in it, and cleaned out the refrigerator.

Jon got a job in a fast-food place and started looking for singing jobs, using his new name, Johnny Vann. Two years of being hustled, learning to hustle a little himself, and finally selling used cars, brought out in him all the latent ferocity his family and Kathy had never seen. He became, in his last wearable black-and-white jacket, a ruthless, effective salesman of dishonestly described cars. To his chagrin, after he thought he had sunk as low as it was possible to go without sucking human blood, his boss fired him for being too laid back, too unwilling to close for the kill on closable deals.

He briefly got religion at a fundamentalist revival in a concrete amphitheater. For a year he sang in the choir of the Rev. Jim Ace Arbury, traveled in a tour bus with fifteen other young disciples of the Church of Christ Optimist, stayed at every mildewed motel between San Diego and Albuquerque, and when the church went bust found himself stranded in San Ysidro on the Mexican border, where he got another job in a fast-food place, his religious convictions flat on all four corners.

It was just after Jon had handed over three specials and double Cokes to a laughing family of three Hispanics and gone back to slicing onions that a grumpy man carrying two guns and a paper sack of ammunition had entered the restaurant and started hosing fire from the Uzi machine gun on his arm. Shrieking customers and employees had hurled themselves to the floor, taken bullets in their heads and bodies, smashed through the plate-glass windows, and splashed their blood on every white surface. Jon had seen a curtain of sprayed blood in front of his eyes, then hit the floor and crawled, taking a ricochet in the hip as he jammed his way through the back door with two others, one of them holding a bloodied face and screaming wildly. The twenty-one left dead inside, the fifty wounded screaming piteously, the final shootout with the cops that killed the mass killer, and the resultant national coverage of the event got the restaurant closed forever. Jon decided it was time to go back east even before his wound was patched. He chose Nantucket because someone told him it was the easternmost town in America, and used his compensation money to fly there. His nightmares, which he told to no one, were all about the little Mexican girl he had handed a Coke to just before he saw her face explode in blood, the plastic drink cup still in her hand.

Nell was still patiently trying to make her books balance, but she was attentive enough to see that Neil's coffee was gone and that it was still pouring outside. She came across the room and gave him a refill without asking and paused before him.

"What did Liam mean by what he said, Mr. Kelly? Are you really some kind of detective?"

"Far from it. Thanks. It might rain forever, the way it looks." He winked at her, finding it easier to slip in to their familial line of light banter. "You know how dependable Liam's word is for anything."

The mild irony seemed to satisfy her, perhaps not. She shrugged and replaced the earthenware jug of instant coffee on the heater.

"Shall we tell you about *all* of us?" she asked simply. "Would you rather hear the stories of our lives or go out in the wet?"

Neil knew that she had asked the question out of a deeper desire in herself to have him listen than she probably knew. He assured her with the quiet seriousness of his Yes that he would enjoy hearing their stories.

"Now you're in for it," Jon called out from behind the counter, where he was crouched counting boxes. "Have you even met us all?"

Neil raised his voice to answer his invisible questioner. "I don't know. How many of you are there?"

Jon placed his chin on the counter and made his hands dance on either side. "I'm just Liam's piano player. You saw my back if you caught his act. Wendy says it's my good side. Wendy over there and I are—were—are—what are we, Wends?"

Wendy tossed a cushion at his head. "Good friends."

"She's the real artist here," Nell said, "the only one from the original group that's still left. We all came along afterwards."

"If you call weaving an art and not a peasant craft," Jon said, throwing the cushion back at her. Fully in the spirit of Liam's this-is-your-life show-and-tell now, he sat atop the counter pulling his crossed ankles into himself and started taking turns with Nell relating a joked-up biography of Wendy while Liam intoned a voice-over weather report from the doorway.

"This guy I knew, another weaver, who admired Wendy's work but already had a woman of his own, introduced us when I was first waiting table and playing a little piano at the Ocean House. And, as usual, scrounging madly to find a place to live."

"The water's still coming down; the water's still rising. The weather is the world; we are all at sea. Every street in Nantucket is a tributary to mighty Main. Every crossing is a crossing. It's pouring ponds."

"She was looking for a used moped, a subject on which I was, ahem, only the world's leading authority. It ran so well she asked me if I wanted to fill in one of the empty places in this collapsing artists' co-op she was trying to keep going."

"The water table is now above sea level. Somebody send out a dove to look for an olive branch. I wonder if the foetuses are beginning to feel the equilibrium now, and are smiling and flaring their little gills, preparing to rule the world of familiar wet."

Neil sat sipping the bitter, lukewarm coffee, substitute father to them, substitute confessor with no power to absolve them from their history, detective most of his own lost connection with their time.

WENDY

Wendy Foster hadn't wanted to be a nurse when she was a little girl, but her mother prayed she would. Her mother was a cleaning woman at the Wilson-Halliday Hospital in Rodeway, Michigan, an upstate farming town. To her, nurses were professional women, always so clean and well-spoken, not tough like the fresh girls in the kitchen.

Wendy became a practical nurse because when she told her seventh-grade Art teacher, Miss Archibald, on whom she had a terrific crush, that she wanted to be an artist, the spinster had looked carefully at the dark-eyed child, shuddered to the depths of her starved soul, and fallen in love. Here in her class was the child she, Emily Archibald, might have been if everything had been different. She had grown up on a scabrous farm in northern Wisconsin, whipped by a father who was always drunk and forced by her whining mother to go to work at fifteen in the commercial laundry over in Barfield. Emily had not got to teachers' college until she was twenty-seven, and in her first job had been made to teach Social Studies and Sewing until grimly earned seniority and circumstances made it possible for her to teach Art two days a week at each of the elementary schools in Rodewell.

She loved Wendy and she swore to herself that she would teach her everything she would need to be an artist. When Wendy told her best friend, Maureen Macauley, that Miss Archibald was teaching her flower arranging at her house, and had let her take a bath . . . "You better swear, Maureen" . . . "I swear to God, Wendy, I'll never tell" . . . "I'll really kill you if you tell" . . . with bubblebath in it and had sprinkled flower petals in the water, Maureen lost no time in telling her sister Doreen. Doreen Macauley was the counter girl at the Nine-Nine-Nine Bowling Alley and she thought Mick Mullen, who captained Kelsey's bowling team and seemed to like her, would get a laugh out of that. He did. So did his helper on the loading dock at Kelsey's, but the born-again stockroom manager was shocked to his skinny soul and almost ran home from work to tell his Alice. Alice was the bloodless spider in each town's web who waits for the likes of Emily Archibald to try corrupting the children so that things can be set right with a maximum of unpleasantness.

After March 1 the Art teacher who came in twice a week was Mrs. Gonnerson, who had been a temp in Gym before. Miss Archibald moved away. Mrs. Foster got permission for Wendy to skip the second term of Art because it was elective anyway, and take Practical Nursing instead.

Wendy won a trip to the state capital in a supermarket coloring contest when she was nineteen because she had put down her age as thirteen, the upper limit. She was so thin and shy no one challenged her, and in Madison she decided never to go back home. She worked as a nurse's aide, she waitressed, she took extension courses in art, and she thought she was in heaven. When Frank Zambini ended her virginity and introduced her to pot and took her with him to a rock concert in Woodstock, New York, and abandoned her there, she hung on to her remnants of sanity and hitchhiked to Boston. That summer she and a girlfriend went to Nantucket and Wendy knew immediately she had come home. Here in this gray-and-white place with golden Scotch broom and purple beach plum everywhere she swore she'd finally become an artist or drown herself. To her complete joy, she had found others to work with who were equally and unashamedly obsessed.

After they had finished hamming up Wendy's little history, all three of them looked half ashamed, as if realizing together that this man who was proving to be such an unaccountably good listener might just be tolerating their group recital. But Nell saved them from their own embarrassment by asking her straightforward question again. This time she put down her paperwork and said, "Shall I tell you about me?" That was the implicit formula they could each hold center stage with for the time it took to tell their story. If the world had ignored their talents, if their little co-op was struggling just to survive, if the customers weren't coming anymore this season, at least each of them could star in a unique life story now. "Maybe not a continuing daytime drama," as Liam said, "but at least a half-hour special."

Neil knew from long years spent listening to students talk about themselves and their troubles how much the young craved validation, feared being simply canceled out by time.

Nell put her hands over her eyes and rubbed them slowly, half mumbling as she talked. "Me and C.J. just kind of arrived here one at a time. Like this girl Linda I knew told me about Faces, which was down the docks then, and we sort of drifted over."

Her singsong, garbled summary suggested the depths of her difficulty in articulating it. Neil watched the others, who seemed to be rooting for her quietly and gently to get it out.

NELL

Nell Vizer, who had been born Ellen Weiser, made jewelry from shells and stones and fishbones. When she was five, she opened her first shop on an upended box in front of her house in Weymouth, Massachusetts. She and her two sisters lived there with their hapless mother, a skinny woman in a loose, colorless dress with her upper teeth all gone, and sometimes with their father, a bony, feckless man who drove a truck and raised chickens and smiled at his kids a lot without really seeming to notice them.

Nell's first stock was all stones, gathered patiently from the edge of Whitman Pond. She sold just one, a flat red one, to Mrs. Juliano from across the street for two cents.

Her second store was a cold-drink stand, going dibs with her sister Patty on the mix (which was Kool-Aid, but advertised as Ice Cold Orangeade) and the work. The first two days netted them a dollar eleven, since there was a heat wave going on, but for Nell it didn't have the same satisfaction as selling jewelry. She sold her share to her other sister, Sheila, for a dime and nagged her mother into sending her to the day camp at the playground, where high-school kids hired as counselors taught her to make gimp chains and shell jewelry. Neil was not stupid, but she was unimaginative and slow, the balance of traits historically responsible for the rise of capitalism but usually called practical and patient. She went through the grades at an average level, learned with average skill the commercial subjects her sisters had, and dropped her hope of taking Metal Shop when her mother decided it wasn't safe for girls.

Nell's sister Patty had asked her at supper one night, "Watcha taking for slurps, El?"

Nell, with a quick glance at her mother, said, "Metal Shop."

"Oh, no you're not, young lady," her mother snarled, sucking away on a tough piece of meat. "That's not safe for girls."

"Oh, cripes, why not, Ma?"

"Don't cripes me, Miss."

And that was that. A fairly typical evening of family chat at the Weisers'.

Nell went from Weymouth High into a cashier's job at

the Savings and Loan. She was contented, even though nothing like happiness ever came her way. She got herself kissed at a party at Monica's house when she was seventeen, then let the same boy get to second base a month later. Her chest had always embarrassed her when she compared it with Monica's, but the boy seemed dazzled by her generous nipples. When Monica's brother Paul asked her to go to Hyannis with him, she was thrilled. She had always imagined that boys like Paul thought of their sisters' friends as just kids.

Paul, unfortunately, was stupid as well as slow and unimaginative. He showed her a single orange contraceptive with ticklers on the end taken from his pocket, while he was driving along Route 6, waving his eyebrows suggestively at her while he did so. No one had ever explained to Nell how condoms worked, but she knew somehow that what she was looking at was dirty and also represented what the trip to the Cape was all about. She thought about it while they drove through the commercial gash that is Hyannis and decided that she was at least partly responsible for her present predicament and that no one was going to help her out of it. In the dirty talk in Girls bathroom at school and from reading "Ask Beth" in the *Globe* she had developed a repertoire of wisecracks about "doing it," but she had in fact joined in with the same mild exasperation she felt in Speed Shorthand or Typing. Sooner or later everybody had to, so just keep calm and try to get passing marks.

Paul, however, got flustered, couldn't get the orange thing out of its case and on in time. Nell sat in the back seat with him in the parking lot behind the supermarket, pants off, watching with some curiosity as he produced his swollen self and told her not to grab it yet, something she had not the slightest intention of doing until she was made to. He had spent the previous three minutes rolling her

97

cotton pants down her legs and sticking his finger into her, a sensation she decided was halfway between needing to pee and having cramps. Now, in this crisis, Monica's brother cursed terribly and spilled everywhere, blaming her with savage ungallantry for causing the whole mess. They drove back to Weymouth without even playing miniature golf, which is what she had heard Hyannis was famous for, and without exchanging a word. Monica told her later that Paul had told her her friend Nell was as hot as a pistol, a confidence that puzzled Nell in the same way an A in Business Machines would have when she thought she was getting C.

If she hadn't worn the shell earrings she had made into the bank one Monday, and if Mrs. Partridge hadn't asked her where she got them and then asked if Nell would make her a pair—*the* Mrs. Partridge whose husband ran the boat club—Nell might have cashed checks and accepted deposits forever. She made Mrs. Partridge her earrings, for which she daringly charged five dollars. After that she made a shell bracelet for Cynthia Young, and then Mrs. Braun, who ran the boutique, and who had been primed by Mrs. Partridge, asked her in the bank one day if she wouldn't make a few things on consignment for them.

In two years she had a modest reputation in Weymouth, and Jenny Filios, who loved Nell's little stone rings, told her she was crazy not to get a place down the Cape summers and make a fortune.

To Nell the Cape was Hyannis and the parking lot behind the supermarket. When Jenny mentioned Nantucket, where she had gone on a day trip with Randy, who had proposed on the ferry, Nell looked with mild amazement at the map and discovered that there were large islands just off the coast where people apparently lived and sold stuff like handmade jewelry.

"I swear, Nell, I didn't see anything there as good as your stone rings," Jenny had said fervently, "and I made Randy take me to every shop there, no kidding."

That was good enough for Nell. Her father, who had hurt his back lifting a coop full of chickens off the truck, was at home every day now, usually in his underwear. The hardest part was quitting the bank. Mr. Barron had chosen her in the first place over Frannie Small, even though Frannie had better marks in Business Machines. She knew that Frannie also had a terrible case of BO, but life was test scores to Nell and so she was grateful to Mr. Barron for his charity. It took all the spunk she had to take a deep breath and go into the upstairs office and tell him she was leaving. His apparent inability to remember her name made it easier. Within a week she had packed her footlocker decorated with decals and moved to Nantucket by bus and ferry. There, to her chagrin, no one wanted to rent her a cheap room in April. The season was just starting, and rooms that went begging in winter cost fifty dollars a night, even with the bathroom down the hall.

Linda Heller saved her life. Linda Heller, whom she met on Main Street and didn't even recognize. Linda Heller, whom she had hated so badly in seventh grade that she had made a pincushion doll of her and stuck pins in it to kill her, the occasion being that Linda told Monica that Neil said she thought Jackie Warren was cute.

Linda Heller knew a bunch of artists who were in some kind of trouble with the bank people and probably the tax people because none of them could do bookkeeping, so all their records were screwed up. When she heard Nell had actually worked in a bank and could do tax forms—
" . . . Well, you know about them, don't you? . . . Well then . . . "—She badgered her into going over to this

co-op these people had and swapping her bookkeeping skills for a place to sleep.

Nell by the next evening was living on Swain's Wharf in what had been a kite-and-sail shop and had the end of the counter reserved for her own work. The other members of the group, who had never bothered to incorporate but called themselves FACES for some reason she didn't know yet, handed over to her their chaotic financial records as if transferring a sick child or a dicey time bomb. Neil looked at the boxes of disordered papers and then at each of them. Wendy blushed. Liam pulled a wry face that made her smile. Jon refused to notice. Nell suddenly felt motherly toward this nice bunch of silly people.

"Gosh, this will take me a week to straighten out," she said. That had been more than a year before.

They had sighed in unison and silently given thanks. Nell was now their resident accountant and a member of the co-op in good standing. She found out FACES meant Fishlots Arts & Crafts Experimental Studio. Jon told her that the first lots of land on Nantucket were called fishlots because they were paid for with a barrel of codfish a year. Liam told her that she was pronouncing her own name wrong, and that she should say "Vizer" and not "Weezer." He was wrong, as it happened, because the name was once Swedish, but she asked him to letter her a sign that said NELL VIZER: HANDCRAFTED JEWELRY. It made her feel professional when she saw it.

Four months later Nell had a seven-year-old daughter. Caroline Jean Jensen was the daughter of a country-and-western singer, the "Swede" half of Swede 'n Low. Rodney Low was bearded and squashed-looking and played Texas swing like a demon and could sing anything he had heard once. Swede Jensen was six feet tall, thin as a rail, white-blond, with braids to his waist and a ropy mustache to his jawline. He played guitar passably and had a tenor wail that could pierce iron, and he could yodel like a hillbilly born, even though he was from Joliet, Illinois.

Swede's first woman had given birth to Caroline, whom everyone had always called C.J., and then started beating the child regularly until Swede threw the woman out of his van in Vermont one night and simply drove away without her.

C.J. struck most people the first time they met her as a pretty typical brat who used too many adult words and needed a lot of old-fashioned home life to calm her down, but Swede said it was just her age. She and Nell became wary friends, and when Swede 'n Low left for an extended shot at Nashville, Nell found herself mothering full time, book-keeping full time, and making jewelry full time. Sometimes that pissed her off, and other times it made her feel important. Maybe Wendy was right and she was letting her-self be exploited, but some evenings when she and C.J. went swimming at Surfside together or just drank tea and talked about TV, she felt like life had really given her a present.

While Nell was still tucking up the loose ends of her halting narrative, a rugged-looking man came in lugging a faded and battered pine panel four feet across, partially wrapped in old sacking. Ignoring Neil, he tore off the covering and displayed his trophy.

"I've decided to share my brilliant find with you all. Isn't that gorgeous? Look at this lovely thing."

Jon stared at the old sign, which indicated a coaching inn or at least an inn, with stage and horses on it. "This is the immortal Guy Furey. Guy's been antiquing again, Nello."

"I hope you found that, Guy," Nell said sharply. The exasperation in her voice betrayed a long history of im-

101

provident actions by Guy. "We can't exactly afford to get any deeper in debt, and the co-op didn't exactly approve any purchase. I know you practically paid the whole . . . "

"Peace." He held up a calming hand. "I got it for nothing. Well, almost nothing. I'm going to do the Greek's sign for him when he opens his sandwich shop. This was in the cellar under there when he cleaned it out. Hey, I could get fifty dollars for it from any antique dealer in town, but it's worth more. I'll restore it, see . . . "

Liam held out both arms in a gesture of resigned suffering. "Guy should really be working somewhere like Colonial Williamsburg. He's a hopeless romantic. Neil Kelly, Guy."

Neil shook the man's extended, unexpectedly strong hand. No aesthete, Guy.

"It's story time, Guy-Guy," Liam announced through his cupped hands. "Neil has promised to hear all our confessions and grant a general absolution. He's heard all about me and Nello and Wends and Jon, so you're the only subject left."

"Sorry, I'm going to write my autobiography as soon as I get time. You'll have to pay fifteen bucks for it. Unless you're a potential publisher," he added hastily, "in which case I'll start dictating now."

Liam sucked in his cheeks and lisped dramatically, "Guy has suffahed tewwibwy. He wants us to think he has post-Vietnam stress syndrome, but he's really just an old sweetie with an eye out for the fastest buck, aren't you, luv?"

"Someday," Guy answered imperturbably, "the awful psychic consequences of my having been an army payroll clerk in Saigon will stop festering in my depths and I'll break out in hostile attitudes and run amok. You will probably get it first, Irish, because you remind me of my sister Vivian. She was a pain in the ass, too."

102

He talked for a solid five minutes about the many reasons in his tormented life why he wouldn't tell anyone his story, and in the process he told it.

GUY

His father, a bitter veteran, had tried to tell Guy to take off for Canada in 1970 instead of letting them draft him for Vietnam. But Guy, in an ironic reversal of the typical American family story of those years, was as straight as an arrow and patriotic. His father, Jack Furey, had let his wife raise the other two children, both girls, and lavished on Guy the kind of time and attention most men give only to their hobbies.

Guy couldn't understand his father's old bitterness at the army. Hadn't he fought in the best war in history? Hadn't the Japs been trying to enslave half the people in the world, and hadn't the U.S. wiped them out and given all those people back their homes and their freedom?

Guy enlisted in the army the first week he was eligible. Like his father, he eventually achieved the rank of corporal, but, unlike his father, he kept it. And unlike his father, who had won five battle stars, Guy spent the whole war in Saigon as a clerk. There he found what so many boys pay so much to learn—that his father had been right all along. War is a scam and the only glory is gain. He organized a system of forged passes, used the money to buy stuff on the black market to sell upcountry through a connection he had there, and to buy into a Saigon brothel that featured twelve-year-old girls.

He returned from the war with $85,000 in cash and another $212,000 in a Hong Kong bank.

He was twenty-two years old, had his father's open grin and winning homeliness and no illusions at all when he enrolled at Ohio State in 1974. He played a little touch football, a lot of pool, and shacked up with three different girls from Shaker Heights his first year. Shagging Shaker Heights girls became his main concern; he wondered how many of them between seventeen and thirty there were and if he had time to screw all of them before the whole next crop arrived in Columbus.

Stacey Lurie put an end to that. He fell in love with Stacey the first time he saw her perform with the gymnastics team. Actually, it started when he saw her picture in the campus paper, airborne off the vaulting horse, those sweet little legs wide apart, right into Guy's cynical old heart.

Stacey was tiny and flat-chested—she would have been chopped liver in Shaker Heights—but wiry and strong as an animal. He got Jimmy Keefe, who was in her Ed Psych class, to introduce him, and poured on the old charm, the same that had shaken Shaker Heights to its erotic foundations. She turned him down for a date. He wondered if it was because he wore army fatigues and bought regular clothes. She turned him down the next time he asked, too. He wondered if it was the Zapata mustache and shaved. He started attending Ed Psych even though he wasn't signed up and sat right behind her. The instructor, a flaccid twerp who seemed terrified of everyone in the class, looked at him once, got a glare for his trouble, and never looked that way again.

Guy watched Stacey take careful notes of all the horsecock the twerp was dishing out, watched her put her pen and notebook precisely away at the end of each class, watched her walk out. For a week he watched. Finally, in desperation, and ashamed of himself for the first time in years, he got in front of her at the classroom door one day and wouldn't let her or the twenty people behind her out until she spoke to him.

104

"Yes. Yes, by Jesus, I would mind. Why won't you talk to me? I bought this swell jacket. I shaved."

Those behind her listened with increasing interest.

"Would you mind letting me get by?"

"Must I say please? Do you like to make girls say, 'Please, may I get by?' What a hero."

"I'll let you by, I swear. Hey, I'll even walk with you. All I want is some acknowledgment that I exist as a real person with inalienable rights you say good morning and good afternoon to."

She looked up at him. She was an even five feet and that was part of what broke his heart about her. "Very well. I see you. Good morning. Good afternoon. Now get the hell out of my way or I'm going to knee you in the balls and you won't ever forget it."

The crowd behind her cheered lustily.

Guy beamed at them all. "She likes me."

She leaned back over her shoulder to make sure everybody could hear. "I think he's a total asshole."

Guy was radiant. This was attention. "I want to buy a new bus for the gymnastics team."

Her heart was moved.

There had been a story running in the campus paper for a week about the scandal of the gymnastics-team bus. It had broken down five times coming back from the Michigan State meet. The administration was digging in its heels about a new bus because the Trustees were already on their backs about sports-program costs and revenues, and a lot of minor sports were going to have to surrender some scholarships to beef up the football team.

The crowd behind Stacey cheered.

She said, "Are you serious?"

When any girl—she could be from Shaker Heights or the Golan Heights—said, "Are you serious?" to Guy, he was home and dry. He took her arm and they walked away in intimate conversation about buses while the members of Ed Psych 107 applauded and whistled.

He bought the gymnastics team a $90,000 diesel bus with options up the tailpipe. He became instantly famous as the first freshman to endow the University. He discovered almost simultaneously that he did not really love Stacey Lurie, he loved Hilaire-Germain-Edgar Degas.

No one had told him before about French Impressionist painting. After all, most American college students never hear about it. But Stacey, who was born to fly and to instruct others (she would eventually become a fine pre-school teacher), made Guy stop smoking pot and start eating yogurt, made him drop all four of his elective courses and sign up for four new ones, including Modern Art.

Guy sat in the dark auditorium and looked at the slides of paintings he hadn't known existed, and he was stunned. He discovered that the University had its own art gallery and went there to see a traveling show of modern masters. He read in a magazine that there were galleries and museums in New York and Boston where hundreds of these French Impressionist paintings were just hanging on walls for people to come and look at.

The realization dawned on him slowly but with fierce certainty that it was the girls in Degas, the tight-bodied dancers bending to tighten the lace of a ballet slipper, lifting an arm to correct a loose curl, whom he really loved. Stacey had been some kind of pointer, a clue to all this. He kissed her chastely on the cheek one morning outside Ed Psych 207, which was even more unintelligible than 107, and without saying a word left Columbus forever. He was a local legend, he was a lot poorer than when he arrived, but he was richer and educated, too, just what he had gone to college for—even if only in a very preliminary way.

In New York he got himself an apartment on the cockroach-infested Upper West Side, enrolled in NYU as a Fine Arts major, and went to a gallery on East 57th Street he had read about in a magazine.

There he explained to the contemptuous lesbian lady who chewed her cuticle and glared at him from beneath reptilian lids painted green that he was willing to pay $150,000 for a Degas.

His first bite of the reality sandwich was discovering that the reptilian lady sold only abstract expressionist paintings. At the place where they sold Impressionists he got his second helping of reality. Not only would all his money not buy a Degas, he couldn't even get into the serious bidding.

More than a diesel bus. These things cost more than a fully equipped bus with options. He was dizzy with shock and joy. Why had he ever wasted his time moving high-grade heroin out of the golden triangle when there was money like this to be made selling paintings, of all things? Legally.

He was delirious with new knowledge. He bought art books. He took five courses at NYU and one uptown sponsored by the Art Students League. He made a vow to screw only girls who could talk about art intelligently and extended his education to unbelievable new lengths discovering how many New York females met that specification and were also pleased to get laid by an artist.

For Guy had begun to call himself an artist and even to paint. He couldn't draw and he had no color sense, but he decided that the act of painting, no matter what the immediate result, brought him closer to Art, whatever that was, every time he did it.

He had come to Nantucket with Celia O'Donnell in the summer of 1982. Celia had a lush ass and a stepmother with a house in Sconset. They stayed a week, then Celia went back without him. There are mornings around six when webs of fog hang in the trees and the sun burning above the moor blurs the white pink and spins blood red and the purple-green moors appear like a painting being unveiled. Besides, Celia's stepmother was a nymphomaniac. Guy stayed. With half what he'd tried to exchange for a Degas he bought a reasonably habitable shelter in Quidnet, on the far side of the island. Kerosene-heated (despite state laws against it) and uninsulated against the hammering onshore winter winds, it was nevertheless at last his home. It was also to become the unofficial winter living quarters of Faces.

Jonathan and Wendy and Nell had just been evicted from the Swain's Wharf place. They and Liam and Guy all got together the same night at a party in Celia's stepmother's house with a dozen other artists and performers. Guy found out conversationally that Liam was a fair carpenter and the rest were willing to work. In exchange for making the Quidnet house livable and with some loose oral agreements to share expenses out of what each could earn, they organized themselves and moved in.

Another group might not have made it, but the threat to each of them that if they blew this they would have to leave the island was a great incentive to reasonableness.

Guy was so dementedly pleased with being accepted as an artist by these people that he began hand-painting T-shirts and visiting real-estate offices. He came in the door one day after a week of looking with a lease for a year, option to buy, on a huge basement under a guesthouse on the corner of Federal and Broad.

They fell on the space hungrily. If eight hundred square feet could have been divided into equal work spaces, it would have been perfect. But by the time they met code standards for support walls, internal doors, exits, ventilation, and sanitary facilities, the best arrangement they could devise was one big open space in front and storage in back.

Fishlots Arts & Crafts Experimental Studio, selling original jewelry, weavings, handmade recorders, and painted T-shirts, was fully launched. Guy's sign, with cartoon faces of all of them and the single word FACES, was hung out front, and they were in business again.

"There you have us," Liam said. "Are we not a living, breathing, singing, dancing, lying, life-restoring soap opera all by ourselves? 'All My Children,' an American five-act farce."

Jon blew a note on his recorder. "Musical comedy."

"And pat on cue like the villain in the comedy, here comes our own child, beloved of us all, Princess Caroline!" Liam bowed low.

A chubby little girl with stringy blond hair to her shoulders, wearing red shorts and a Snoopy T-shirt, wandered in from the back and tipped up the wicker chair to dump an orange cat onto the floor. She said, "Rotten fucker" to the cat and sat in the chair herself, drawing her bare feet up under her and glaring at Neil.

Everyone but Nell ignored her. Nell took a pencil from between her teeth and spoke to her in that tone only a mother uses. "You sound pretty rotten yourself, young lady. This is Mr. Kelly. This one's C.J. She's mine."

The child, who busied herself picking her knee scab after the first look, said, "What's his first name?"

"What do you care, pest, to you he's Mr. Kelly," Jon said.

"Well, how come he gets to know my name, but I'm supposed to call him *Mr.* Kelly? What am I, catfood?"

Nell rolled her eyes upward and then looked at Neil. "C.J. has these days."

"Besides," C.J. continued relentlessly, ignoring her

109

mother, talking to Neil, "C.J. isn't my name to strangers. It's what only my intimate friends are allowed to call me. My *name*—" she spoke lockjaw—"is Caroline Jean Jensen."

"Oh, yeah?" Neil said. He had raised two daughters and was not fazed.

Her mother spoke to her sharply. "Miss C. J. Jensen, did you eat anything after school?"

"I'm dieting," the child announced loftily. "I'm sick of being a fat pig." No one commented. C.J. was obviously taken for granted in all her dramatic moods and used to being accepted as something between another adult and furniture.

Then Liam solemnly waddled across the room, acting out C.J.'s self-description, cheeks bulging.

C.J. clearly wanted his attention. She yelled at Liam, "Cynthia Johanson had to go to the hospital, you know, Liam."

Nell rolled her eyes up again. "Oh, God, what's she got now?" She added a *sotto voce* comment for Neil's benefit. "Cynthia is also the world's biggest hypochondriac."

"If there's an outbreak of cholera in Bangladesh on the evening news," Jon said sarcastically, "Cynthia will have it in the morning."

"Bad news travels fast, right, C.J.?" Liam said to her with a pally wink. "Careful what you say, this fellow Kelly is a famous detective."

"Well, I'm not lying. I don't just make things up, you know, like some people," the girl said with grubby dignity. She turned her chair backward to them and took a comic book from under the cushion to read. "Not like those movie guys."

"What does your friend Cynthia have?" Neil asked politely.

The child looked over at him as though he were disgusting. "Cynthia Johanson. She likes to be called by her

110

full name, not some nickname. Her father is a Norwegian sea captain whose luxury liner cruises the breathtaking fjords of Scandinavia twelve months a year, often risking collisions with ice floes," she explained calmly.

"I've sailed in those waters," Neil said seriously. "You're right, they are beautiful—breathtaking, as you say. What did you say Cynthia Johanson has?"

Raising daughters, like riding a bicycle no hands, is not a skill one loses for lack of continuity. Neil was sure the child wanted to tell them something and that the group's routine of banter and oblique insult made it difficult for her.

C.J. looked at him over her *Adventures of the Superheroes* with fresh interest. "Poison ivory," she said finally. "It will probally keep her from being the child star of the film."

Neil wasn't about to risk patronizing this moppet by humoring her mispronunciations. "Poison ivy can be a serious business. Probably not, but you never can tell."

"Taxi dendron," C.J. said airily. "I looked it up in the school library. Rahoos Radickens."

Nell said to Wendy, "God, she's in seventh heaven, look at her. She's got someone new to tell all her lies to."

C.J. didn't bat an eye. She was hanging onto Neil's attention like a leech.

"Your Latin isn't quite right," he said. "*Toxicodendron* is the general name in Latin, and you don't try to pronounce the 'h' in Rhus. *Rhus radicans*."

"Roos radicans," she said carefully. "We took a pee in the brush and she used the leaves to wipe her thingy. She may get convulsions and a temp of one-oh-five. I read that in Wendy's medical book. And you're quite right, Neil, poison ivy—" she pronounced it casually, she had never said it wrong—"can be a very serious business. Grown men have died of it."

111

"Cynthia Johanson sounds pretty dumb to me," Wendy told her. "Did *you* get any, C.J.?"

"Of course not," the girl exploded. "Do you think I'm stupid? Boy!"

"I think you're too lippy," Nell said sharply.

Jon barked at her in mock seriousness, "You been practicing on your recorder?"

She made a horrible face at him. "I stink. I don't see the point of practicing, all it does is make me stink worse."

"You're not supposed to practice getting worse, dopey," he said.

"Cynthia Johanson never practices. She just picks up any instrument at all and plays perfectly the first time. Her mother says she has perfect pitch and a God-given talent. I'd rather listen to her, so if you want your old recorder back, take it."

Nell offered a word of explanation out of the side of her mouth to Neil as she started pinning earrings onto a felt board. "Cynthia Johanson is her imaginary friend. She's perfect at everything. So's her mother."

C.J. bristled. "Oh, yeah?" she yelled over her shoulder. "Oh, yeah? Well, it must be great is all I can say to have a mother like that instead of some old weezer who collects shells on the beach like some stupid coof."

"Button your lip," Nell said sunnily.

"Where'd you learn a word life coof?" Wendy asked her.

"I have friends who don't all talk like people from the Great Lakes, you know." She managed to make that a pretty negative epithet. Neil silently congratulated her on her originality, but he was old-fashioned enough to think she also needed a little discipline.

"It means some jerks who are from off-island," she

yelled over her shoulder, volunteering since no one had asked her.

"We know what it means, sweetie," Guy said, popping a scrunched-up ball of paper in her direction. She batted it away angrily.

Nell was losing patience. "Go do some homework. Have you worked on your Social Studies project for school?"

"Of course not, do you think I'm stupid?" The child tossed her magazine on the table and raced out the back door yelling.

"Last week the Johanson kid had cancer of the uterus, no less. C.J. read an article in my *National Enquirer* and it said if your mother put talcum powder on your bum when you were a baby, you could have asbestos fibers up your thingy, as she calls it. Bam, Cynthia Johanson, that little pain in the ass, has asbestos in her uterus. God!"

Wendy said, "You want me to look at her, Nell? If she's got PI on her little wahoozie, it can be painful as hell. Sometimes kids tell the truth, you know."

"You never have to worry about that with C.J. More likely she's been playing with herself and got a rash. I'll check."

Liam returned to his attempt to divine from Neil whether Marjorie had sent any money. When Neil finally realized what he was after, he lost no time assuring him that he had come only to say hello and see Liam with his own eyes so that he could assure everyone back in Kent that all was well.

"Your correspondence, what there's been of it, seems to have conveyed a sense of doom that has your stepmother concerned."

"Ah, sure," the Irishman said through pursed lips, "it's all a lark. If starving and being in debt is ever a lark." He smiled genially.

113

Neil studied the ominously handsome face as the young Irishman chatted and clowned.

The rain had stopped and a bright, hot sun was making everything steam.

C.J. aimed a hard kick at the orange cat, took a running jump over the crates lined up outside the back door, and landed in a puddle with a swear. She had watched the tiny American gymnast take the gold medal at the Olympics on TV in Eddie's shack and had for almost two months planned her own future as a champion gymnast. She had stood on a bench practicing balance. On the beach she had paraded in the stiff-legged victory walk, arms extended above her head, hands spread. She had just *nailed* her vault and every judge had given her a ten, even the Communists. The crowd chanted "U.S.A." over and over, and "Cee Jay, Cee Jay!" She was dewy with sweat, but poised and gracious; she would not wipe it off. She knew that the TV cameras caught her radiant glow and that back home everyone at Faces was marveling at her posture, her sheer athletic grace.

Her Gym teacher had not been impressed with her forged-by-Liam excuse from school Gym class because she was training with a special gymnastics teacher—a Rumanian, as it happened. Nell had given her hell—worse, had laughed at her silly pretensions to an athletic ability her awkwardness wholly contradicted. Liam had taken his bawling out and given her a hug.

Eddie had told her that all those girls got doses of male hormones to make them jump higher, and when she asked him if hormones were like vitamins, he had grinned and told her he'd tell her when she was older—the most hateful answer in the world.

Then he agreed she was probably old enough, and that

week after her sailing lesson on board the *Hi Hattie* he showed her how to get male hormones.

Eddie looked like a door-to-door Mormon missionary— sincere gray eyes and a face so symmetrical, a nose so sweetly snubbed, that many people failed to notice it lacked character completely. Was, in fact, a mask that would never betray his character. He had read a book once about a man who kept a picture of himself in the attic; the picture got old, but the man stayed young and smooth-looking. Eddie liked that. His own picture of himself he kept locked inside himself, a pitiful little boy who still wet his pants when he was eleven and whose only childhood pets had been the bugs he caught and slowly killed in the two-room apartment where he was left every day to wait for his mother to return.

He knew his mother was what people called a good soul, a forever hopeful, wan, religious woman who lost her husband in a mining accident in West Virginia, then fled north to work as a waitress when Eddie was four. She got as far as Gary, Indiana, where she got the sort of job she was willing to take and the rundown apartment where they lived. She spent most evenings at the Pentecostal church where she ran the mimeo machine, turning out the thoughts of Rev. Billy Powell, collating and stapling them for women like herself to hand out door-to-door in the black districts. Billy Powell had faith that God was going to reform the blacks through him, bring them to white Christian values. The river of his rhetoric was as mighty as the Jordan, although no blacks ever came to services.

Eddie ran away at thirteen and led the miserable, battered, useless life of a street hustler and petty criminal until he was sixteen. He had got to New England by a fluke. A trucker out of Cleveland picked him up on a wet, filthy night and gave him ten bucks to ride with him all the way to Boston. He had to take care of the man, but he was used to that. In Boston he wandered around the Combat Zone, got chased by two guys, and ended up on the waterfront, where he slept in some canvas. In the morning he met another wharf rat, Gooly, who was just getting ready to wash down a boat that was going on a harbor cruise with a bunch of gay guys in advertising. They already had five or six kids lined up, but when they saw Eddie he was more than welcome to join.

He went out on boats as often as he could after that, and by the end of the season he could pass for an experienced sailor. He knew about Provincetown by then—"the fag capital of the world," Gooly called it—and the next summer he crewed for a guy who unwisely let Eddie take his boat out alone one August Monday while he was back in New York taking care of business.

Once Eddie had stolen the boat for himself, he promptly left the whole gay scene behind him. He would never know that his recent lover had died in a car crash that week after lying comatose for three days. Or that the man's wife had no idea he had owned a boat in Provincetown. It was just one weekend's work to rename and repaint the eighteen-foot cutter, and since there were approximately a thousand like it along the coast, changing one digit in the number seemed a pretty safe way of avoiding the police.

The *Don Q.* became the *Hi Hattie* and Eddie became straight. In five years he was a good sailor. In six he had settled in Nantucket because it seemed to him the straightest place he had ever been. He set himself up to give sailing lessons to kids and run fishing trips for small parties, but only mixed couples.

The mothers whose kids he taught loved him because he would do so many extras for no fee. He'd pick the kids up in his truck, drive them home after lessons, and even lend a hand on the family's boat, scraping and patching, when they needed it. He was so cheerful and easy-going and so good with boats that everyone trusted him.

C.J. was the seventh child he had abused sexually. Like the others, she believed she was the only one, and she would rather have died than tell anyone.

C.J. loved Eddie because he had taught her to sail and it was what she did better than anything else. Having learned mostly on his own, he recognized a born instinct for sailing when he saw it. C.J. remembered everything he said, thought he was infallible. She checked the boat out every time she boarded, because Eddie had said to. The spreaders, the navigation lights and battery, the rigging screws, warps, and heaving lines had to be ready for use. She learned how to take *Hattie* out of her berth and berth her in stern-to, even in a fair beam wind. She could tack up a channel with a kind of fidgety touch and perform half a dozen other tricky maneuvers Eddie had taught her. She could tie the six basic knots a sailor needs, and would no more use a rolling hitch where a clove hitch was wanted than she would tie a sloppy bowline. She knew and felt it in her bones where it made her sing that running before the wind with the sail out at right angles was a different kettle of fish from reaching across the wind with the sail half in or beating right into it buttoned up tight. Eddie knew that she could feel the tension lines of the boat in her hands, as he first had, and he was happy for her. She was like a new boat herself, always eager, tense to please him.

When he had first beckoned to her to come below into the tiny cabin, she knew it would be some surprise, because Eddie always got bright-eyed when he had a great idea. C.J. had been sailing on the *Hi Hattie* since spring and he had told her the previous week that before they put the boat up for the winter he was going to let her be skipper once and he'd crew to her orders.

She had ducked partway down into the cabin and stopped.

"Hey, I thought you said to come below, I'm sorry . . . "

Eddie was lying naked on the bunk with his thingy in his hand. "I did. You wanna see how they get male hormones or not?"

C.J. felt sick in her stomach. Did she? She half-remembered a dirty joke she had read in Guy's *Playboy* once and hadn't quite understood. It had made her feel funny. She stuck her head back out of the gangway again so she couldn't see him and called back, "Whaddya mean? I better finish up on deck. You said."

"I said come down here, C.J. Hey, buddy, if we're going to be shipmates, you've gotta trust me. Hey, come on. All I can see is your big feet. Cap'n's orders, C.J., are you scared of what you'll see?"

"I'm not scared of anything, stupido!" she yelled down at him.

"You don't even have to come in off the ladder. Just sit there and I'll show you what I promised."

She peered down into the little room hesitantly. Lorna Porvu had said at recess one day that she had seen her brother make his shoot by pulling on it. If Linda Porvu could do it, so could she, but, boy, she wasn't going to move off that ladder for anyone.

She set herself awkwardly on the narrow stairway and peered down at Eddie on the bunk uncertainly. Eddie was over twenty, she knew that, so he was probably plenty experienced.

He was masturbating slowly, a huge grin on his face. "Do you know what this is called, C.J.?"

He called out in the exact same voice he used to quiz her on the parts of the boat. She didn't know now if he meant his thing or what he was doing, so she kept quiet.

118

"Do you ever play with yourself, C.J.?"

She flushed. Nell had been after her about that just last week. "I don't want to watch anymore, okay, Eddie?"

"Sure, C.J. That's okay with me. I was just going to show you the male hormones. They'll be coming out any minute now, but I'm sorry I scared you, honest, and it's okay if you aren't ready to see them yet."

She thought feverishly of those little American gymnasts in their red-white-and-green leotards on TV, hugging their fiercely mustachioed coach when their scores came in. So that was it. A link formed in her mind. *He* gave them his hormones. She knew the Olympics people had said it was illegal, but everyone said they all did it anyway. Sex. She watched Eddie with unblinking dread, rapt, and saw what suddenly happened. She let out a yell and banged her head on the overhead getting out onto the deck.

Fifteen minutes later Eddie was scrubbing woodwork beside her, giving her a familiar nudge with his hip and a wink. Not a word was said. Her heart had stopped hammering, and she felt ashamed of being such a baby. So now she knew about that, and all that male-hormones stuff. She didn't mind when Eddie spontaneously reached over and gave her a quick hug and felt her fanny. He was by far the nicest man, as well as the best skipper, she knew.

The seduction of C.J. by her sailing instructor continued step by step and confidence by confidence, for two months, until he had convinced her that letting the hormones go right up inside into her nervous system was the healthiest thing in the world. Sure it hurt at first, he agreed, but did she remember how much her hands hurt when she first started hauling sail? And her back and legs when they hauled anchor together, even with the winch? He taught the child to perform the work of sex in the same joking, loving, bullying, Big Daddy way he had taught her sailing. He stroked her and told her she was wonderful. He was the one who told her the secret that this movie these guys were making on the island was going to be a porno movie, and he showed her a porno movie magazine he had that showed little kids doing it. He told her that if she ever told anyone all their secrets, Nell or any of her school friends, he would never hug her again and he'd tell all the other skippers to put her on their shit list, which meant no one would let her sail with them.

To crew a whole season on a regular boat was C.J.'s dream of glory and her hope of escaping from everyone at Faces except maybe Liam, who really was funny. She'd rather die than get on every skipper's shit list, because that meant she'd never get away from Nantucket and go to Nashville. She hated Nantucket and loved Nashville with a passion and sharpness that brought the taste of blood to her mouth when she thought about it.

Now all of a sudden Eddie was talking about putting the boat up for the winter and maybe going to live in Florida until next year. She was furious at the betrayal.

"I haven't even taken her out yet. You said I could, you liar bastard. You rotten fucker." She glared at him helplessly through her tears. She hated him and she didn't care if he went away forever, but she loved him, too. No one else had ever been so good to her. Now he was going to leave her on this putrid island while he went to Florida. Right next to Nashville, Tennessee, or near it anyway. She wanted to kill him she hated him so much. He'd be sorry when she got dead this winter from cancer of the uterus.

"Neil Kelly says I probably have cancer of the uterus!" she hollered at him and stuck out her tongue. "And he's a detective from Scotland Yard."

"Hey, none of that imaginary stuff, I told you I don't like all that." Eddie had lived once on a correctional farm for

120

delinquents in Florida and in his nightmares he was back there.

C.J. was glad he was scared. She saw him shiver. "He's not an imaginary guy. He's a real friend of Nell's, and Liam says he's the most famous detective in England, and I showed him my rash and Wendy said . . . " She was crying hysterically, babbling and spitting and coughing.

Eddie went cold, then hot. She had showed somebody that rash of hers. Jesus, and a detective, some boyfriend of Nell's. Eddie wasn't smart, but he wasn't dumb enough to stay around and let them catch him again and stick him in Walpole this time where some big coon would make dog-meat out of him.

"Off." He jerked his thumb toward the dock.

"Oh, yeah?" C.J. knew she had gone too far. He looked really mad.

"Get off my boat and don't come back. You're a little fink bastard. We made a deal and you broke it. No more friends. Off." Even while he was yelling at her, he was looking up the wharf to see who was coming. Except for Dan Molinas painting *Flicka* and a couple of old wharf rats who fished with string there every evening, no one was in sight yet.

C.J. kicked the canvas chair across the little deck and jumped to the dock, still blubbering. "You think I care, you rotten, stinky fucker?" She turned and ran as fast as she could off the wharf and across Whale Street and toward the A&P parking lot. She stopped and squatted behind a high-wheeled Bushwhacker and looked back and watched Eddie cast off and steer the *Hi Hattie* out into the channel. She was madder at herself than ever then, for thinking that maybe he'd yell after her something like "Aw, come on back, C.J., old buddy, I know you were just making your mouth go."

When *Hi Hattie* had made the turn, C.J. edged back

121

down the dock, stretching her neck to see if they were still in sight. She went all the way to the end, past the wooden barrier that says ONLY YACHTSMEN AND THEIR GUESTS. *Hattie* was gone, all right.

Jake Jones was sitting on the flying bridge of the *Lucky Oldsun III* photographing the ragged, dispersed rainclouds in the sunset sky when C.J. came mooching back along.

"Hi," he said, "thinking of buying yourself a boat?"

She looked at him disgustedly, but kept on walking. If he knew how much she loathed and despised those big, clunky power boats, he'd just keep quiet. Five minutes later she was back, pointedly ignoring Jake.

"Find anything you like yet?"

"I wouldn't want one of these junky old things if you paid me!" she yelled up at him. "Besides, you coiled that rope there backwards, stupid." She pointed to a coil on the cockpit deck.

"I'll bet you're one of those old-time sailboat sailors," he called after her, but she was already flying off up the wharf.

The next evening at sunset she was back on patrol, but this time when she saw Jake she looked at him, even if she still had too much pride to wave or speak.

He saluted her British style, palm out, very formal, said, "Evening, my lady. How are you this evening?"

"Fine." She looked everywhere but at his clunky boat.

"*Are* you?"

"Am I what?" She hated sarcastic people and he sounded sarcastic.

"I asked you yesterday and you never answered. Are you one of those sailboat people who think monsters like this are just a pile of junk?"

"I used to sail a lot," she said casually, "but Cynthia

122

Johanson, my best friend, had to give it up, so I did, too. We're going to learn to fly instead."

"You don't say. What did you mean I coiled that rope backwards? I've been looking at it ever since you said that and it looks fine to me."

Boy, some grown men were stupido. "Counterclockwise is backwards."

"I'm left-handed, is that way okay for lefties?"

"Makes no difference. Ropes are twisted clockwise when they're made, so you should always coil them that way. It's just the right way to do it, that's all."

"Sez who?"

Sez Eddie. "Sez anybody who knows anything about sailing."

"Anything else wrong?" With a sweeping gesture he invited her to inspect his premises.

She stood for a moment uncertainly, hands on hips. Then, tempted beyond endurance by the chance to get on the boat, she stepped over off the dock onto the rail and down onto the cockpit deck. She immediately spotted something else to correct. "Sure. That coil should be made up with a buntline hitch, not just hung over a stupid cleat."

"Oh-oh. You are sure hell on ropes. Want to see her bridge? Enough electronic stuff up there to run an aircraft carrier. Do you use radar, or is that against your religion?"

"I don't mind," she said dryly, "but a real sailor should be able to navigate without it. Without no mechanical help," she added emphatically. She scampered up the ladder, but stopped, remembering her main reason for stopping in the first place. The toilets on Straight Wharf were locked after the last ferry left. "Can I use your head?"

"The john?" Jake said with maddening deliberateness. "Sure. Lefthand side there behind the little blue door is the

123

one for the crew. There's another one for the guests inside, but Mr. Olds doesn't like anyone but himself to use that one."

Her look of pure disgust at everything he said in his landlubbery way was a pleasure to see.

"Oh, I know whose boat this old thing is," she said to reassure him. "And—" she paused dramatically before going into the little head—"someone told me what kind of movie—" she drawled the word as sarcastically as she could—"you're making."

"Well, you just have your pee and keep everything else to yourself, then. It's supposed to be a secret."

He leaned over the rail and thought of the kids growing up on this island, probably into boats before they could walk, like Oklahoma kids and horses. All that stuff about knots and tides and chart reading that he had learned in an adult education class in Santa Monica, it made him laugh, these kids knew it before they went to school. He was actually a pretty good power-boat sailor. Before he had got roped into that stupid trip to Israel and gotten their boat wrecked, he had never been to sea, but, against all his expectations, it was probably the only time in his life when he wasn't scared. He had come back determined to learn how to sail properly. If anyone had told Jake that he would be more excited at getting his first pilot's license than by his first Academy Award for best supporting actor in *Kiss of Truth*, he'd have thought they were insane. But that's just how it had been. He had started with the books and worked his way up through small power boats—no sails for him, thank you—had crewed for anyone who'd let him on board, had finally bought himself a little Chris Craft and learned enough so that Billy O. hired him to skipper the *Lucky Oldsun I*.

124

He hadn't told his employer yet, but after this Nantucket project was launched, he was out of it. Jake Jones knew where he wanted to settle, get himself a little twenty-four-footer, and just cruise. Billy O. could try making Nantucket into a soap opera if he wanted to; Jake Jones was going to make it home.

The lippy kid came out of the head scrunching her shorts around right and said grudgingly, "I'm C.J. Jensen."

"I'm Jake Jones. Welcome aboard."

"My friend Cynthia Johanson said she'd meet me down here, but she hasn't shown up yet." She skipped up the ladder to the high bridge and sat herself in the chair, squinting to see how far she could see in the fading light. Pretty far.

Jake just watched her. She looked at the array of sophisticated electronic gear on the console. "Cynthia Johanson's father's ship is propelled by solar energy exclusively."

"Is that so?"

"Yes, the Scandinavians are heavily into solar."

"What do they do when it rains?"

"He switches on his nuclear backup engines, of course."

"Of course. Do you want me to give you a tour of the inside?"

She jumped up from the chair. "No thank you. I don't think I really like big clunkers like this." She was suddenly very anxious to get off and go home. She rabbited down the ladders and jumped from the rail onto the dock while Jake was still standing on the flying bridge. She raced up the dock, hair flying, yelling back over her shoulder, "S'long, Jake!"

The tide was right and there was going to be a moon when Eddie had sailed off. He knew that if they were really after him the Coast Guard wouldn't have that much trouble finding him, but he was at least going to make them work, not sit in Nantucket on his butt.

Damn kid. Rotten little bastards, all of them. He never did have any real friends on this lousy island. Bunch of stuck-up pussies thought they were all better than him. Nell hated him, he knew that. Him and Swede could have been really good buddies, but he knew who had broken that up. And that big psycho Jack Darling he had the jam with who sucker-punched him that night. Jack thought C.J. was the goddam cat's meow, like he was her goddam daddy or something. He'd probably break anybody's spine if he found out they was fooling with her. Every goddam time Eddie went somewhere, somebody had to spoil it for him. Stupid C.J. Kids suck around and suck around, just asking for it, and when you give them what they want, they all turn on you. He hoped she did have cancer right up her little twat, serve her right. Let them try and find him. He saw on the TV news when they grabbed all those teachers at that school in California who were cornholing the kids and this psychiatrist said they were all sick, anybody who did that to kids was sick. Maybe he was sick. If he was, they couldn't stick him in Walpole, any lawyer ought to be able to get him off. He hadn't done anything to her for Chrissakes that she didn't enjoy, the little bitch. Florida, here I come. He leaned down and took a cold Diet Pepsi from the icebox and turned on some country, got a good strong signal. He felt good, let out a happy hoot, and gave a wave to some late fishermen coming back in. Goddam. Yahoo.

7

It wasn't until a week later that C.J.'s infection got complicated by her refusal to take showers and Wendy and Nell got to look at it carefully, and by then her tormentor was far away. It wasn't any poison ivy, the women knew that. Wendy was pretty sure it was a yeast infection, but when they asked C.J. where she got it, all she'd do was blubber and scream that she got it from that dirty pig Cynthia Johanson, who had VD from making porno movies with all those guys from Hollywood. She was at first incoherent, then silent, and to Nell that was the scariest of all.

The doctor gave her tranquillizers to examine her, then they rushed her in a plane over to the Hyannis hospital, and then in an ambulance up to the Children's Hospital in Boston. The infection was readily treatable, but C.J.'s furious withdrawal and occasional outbursts of screaming yielded to none of their techniques. The doctors knew she had been sexually abused, but she refused to help them when they tried to pry information from her.

While C.J. stayed in Boston and a therapist who reminded her scarily of Nell showed her puppets with thingies on them and tried to get her to put them on her own hands and make them talk about what they did, C.J. sat with her hands folded and said nothing.

Nell, stunned, wondered if Swede would blame her and

tried to imagine who would abuse a child so savagely, drive her like that into a corner of herself.

Faces was like a morgue all week. The therapist was finally able to tell Nell and Wendy when they came up to Boston the little she had been able to decode from the girl's hysterical outbursts of swearing and sullen poking at the puppets. Whatever had happened to her, it seemed to be connected with making porno movies on a boat.

The regular drinkers in Cy's all had to keep edging away from Jack Darling. By the time he found out from the gossip around that Nell's little girl had been raped by someone, he announced to Danno and Pork and anyone else listening that he would find that sicko bastard and he'd never live to stand trial. When Danno said that it had to be one of those weirdos from Hollywood, that made a lot of sense. Pork said he saw C.J. running like hell away from that Olds' boat one night yelling like a banshee, and asked the other guys if he should tell the cops that. Jack put a hand on his arm and said, "Don't you say nothing to nobody, Pork. Gimme a chance first, then you can call in the goddam FBI if you want to." That lousy Jew skipper, Jack was sure he needed to be talked to; maybe all of them needed it, including that pretty boy Olds.

Everyone in town was speculating about it one way or another. Nothing like it had ever happened there. No one even thought of Eddie Dallen in connection with it, partly because he wasn't around and someone said he had talked about taking off for Florida a month ago. Besides, Eddie was so good with kids, and no one had ever said a word against him. He would be as mad as everyone else if he knew what someone had done to C.J. Linnie Albani told her mother that Mr. Porson, the elementary-school principal, had touched her in his office, and Mr. Porson was questioned discreetly by the police. He said yes, he had held her by the wrist a moment when she refused to pay attention to him, but that was all. Three other teachers were questioned, but refused to talk about it even with each other. The two old winos who lived together someplace down behind Washington Street and fished together off the dock were watched closely for a while and taken in for questioning, but there was no evidence that they had been fooling around with anyone but each other for years. Even the youth-group minister who among other follies had tried to introduce aerobic dancing to a mothers' group was suspected.

Jack Darling was a big, fierce, glaring man with a haystack of bleached reddish hair. He braced himself in the doorway of Faces as if poised to attack or escape. It was his habitual stance; Jack was ill at ease everywhere and he had the unhappy gift of making everyone around him edgy. As a schoolboy he had been instantly suspected of being up to no good by all his teachers. People moved away from him in bars, away from the aura of simmering violence. The skin on his face seemed raw or boiled, shiny and scarlet. His startling blue eyes seemed without depth, his lashes were invisible and his eyebrows almost so—whitish streaks.

Whether his looks had always been an index to the core of violence in him or whether, more likely, he had simply learned what the world expected from him and how to oblige, he was in fact a troublemaker and a savage, habitual fighting drunk.

"Any a you seen Nellie?"

"She's not here, Jack. Try Apple's," Guy said, looking up from repairing his sneaker lacing.

"She said she'd be here today." He pointed at the floor with a thick, stabbing finger.

Guy did not bother to look at him again. "Tough."

129

Wendy intervened with an almost audible sigh. She knew Guy's fascination with baiting Jack and his skill at it. He teased him like a big dog. "She had to pick up some beads Apple promised her from Boston, Jack. He called her half an hour ago, so she went right over there. She's making you that beaded belt finally, right? So be happy, she's getting it together."

The scarlet face paled—it was what Jack did instead of blushing—and he reached under his shirt and scratched his belly nervously. Wendy knew Jack's great secret, that he was mournfully in love with Nell. Nell knew it, too, of course, because the big, doggish man had been not so subtly following her around town for weeks and had recently begun sending her big, florid Hallmark cards with poems with words like "supernal" and "yesteryear" in them. Once, to Nell's combined hilarity and groaning distress, an inspirational verse by Maltbie D. Babcock, D.D., copied out of some godforsaken book by hand and printed on the back of a poster of a wide-eyed child. The knowledge that she could run him like an obedient puppy did nothing to allay the nervousness Nell felt about his goony attentions. Wendy, who had the real power—being able to understand him without being responsible for him—glorified in gently teasing them both.

It made Jack mad. He felt like taking back the shark's teeth he had given Nell, which she kept on display but didn't even make a necklace or something out of.

"I'll tell her you were here, Jack," Wendy said, winking.

Nell had turned to her friend once and said bitterly, "Okay, Miss Smartass, when he comes around here some Saturday night full of Early Times and hauls out that thing of his and proposes to stick it in yours truly, I just hope you're around to offer yourself as a substitute stickee, because I'll shoot that crazy bugger."

130

"Aw. Nellie, sweetheart—" Wendy knew that no one but Jack Darling called her Nellie—"Bill Donlon told me Jack's isn't any bigger than anybody else's. He says they've taken him in three different times drunk, twice naked after fights, and that he's just your average, ordinary-endowed man."

Nell threw a cushion at her to shut her up. "Just be here, that's all. Maltbie D. Babcock is all yours." From that hour poor Jack was Maltbie to them all.

Liam, who had composed hundreds of variations on the theme from the Archie Bunker show, crooned, "Mister, we could use a man like Maltbie Babcock again . . .'"

Jack lumbered away seething. He knew Guy thought he was stupid and it really burned him off. Some of those people there at Faces maybe ought to have the cops talk to them, some of those fancy-talking sonsofbitches like that Guy and that Irishman, the comedian, and that musician. Jack would bet anyone *he* was a fag wierdo, damn musicians all were. Damn cops ought to talk to themselves, come to that. You were always hearing about cops doing crimes, maybe that fat bastard who'd busted him that time at Cy's and put the knee into his nuts liked to make it with little kids.

With Jack Darling shooed off, they returned to their odd jobs and bickering. Independently each was trying not to notice how long it had been since a real customer had come through the door.

Guy surveyed his wrecked running shoes ruefully. "I paid twenty-four bucks for those on sale. I don't think they'll ever dry out."

"Nature's revenge." Jon smiled falsely at him.

"Don't give me any more of that Nantucket-the-beautiful crap," Guy snapped. "You can carry that damn petition around until your arm falls off, but why don't you ask yourself what it is precisely that you're trying to save?"

131

"I'm trying to save, brother Guy, what we all came here to enjoy. Is that so hard for your primitive, battle-scarred brain to grasp? A beautiful, livable, happy island."

Guy made a rude noise.

"Oh, Guy, you're such a cynic. Jon is only—"

"Stay out of this, Wendybird, or I'll run right over your frail body with iron wheels. Look at my damn shoes and weep."

Nell peeked through the curtained doorway from the storeroom.

"Maltbie the beautiful was here, Nell, but we told him you were out."

"God, thanks." She was wan, only half aware of them.

Wendy asked her if she had eaten aything yet, but Nell didn't answer. They all watched covertly as she picked up a small file and abstractedly began smoothing down a half-finished ring. An unnatural silence hung like fog over the big room that was usually crackling with vulgar talk and work noise.

Wendy could hear her own falsely cheery voice, but someone had to say something. "Did Guy show you the gorgeous plant he scored out in the swamps today, Nell? Show her, Guy. It's really fantastic, wait till you see it, Nello." Wendy encouraged Guy to produce his find with lots of eye action and simultaneously shot Jonathan a venomous glance that told him plainly: *No more talk about endangered species, pal.*

Guy went behind the screen masking his painting bench and lugged out the four-foot-high plant in a wooden tub. It had six-inch pink flowers against dusky olive leaves. "Isn't that spectacular? It's hibiscus. They grow right here on Nantucket. For those of us who don't mind wrecking a perfectly good pair of running shoes wading in bogs to dig 'em up."

132

"It's an endangered species," Jonathan said flatly. "It's against the damn law to dig them up."

"Fuck you. I got it for Nello."

"Anyway, it's not a true hibiscus, it's swamp mallow."

"Jon has appointed himself curator of Nantucket to prevent vandals like me from despoiling it."

Nell stared at the lovely plant, not really seeing it. "It's beautiful, Guy. I didn't know hibiscuses grew around here."

"They won't if enough vandals dig 'em up."

Guy mouthed the familiar epithet silently in Jon's direction. There was another appreciable silence while each of them got busy with something at hand.

Nell said, like someone doing her part to restore normalcy, to avoid avoiding the subject of C.J., "How's the petition drive to stop the movie going, Jonathan?"

Jon eyed her warily. It was almost impossible to say anything about that topic without implying something about C.J.'s—what? Wounds? Injuries? What do you call it when a child is savaged and degraded by some freak?

Guy thought a good old-fashioned screaming argument like the hundred they'd had before might be the best thing to break the awful tension. He let a few sparks fly to see if anyone exploded.

Jon was happy to oblige his instinct to start a quarrel. "This lovely island town . . . our home, I remind you, GI Guy . . ."

"This island town that keeps the whale as its totem? The cutified, frisky whale on all the sweatshirts and belts and umbrellas and jockstraps and God knows what else that it slaughtered for a century to light the parlors of New York mansions and make scent for rich, fat women in Boston?"

"Killing whales in 1840 for fuel oil is not exactly the same as killing them now for whatever the hell it is the

133

Japanese keep doing it for. These people worked like dogs at what was as honest a trade as raising beef cattle or mining coal . . . "

"Ask yourself, Jon. Has any other comparable population ever so tormented itself, so depleted its menfolk and left its women lonely for so long in order to devote its extremest energies to the slaughter of an intelligent, beautiful creature for so little reason?"

"I sure wish Swede would come back," Nell said. " 'Cept he probably wouldn't know what to do either."

The argument died for lack of support. It was Wendy who asked Guy if he had enough money stashed away somewhere to take them all out to dinner. They had all sworn they'd ask no more from Guy after he had financed their space, but this seemed like a good time to make an exception.

"Did I ever tell you people," he said wistfully, "about the time I bought a bus for ninety thousand dollars? Well, by Jesus, it's time you heard about it, and I'll tell you during dinner at Obadiah's. On me. Move your ass or be late to class. We eat gourmet tonight, *mein kinder!* Whale steaks for you, Jon."

Getting spruced up and eating out for a change really did seem to help. Wendy, who shared the south bedroom with Nell, was the only one who could hear her cry into her pillow all night.

About five in the morning, just as the first light was beginning to eat at the edges of the windows, she whispered, "You awake, Wen?"

"Sure." Was she? She tried to be.

"Do you think Liam did it?"

"Liam?" She was now. "No, never."

"He's so weird. And now he's hardly ever around anymore."

"Aw, Nell, you know Liam . . . "

134

"Yeah. I sure wish Swede would come back. Or write or something. I'm not her mother, Wen, not really. He's her father at least. You'd think her father would at least . . . "

What would he?

"Men," Wendy said.

"Yeah, you said it."

8

———

As Neil walked for the second time, reluctantly but doggedly, toward the club where Liam was performing, he worked over in his mind the problem of what to tell Dolly so that she could relay his assurances to Marjorie. He had been writing bland reassurances, but he knew that his words probably were as ambivalent as his feelings.

Liam was not obviously a burnt-out case, but neither could Neil say with conviction that he was a satisfactorily stable young man just temporarily down on his luck. There was enough volatility in the Irishman to make him either a suicide or a sober citizen at any point in the near future, depending on such casual and weighty matters as whether anyone recognized his unique talents and offered to support them or not.

Being a friend is not unlike being a parent or a lover, and being both a friend and lover was something like the act of poetry. Make it new, the best critic had said, meaning make it news. But make it real, too. To match the word to the parent feeling, that was the rub. To say the thing that made it not only new but real. The metaphor the dizzy volunteer reaches for might become the trope of self-incrimination. The careless translation of feeling into the new and real must always pass over the bridge of disconnection in danger. Beneath runs cold drowning and the extinction of friendship; beneath is nothing, what was there before love. Guilt, that gray presence slinking along the edge of visibility, waits for a single slip. A fiery finger for you, old wolf. Men hang themselves choked black every day with the rope that language gave us to climb to glory. I'll see him once more and say what I think, Neil decided.

Liam was on, doing his stand-up comic routine for the late crowd. Someone over in the corner behind the stairs had started a chant for him while a fill-in piano player was tinkling out some Cole Porter, and when he came on for his second appearance, Liam was greeted with the yells of his fans immediately asking for some of his established bits.

"The Neanderthal Tourist!"

"Dr. Scalpéll!"

"Archie Bunker!"

"All right, all right, you idiots," he greeted them, "*I'll* decide what you'll hear, you fools, and anyone who doesn't like it can . . ."

They were well trained. "Can what, Liam?" they chorused.

"Can," he crooned, breaking into maudlin song, "kiss the place me mother used to kiss me when my socks were falling down . . ." He was wearing no makeup tonight except for something dark around his eyes. "I was reading bumper stickers downtown today. Yes, you cry, tell us about them, Liam, love. I like the ones with pictures for the key words. 'I Heart My Schnauzer.' 'I Spade My Cat.' You won't believe this, but I saw one on Main Street today—this Neanderthal tourist in shaggy fur slacks is driving his crude stone vehicle over our crude stone streets . . ." cries of glee and booing . . . "and his vehicle, mind you, is drawn by this monstrous forty-foot-long creature with a sawtooth back. Yes, he had

137

a bumper sticker on his wagon. What did it say, you ask? . . . " They recited the question in chorus. "It said, '*I Club My Brontosaurus.*' "

He grinned evilly at them, pointing wordlessly to this one and that one in the audience, bowing deeply to the table where Billy O. and his entourage sat.

"I want much more noise than that in here. Remember that all art is a guerilla expedition against the chaos of experience and the silence of death." He rattled it off so quickly that most of them thought it was just a one-liner they had missed. "A smart lady said that, not me, so it's all right if you don't applaud, you louts." He reported on the latest doings of a criminal syndicate of priests called the Pater Nostra, then he launched without transition into his doctor bit. "I have a doctor you may know who specializes in unnecessary surgery . . . "

Raucous yells of "Dr. Scalpéll!"

"Dr. Scalpéll, yes. You've been to him, some of you—you over there with the prefrontal lobotomy and your moronic friend with no brain at all.

"It's a great specialty, the fastest-growing field in medicine. Well, are you sure it isn't a good thing? Before you leap to join the good doctor's critics, ask yourself if it mightn't be a very good thing. He has some interesting theories . . . "

"Tell us about his theories, Liam."

"Ah, I see the Neanderthal tourist and his lovely brontosaurus are here with us tonight. If she speaks without permission again, club her . . . As I was saying when prehistoric woman there interrupted me, that's how Freud got started, right? Dr. Scalpéll said to himself one day in his lab-oh-ratory, Why should we take the total of organs we're born with as the right number? Why not experiment? Isn't that what science is for? Here, cut this off, man, and when

138

you heal a bit, we'll see what happens without this long thing over here. Then we'll do a little trimming along here, maybe chop these off. God, look at those ugly things just hanging there. Off. What would anyone want two of those for?" . . . hands them to a man . . . "Can you use these?"

He hummed and hemmed and sawed away in mime, discarding things over his shoulder in the direction of his listeners.

"Are you sure politics isn't an aesthetic activity? What makes you think flowers have sex exactly the way you were taught in school? You think after we go to sleep at night the rho-do-dendrons aren't racketing about, ripping off a few stamens and pistils on their own? Why do we teach our kids in school that the death penalty doesn't cause television?"

There couldn't have been three people in the place who had the slightest idea what he was on about, but he didn't switch them back to the doctor bit until he got some sense they were uneasy.

"Let's stop just cutting off the outside stuff and get down to the important stuff inside everybody," he said gleefully in his crazy-doctor voice. "What's all that gurgling after you eat?" He had his ear against the stomach of a woman sitting near the piano, who screamed with laughter. "How come, you may ask, there's nothing under 'gurgling' in any of the science textbooks? Look, darling, just sit still for a minute, we can get rid of all these stupid connections and . . . God, look at all this red-and-brown stuff you've got in you . . . Doesn't that feel terrible to have that in you? . . . You don't need that . . . We'll just cut all this crap out . . . " He was manhandling the woman, whose husband was convulsed with amusement . . . "and run a nice plastic tube from here to here . . . " he wiped something off his arm and wiped it on her . . . "Would you mind not moving around and giggling while I'm working, please? . . . Your saliva is running down my sleeve . . . Are you absolutely sure menopause isn't a form of communication? There, finished . . . Now all the clothing you really need are a hat and shoes. Big savings . . . year after year, it will add up, you'll see. I'll just have Nurse dispose of all these extra garments you had when you came in . . . Next."

Liam pressed on for another forty minutes, getting wilder, calming down, becoming almost untranslatably literary for a few moments, then segueing into new vulgarities, handing around imaginary mystery substances for the audience to guess at . . . telling them about the time Neanderthal Tourist went swimming at Surfside with his beast only to have some wooden-legged nut come after them in a dory yelling, "I have you at last, Moby Dick," and trying to stick a harpoon in Bronny, and the time Neanderthal Tourist thought he'd go whaling and took off after a real whale with a stone spear yelling, "A dead whale or a stove boat," and ended up steering a GE electric range back into the harbor.

"The kid's not bad, but he could take lessons from John here." Olds spoke into Neil's ear through the cheering and applause for Liam's exit.

Neil had come in too late to get a seat at the bar. While the hostess was still trying to find him an empty seat at any table—an old Ocean House custom—John Finn had come over and insisted he sit with them. The other patrons, more of whom had come to ogle the celebrities than to see the show, now ogled Neil, trying to place the half-familiar figure they had seen around town. God, they had thought he was just some harmless academic, but he was apparently big buddies with the Olds crowd.

"I should have guessed you'd be a comedian, too," Neil said to Finn.

"Comedy, tragedy, songs, dances, recitations of popular

140

old-time favorites, available for baptisms, Bar Mitzvahs, brisses, ship launchings, first nights . . . "

Goldie lit a black cigarette and blew the smoke at Finn. "John, we'd all be grateful if you would fuck off." The real venom in her tone, coming from the smiling madonna mouth, was like a tiny lick of fire. Goldie was no lady.

"Ah, think of it as a plaint of pain only, Goldie, darlin'. Pity the poor, drunken helot and profit from his experience and horrible example."

Olds admonished the little actor as though he were an unruly child. "You're giving the wrong impression by saying that, John. We're not drinking any alcohol at this table, Neil, that's my rule. Goldie and Panda insist on smoking those poisonous Sobranies, but that's as far as I'll let my little family here go in the direction of debauchery. What'll you have to drink, Perrier or ginger ale?"

"Jack Daniel's, neat, water on the side," Neil said to the waiter. "I didn't ask to sit here," he said to the obviously offended star. "You sent your troops to steer me over. If you're an alcoholic, I'm sorry, but maybe you shouldn't hang out in nightclubs. I'll drink what I please."

Panda took a black Sobranie from Goldie's box and eyed him speculatively. "You must think you're some hot shit, Farmer Brown. Do you think *we*—" she gestured around her with the cigarette, accepted a light from Milo—"need you that bad? *Want* you to work for us that bad?"

"I don't think you need me at all. But, yes, I think at least some of you want me, for God knows what ultimate reason, and I think some of you are pissed off that I'm not groveling with gratitude to have all you Hollywood movie mavens crooking your finger, saying, 'Come over here, peasant.' "

"Tonight I am John Furriskey," Finn said impressively.

141

He hadn't been drinking only Perrier, Neil could tell that much. In fact, they all knew that William Olds' injunction against liquor need be observed only ritually. The waiter had ferried a steady stream of gin and water to John Finn all night and charged him for Perrier on the bill, but two-fifty a shot. Neil was simply the only one ordering liquor aloud.

Neil turned to the little man. "Who was it, Mr. Furriskey, sor, called Ezra Pound a drunken helot after reading his early poems?"

John looked at him aslant. "Boys, you are awfully well read for a professor, Kelly. Watch this man," he growled hoarsely to Olds, tugging at his sleeve. "He's too smart to be a teacher—an impostor wrapped in the specious garb of truth." He patted his employer's jacket smooth and produced an eructation of excruciating amplitude, sewery and vile even at some distance.

"Oh, for God's sake, William," Goldie said, fanning the air viciously, "I'm not staying here to smell this old creep all night. You stink, John. I hope all of you wash before coming back to the house. You'll be contaminated from Stinky there." She gathered her things from the table and made a sensational exit, watched by every male in the place and one or two females.

"Boys, she must be having her period with bells on it, that one," her offender said admiringly. He beamed at his companions as if inviting a second opinion of his shrewd diagnosis.

Panda Olds spoke to Neil as though nothing awkward had been said. "I found out you grew up in China, Kelly."

Neil wondered again why he was worth all the research. "That's correct, I did."

Olds mimicked him again, shaking his head in sarcastic amusement. The relief pianist was taking requests. Somebody slipped a dollar into his tips glass and said, "Misty," and he began to play "My Funny Valentine." " 'That's correct, I did.' You kill me, Neil, kill me. I don't know if you sound more like the Duke of Cashmere handing out the prizes at Wimbledon or old Judge Hardy—remember Lewis Stone in the old Andy Hardy series?—fixing a stern eye on Mickey Rooney before he let him take Polly to the prom. Panda's right, you're some kind of an archetype of the shrewd old bastard. You really *should* play a judge."

A woman from another table with a few drinks in her came over for an autograph. The waiter skillfully shunted her away, explaining that Mr. Olds didn't want to be disturbed.

"Well, then, why is he disturbing us with his damn movie?" she barked over the waiter's shoulder at Olds. "I don't want his damn autograph, I want him to sign my petition to block this stupid movie from being made here."

She went back to her table to sarcastic applause and comments from her friends.

"Kelly probably would have signed it," Panda said acidly.

"Kelly, as you call him, daughter of mine," Olds said, giving her shoulder a squeeze, "is coming to work for us and he is going to give this whole project the one ingredient it has lacked till now—class. Class, am I right, Neil?"

Neil had known for a long time that there are certain kinds of pushy people—door-to-door salesmen, Bible students who want to discuss your chances of salvation, politicians needing your vote—against whom normal rudeness is a paper sword. The secret weapon decent people must use against such solid brass chutzpah is a kindly concern directed at some weakness. Such people are all overcompensating for some mortally felt inferiority and are somewhere in their egos quite easy to hurt. And deserve to be.

"Tell me about the terrible scar on your neck," he said

143

suddenly to Olds, leaning to one side the better to see the livid cicatrix. The scar, after all, represented the beginning of the end of Olds' acting career and the death of his wife. It had to be some kind of boundary line in the man.

Olds sipped his drink and fingered the scar casually, apparently not in the least upset by the question. "You mean you haven't read about this famous American benchmark in any of the thousand movie magazines that mourned the end of my acting career?"

"Not to mention Tara's," Panda said sweetly.

"Of course you wouldn't," Olds continued as if he had not been interrupted.

Neil knew when he was being asked to change the subject. He chose not to. "How far down does it actually go?" he asked naïvely.

The first flicker of annoyance clouded Olds' face. "Why the hell does everyone want to know how far down it goes? What if it goes all the way to my frigging big toe? Who cares if it's actually put on with studio makeup as a publicity stunt? I have never been able to fathom the public fascination with what is, after all, a blemish."

"Haven't you?"

"Oh, sure, devilishly handsome star gets his goddam head ripped open and manages to kill his gorgeous wife in the same accident . . . you see, Pamela, I do remember . . . one beauty dead, one ground up into dogmeat, good God, maybe he'll be a beast the rest of his life . . . America holds its breath . . . the medical miracle . . . music, please, something from Handel . . . He Lives! . . . the immortal Billy O. profile is salvaged . . . the smile that launched a thousand orgasms is meticulously scraped off the freeway and pasted back onto the brain that dare not speak its IQ. The miracle of Sinai Hospital . . . he can play the violin again . . . "

144

"I didn't know that." Neil had probed a more sensitive fault line with that remark than with the original question.

Olds was clearly indignant. "You trying to con me? You really didn't know all that? Christ, what do they teach in our colleges these days, John? I thought every American child had to memorize the Olds medical history and be ready for three questions about it on the College Boards. Hey, my accident put the Vietnam War off the front pages for four days once." His voice was actually a little hysterical. "Are there a lot of people who don't know about me, do you think?" It was a naked question, and he caught himself. "No, wait, don't tell me. If there are, I don't want to know. I came ahead of Pete Rose, Howard Cosell, Robert Redford—you name him—in name recognition in all the polls for years . . . ahead of Muhammad Ali, for Christ's sake."

Panda patted his hand. "Never you mind, Billy, we all know it by heart, even if everyone else forgets."

"No shit, Johnny Carson and I tied. And he was on the tube every night."

Pathetic celebrity man. Terrified of being unknown, unfamous. He kept talking insistently to Neil. "Someone put you up to that, told you you could get me pissed off that way. I'm right, right? Who you been talking to? Jake? Not my Panda, I hope. Goldie wouldn't tell him a thing like that, would she, Milo?"

Milo shrugged, continued to say nothing as he listened to the piano with his eyes half closed.

"You're one of these people that people tell things to, aren't you, Neil? Should have been a psychiatrist or a bartender. It's the Judge Hardy thing again . . . interesting . . . You're an interesting guy, Neil. Please, get yourself an agent and let me hire you at some goddam inflated salary and even if you never write a line we film, we'll have good times

145

talking. You can teach me . . . He'd like that, Pan, wouldn't he? . . . Can't you just see him smiling like a shark and giving me lessons in nasty? Hey, you can always write the Ben Jonson story or whatever it is. That's waited what, four hundred years—is a little more delay going to matter? Hey, Milo, wake up. You're not paid just to make movies, you know, you have to listen to me, too . . . I've got a great title for a film . . . *The Ben Jonson Story* . . . Like it? We put this Jonson in blackface, see. He sings. Ben Jonson sings!" Olds got down on one knee next to their table and extended his arms wide and sang "Drink to Me Only with Thine Eyes" as if it were "Mammy." "Get it? Hey, just having fun with the serious there, Neil. You grew up in China? Jesus, that's wonderful."

He was rolling now. Some people really can get drunk on the adrenaline generated by their own ego trips and fears. Olds pulled sweat from his nose with his fingers, kept improvising. "These Nantucket sea captains all sailed to China, am I right?"

"Actually, no. The Pacific islands, yes, but rarely to China. You're probably thinking of the Salem traders."

"Fuck it. We'll have a branch of our family from the bank . . . the Coffins or the Starbucks . . . don't you love those goddam names? . . . live in Salem and sail to China. We'll do a whole parallel story takes place there . . . all Chinese actors. God, those Commies would love to get their hands on that much U.S. currency. Our hero . . . hey, we'll call him Neil Kelly if you want, how's that for a sweetener? . . . has one family, household, you know, seven, eight kids, here and one in China . . . this little golden concubine there. She dreams of going to America, where this Kelly, she thinks, is some kind of king or warlord . . . His wife in Salem meanwhile is always nagging him to take her to China, where she thinks he is dying of loneliness for her while he's

146

away . . . We'll have his oldest boy ship out as first mate or some goddam thing . . . cabin boy . . . fall in love with the concubine . . . Oedipal stuff, you telling me that's not good drama? Read Freud . . . They've got two hundred million TV sets in mainland China now, we can crack that market and triple it, quadruple it . . . "

He stopped in mid-sentence. His energy seemed to wane completely. He turned away from Neil without another word and spoke gently to his daughter. "Am I making a total ass of myself, Panda? Are you getting ashamed of your old Dad?"

"You sound like some broken-down bit player teaching an extension course in screen acting at Hollywood High night school," she said flatly.

"Do you want to know the magic key, Professor Kelly?" John Finn asked easily, taking the focus away from the brittle connection between father and daughter. The waiter cleared the empty glasses and set refills all around.

"The magic key—to entertainment, mind you, that is what business we're in—the magic key to entertainment is imagination. That's what locks in the public's attention. I deal in it, and so does my maker here, all of us. We imagine and create for the omadhauns—" he indicated the rest of the club with a gesture of his head—"what they never could imagine for themselves. It's as William the Blake said, isn't it? 'To see the world in a grain of sand.'" He fished in his pocket and handed Neil a pebble from the beach.

"Isn't it a much greater feat, John," Neil said, holding the tiny stone between his fingers, "to see the grain of sand in the grain of sand, the stone in the stone?"

"Ah, you're talking about science or something," Olds interrupted. "John's talking about art. Small a, mind you, small r, small t."

"No imagination so quick, I think," Neil said, holding

the tiny stone flat on his extended palm, "that the plain view can't hoodwink it in a second. There's plenty out there, but doesn't our eye learn early on not to try to endure it all, so we choose to see little, the part we can manage? Then self-appointed seers like you Hollywood people come around and say, 'Rely on us, we'll tell you what's worth seeing.' And confused people—the poor idiots—get frightened into hiring you to sort out reality for them, confront it, get it down to some gritty common denominator real in its own pathetic way, but essentially worthless."

"He thinks we're selling sand, Pammy."

"I think you're selling sand and telling your customers it's gold dust, Olds."

Panda dumped ashes from her Sobranie into Neil's hand, which was still extended with the pebble in it. "If they think it's gold dust and it gives them the same pleasure gold dust would, who's getting hurt?"

Neil blew the ash off his hand. Unfortunately, it went all over Panda. "The truth is getting distorted, and if the truth is good for us, everybody is getting hurt. And you, Miss Olds, can't know what pleasure real gold would give them because you've never offered them that, only the illusion. There is a Sufi proverb: *There must be real gold or else there would be no counterfeiters.* The difference between a William Olds epic and Ben Jonson is the difference between real sand and real gold. That is why I prefer to work for him and not for you."

"Except for Doris Day, you're the first adult virgin I ever met, Kelly," she said sweetly.

"You'll keep thinking about it, though, won't you, Neil?" Olds asked him.

"Thinking about things is what I do for a living. I can't really help myself."

148

"Milo—" Olds gave his cameraman another nudge with his foot—"we better scamper. Where's Jake? I told him to be here with the car by eleven, it's way after."

"Isn't this week Yom Kippur, Bill? Maybe he's mourning for his sins someplace."

Olds glowered at him. "Tell him he'll mourn for his ass if he doesn't get over here with the car."

Milo slid out of his chair, raising a hand to fend off his boss's wrath. "I'll call the boat. He probably fell asleep."

"God, did you know the cops were all over my boat, questioning Jake about that kid, the one who got mauled by some pervert? Poor old Jakie, my Yiddisher sailor, solid citizen, Mr. Bonds-for-Israel Middle-class Jewish Morality. My father should have been as straight as Jake is. Get this, some schmuck of a town cop told Jake this kid said we were making porno chicken flicks on the boat. Jake told him to get lost, get a warrant, whatever. Some kid . . . " He sighed, a man beleaguered.

He signed the bill in his inimitable scrawl, handed the waiter a ten with a wink, and looked at Neil speculatively.

"Okay, let's agree for now you don't give a damn about the historical angle here. But I can read, you know, and I read the R-and-D report on you; you're a pretty well-known detective."

"I'm no more a detective than you are a yachtsman. I've been close to some sad events involving crime and the police. I suspect that most Americans have by the time they're my age; it's a violent country. Once or twice I was able to suggest something that *might*—get that, for the record, *might*—have contributed to a quicker understanding of the matter. That's all she wrote."

"Beautiful." Olds nudged his daughter, raised an expressive eyebrow at John Finn. "In other words, you've

149

solved half a dozen mysteries that the cops haven't been able to. Am I making that up? You've been in the papers more than some movie stars, for Christ's sake. FBI, CIA? . . . Scotland Yard in England? . . . Half the police departments from here to Santa Fe . . . "

Neil listened to the piano and said nothing. There is much of the past that any prudent man chooses to let fade away with its pain. The relief pianist was obviously drunk.

"So here's my final proposition." Olds was undeterred by any sense of tact. He was sure he had the hook in now. "We've got a crime here—not a big crime, a little bank robbery—but we want to use it as a cornerstone to establish the series. Bank robbery, bang. Town splits into factions, family against family, lovers and brothers and God knows what at each other's throats—like a little civil war right here in Nantucket. Now, that's all dandy, but research has come up with an angle, and, frankly, I like it. A nice little mystery we can milk here. Are you listening? Hello, Kelly . . . are you still with us or did you die and go to Irish heaven? Did you ever hear the definition of Irish heaven? The Protestant prohibitionists' hell." He waved a hand in front of Neil's eyes.

"I was listening to the music. Did you say something?"

"Good, because that was all prologue. Shakespeare. Here's the punch line. They never found the loot. Those bozos kept coming back here after the heist, didn't they? How about this? . . . They buried the gold here, on the island . . . too heavy to carry . . . God knows how much . . . maybe more than the owners ever let on . . . What if the last British ship carrying all their money out of Boston before they surrendered in the war sank right around here . . . hold it, hold it . . . and what if all that was found and stashed in that vault? That wasn't any nickel-and-dime caper, Neilo,

150

that was the heist of the century. And it's still here somewhere.

Neil yawned. "I'm glad someone asked him to play Fats Waller."

"Aw, c'mon, Kell, you're not that *blasé*. Or, as my daughter's funky friends say, 'blaze' . . . you're not that blaze . . . big mystery like that . . . ?"

"You're talking nonsense and you know it. This is all something concocted in your studio think tank. You're trying to hype an idea you don't really believe in."

"Would you believe proof? Not believe in it? My heart and my soul I put into something I don't believe in? Proof? How about we dig up some old coins? . . . Where's that list we had, Panda, of the coins . . . ? Anyway, how about some *Spanish pistoles*? Thousands of French crowns . . . "

"That's called 'salting the mine,' Olds, and it might lure a few yokels, but it won't lure me."

"You think this is a set-up? He thinks this is a set-up!" he said with grotesque amazement to Panda.

"By George, Bill, I think you've got it. I think he really does," she drawled sarcastically.

"This isn't *Masquerade*, you know, where the Englishman buried the golden bunny and wrote all the clues in a book. Well—" he grinned his aw-shucks grin—"maybe he did give me an idea. But listen to this twist . . . *we* discover the treasure, in the course of our shooting . . . *we leave it there* . . . say a million dollars in old coins . . . then bit by bit, on the program, we reveal the clues . . . takes maybe four, five years to get them all. Like it?"

"I hate it," Neil said flatly. "You all live in such a bullshit and cheapshot world that you are contemptuous of everyone else. No, I don't want to be jerked around and made an accomplice by rich idiots playing rich-idiot games.

151

My time is valuable. My scholarship, my skills, my ingenuity —whatever it is you imagine you can hire—none of it is for sale or rent."

Milo came back to interrupt his speech just as he was really getting mad.

"I woke Goldie up, boy, is she pissed. She says Jake's not at the house, she says she even looked outside. Boat phone's out again. Maybe he'll be along eventually."

"I don't pay him to be along eventually. I want him here now."

"For Christ's sake, Bill," Panda said, grabbing her shoulder bag from under her chair, "I'll take you back. Let Milo and John jog or get a cab or whatever they feel like."

"Okay, love, but that little sports car of yours is not my ass's idea of heaven . . . Hey, Neil, did you ever hear the definition of assholes' heaven? Queers' hell . . . You're supposed to say, 'No shit?' Then I say, 'That, too.'"

Neil stayed while the beautiful people left. There was a riff on the piano, the theme from *Remember Love*. The Billy O. million-dollar smile flashed, there was scattered applause and one wet Bronx cheer from the far corner. Ah, fame.

9

The police arrived in force at Olds' rented mansion on Cliff Road above Jetties Beach early Saturday morning. A State Police captain, a lieutenant from the DA's office, and two cops from Nantucket, a lieutenant and a sergeant. Olds' attorney had flown in on the a.m. commuter plane from New York.

The Billy O. of charming legend greeted them and asked them into the massive white-and-blue living room, its wicker furniture set so that every seat faced the sea. With the northwest wind clearing the storm out, the Sound was brilliant blue, racing whitecaps everywhere. The incoming eleven-fifteen ferry ran like a white-and-red toy toward Brant Point light.

Their world-famous host was all affability. No, gentlemen, he hadn't the least intention of impeding their investigation. Yes, he understood fully the gravity of the allegations, even if they came unsubstantiated from a hysterical child. Of course they could—and *should*, he insisted on it—search the boat and the house. He gestured broadly, vaguely, as if to say: Send divers down to my beach if you wish . . . anything at all.

When the police, who kept deferring to each other and to Olds in their evident zeal to be fair, got themselves organized to leave an hour later, after a courtesy tour of the twenty-four-room house, the basement and outbuildings, Milo nervously accompanied them down to South Wharf to search the boat again. They had a theft to investigate there anyway, the town cops said; someone had reported an outboard missing.

Billy O. told them—just frowning attractively, the concerned employer—that as a matter of fact he hadn't seen his skipper, Jones, since yesterday. He suggested they'd probably find him on the boat, sleeping . . . he was a fanatic about the boat . . . sure . . . Milo had better take the extra set of keys, just in case . . . no problem . . . *nema problema* . . . Go easy on Milo, though, he went for a moonlight swim in the surf last night and it knocked the crap out of him . . . "I told you, this ain't Malibu, Sidney . . . " They all got a laugh out of that.

The lieutenant from the District Attorney's office, sotto voce, told Billy O. that his wife had made him promise to get an autograph . . . you know . . . He mumbled with embarrassment, alone in the big hall with the star, but Olds gave him a wink. Hey, he understood completely . . . slipped into the study and signed a picture, put it into a manila envelope for him. "Give her a big kiss from me, Lieutenant . . . "

The seven cars and three recording trucks waiting outside for the police to leave all belonged to reporters. A cameraman was set up on the lawn filming as they all shook hands on the porch and two others frantically ran for positions with hand-held cameras as they filed out between the manicured flower borders.

Olds hailed them like long-lost friends. If it was merely a chore to charm the cops and turn their questions aside, it was pure pleasure to butter up reporters, especially since a quick survey had confirmed his guess that the media would send their arts-and-entertainment people, not their crime reporters, for this.

154

He led them over the crushed-clamshell walks around to the back patio. Give them a taste of Neil Kelly–type hospitality, al fresco . . . let the poor bastards stand in that northwest wind for a while and they'd get to the point faster.

"No, no, of course not, Peter . . . no substance to it at all. God, I would have thought that would go without saying to someone from a sophisticated magazine. Hey, Alan, I thought the *Globe* was a family newspaper, what kind of a *National Enquirer* question is that? Annie, good to see you . . . my favorite interviewer, ask me anything. Sure, I'll stand over here with the Sound behind me . . . is the light okay this way . . . ?"

They jostled good-naturedly and recorded the brilliant moment, the smiling superstar, for waiting readers and listeners.

Olds' legal counsel, who also represented an indicted state senator these days, remarked to himself on the similarities between the two men and their styles. The senator had taken some very large kickbacks on a state construction project in his district, unfortunately from an undercover FBI agent. The attorney watched Billy O. and wondered what *he* had actually done.

They were halfheartedly taking end-of-season inventory and competing to recall most accurately the smell of the studio they had first shared on Swain's Wharf.

"Pot and urine," Guy said flatly. "Who could forget? I remember how relieved I was when I heard you all had just been evicted when I arrived."

"Jonathan's dog, Mandrake, and urine," Wendy said. "Both left at the same time unless I'm mistaken."

"You've forgotten that Persian restaurant with the huge vent fan on the corner, never mind old Mandrake," Jonathan told her. "Burnt lamb and urine."

155

Nell thought a moment before answering. "Wendy's patchouli and urine."

Wendy sniffed. "Why do you think I wore the patchouli? Maybe it was just urine and urine."

Guy took a deep breath and broached the subject of finances. It took some accident of humor these days to loosen everyone up enough to talk about much of anything in front of poor Nell.

"I know it's a dirty word, folks, but it's something you need to get through the long Nantucket winter. What about our profits on the season?"

"Ah, Christ, Guy . . . " Jon began, then subsided.

"We all agreed to have a meeting in early October to talk about possibilities. Okay, *kinder*, the season ends technically on Columbus Day, the middle of this goddam month. Are we viable or not? Did we break even or take a bath or make a fantastic profit or what?"

Jon looked up from his tinkering with a squeaky recorder long enough to speak again. "Do we have to have a town meeting, Guy? We don't need Roberts' Rules of Order just to discuss the business, do we?"

"Jon," Wendy snapped at him, "that's not exactly fair. All Guy's saying is we need a business meeting. Are we a business or not?"

"My deepest apologies, Your Highness. I guess I thought we were just one big, happy conspiracy against the enemies of art."

"Nell," Wendy said encouragingly, "you keep the books. Could you give us a sort of state-of-the-studio report?"

Everybody waited a full beat. Nell finally said, "Gosh. Shit, I don't know."

Guy was gentle but persistent. He had started this for a reason. "That won't do it, Nello. I mean, as our accountant, you can't very well tell the bank, 'Shit, we don't know' when they come around to check their collateral. The IRS won't think that's too hot an answer either. We're all with you on this whole terrible business with C.J., Nell, but I think we all need to concentrate on this other thing for a while."

"Listen to our international dope smuggler worrying about penalties on his income taxes." Jon played a swift obbligato on the recorder he was repairing, hit a clinker. "Damn."

"If I'm not mistaken, Jonno," Guy reminded him, "my Moby Dick dolls kept us in the black this summer. Your wind-instrument hospital sure didn't."

Nell joined the argument as if she were coming back to consciousness after sleep. "Guy's not exaggerating, Jon. God, if he hadn't invented that doll, we might have folded in August. My jewelry inventory is way up, never mind my famous thirty-percent-off sale. Wendy's flowers under glass helped, but not that much." She made a mournful face as the tears started to brim again. "Hey, I'm okay, everyone, really. I was just thinking, if Guy hadn't come up with the money for C.J.'s hospitalization, where would she be?"

"No one will hear me mention the three-eighty a week coming in from my job at the Ocean House—and while you're doing sums, Liam's nine hundred that he kicked in . . . "

"Where is that black Irishman, anyway? He missed his turn at the register." Guy looked under the straw rug.

"Typical us," Wendy said with a laugh, "we're having a meeting, but no one's taking notes."

"Which means we're having a really swell heart-to-heart talk," Guy complained disgustedly, "but we still don't know if we are going to be able to continue." His voice was rising as he stood up and spread his arms histrionically. "Am I going to have to sell my sensational Moby Dick doll to this gigantic toy-store chain that wants to buy it in order to pay off the mortgage and untie us all from the railroad tracks before the Toonerville Trolley runs us over?"

They all came to life, cheering and clamoring for details. It was true, and what Guy had been trying to get them around to. He was reluctantly beginning to believe nature had made him a successful businessman, and not that great an artist. He had invented a foot-long fabric whale doll with a zipper mouth. When unzipped, the whale could be made to disgorge a fabric Captain Ahab, thereby shifting the pebble filling so that in the end you could stuff Moby Dick inside Ahab and zip up the captain's mouth, which had stitched across it: I'VE GOT YOU NOW, MOBY DICK.

Wendy had been his partner on the doll, suggesting the final expression they chose for Ahab's face and actually stitching the first few samples herself. He had phased out his line of T-shirts and got a jobber to sew one hundred dolls, which they sold for thirty dollars apiece. Then in late September a buyer from Boston had seen the doll and talked to Guy about buying the item outright. Guy waved the letter he had received above his head gleefully. An order for four thousand dolls and a possible deal for outright sale plus a percentage.

They pummeled his back and kissed the toy and threw it at each other and laughed at their worries. They solemnly argued royalties vs. supplying the dolls themselves. They hadn't any idea what they were talking about, but they were delirious to have some unequivocally good news to kick around.

"Listen, can we do Captain Hook and the alligator?"

"How about Captain Cook and the cannibal?"

"Captain Bligh and the whole crew of the *Bounty*!"

"Queequeg and the quahog! What are we talking about?"

"Liam, my man! Where the hell have you been?" They greeted their missing colleague with rebel yells.

"In jail, actually. Spelled g-a-o-l, actually. What are we celebrating?"

They told him in terms half ribald, half economic.

"Marvelous. What's to eat? I'm starved."

They broke out the Stroh's and Ritz crackers. Liam explained that he had spent the night in the old jail on a bet. The original Nantucket jail, spelled g-a-o-l on the sign outside, is a tourist stop on Vestal Street, and almost any time of day you can see people in Bermuda shorts having their pictures taken in the stocks or peering out through the barred windows of the old log structure.

"Ah, Liam," Wendy said, shaking her head, "with you I never know what to believe." She added with no real bitterness, "You missed your turn, you know."

"Those prison clothes you're wearing?" Jon asked him. "I don't think I've ever seen you before in green running shorts and a Georgia Tech sweatshirt."

Liam held the sweatshirt away from his body as if trying to read it upside down. "Trifling problem with my own clothing involving large quantities of bilious puke. Found these hanging on a line in the backyard next to the gaol. Bit easy to identify if the peelers come round, aren't they?" He peeled off both garments, which were all that he was wearing, and threw them at Guy. "Now," he said, nonchalantly standing there naked, "who has something trendy I can wear until I get back to the house?"

It was well they enjoyed their impromptu party. It was to be the last; the co-op was already inexorably unraveling.

10

"Do you know the expression 'crossing the bar on a camel'?"

"Anyone who knows Nantucket history does."

"There you go again. That's my point. *I* didn't know it . . . it sounds like some damn party game, or one of those Hindu sexual positions in the *Kama Sutra* . . ."

Olds was back on Neil's deck. For the last half-hour he had been selling, selling, probing, and selling, trying to get Neil to evince the slightest interest in his TV soap opera.

" . . . against all the odds, for God's sake. Here you have, what—the greatest whaling port in the world at the time, and when the whaling ships get home with a full load of oil, they find they can't get into the harbor because there's a goddam sandbar out there that makes it too shallow for them . . ."

Neil had been courted before. By people who needed him, by people who were just curious about him, and by some who had admired, even loved him. But, for the life of him, he couldn't fathom Olds' fascination with hiring him. Was it just that this spoiled brat of an adult couldn't bear not to get his own way, so that every denial of his least wish instantly became his most passionate desire? Infantile, but not that uncommon even among that majority of the population who had never been idolized, adored, and cosseted.

Olds wouldn't stop talking—couldn't, Neil realized. He was driven by his compulsion to get an agreement from Neil to something—perhaps to anything—just so that his ego could stop hurting. " . . . so they have to invent this—thing—to lift the ships over the bar . . . " He hooted at the absurdity.

" . . . Well okay, let's say for now that you're not thrilled with the historical angle. But, Christ, Neil, you should be. What a consultant you'd make, keep me from making some gigantic boo-boo that would have the critics licking their lips with glee." He fluted in the girlish tones of a self-satisfied TV reviewer: "William Olds' new TV soap epic, 'Nantucket,' had a real howler in its opening episode this week. Olds, who should have done his homework better, had an actual camel carrying the whaling ships into the island harbor. Even my twelve-year-old daughter laughed. *She* knows what 'crossing the bar on a camel' means, and so should you, Billy O."

Neil wanted with one part of him to throw the handsome superstar off his deck and go back to work, but winced inwardly, because he knew that was the rub. All this nonsense of Olds and Panda and their projected soap opera was a convenient distraction. He didn't want to face Ben Jonson just now. Old Ben on more than one noted occasion in his boozy career had failed to show up for a scheduled appearance and he was doing it now to Neil.

" . . . It was Panda's idea, really. Right through the opening credits, run a film of the car ferry there unloading, people coming back here from Yarmouth or wherever the hell they go in the morning, six o'clock at night, just like the commuters getting off the New Haven Railroad at Greenwich. Car comes slowly down that big metal gangplank, we zoom in on the bumper sticker: IT USED TO BE NICE IN NANTUCKET. Have you seen those on all the townies' pickups? Beautiful. The paranoid hostility of this place in a nutshell. Then we fade fast . . . " As Olds droned on, acting out his tireless sales pitch, Neil let his mind wander over his own concerns.

He couldn't even finish the letter to D without losing his composure and making an ass of himself over this Humbles. As for Liam, Neil had been asked to reassure his stepmother, but what was he supposed to say? He had talked with the mad young Irishman twice now, but had only discovered that conversations with him were likely to segue into comic routines without any clear punctuation. Liam had clearly been in a black Irish rage after the discovery of C.J.'s rape, cursing and biting off his words in pain. He had sworn he'd personally find who had done it and kill him, then take off for South Africa or somewhere, and now Neil had heard from Nell that he had missed his turn minding the store at Faces and no one there knew where he had gone.

" . . . and you're probably curious about that, am I right?"

Neil, who hadn't heard a word for several minutes, nodded absently.

Olds laughed, undismayed. "Sure, you're fascinated, I can tell. Jesus, Kelly, you must be aware that you are the only one—the *only* one on this island who isn't waiting for me to ask them to dance, no matter what their petitions might say." He waved away any random dissidents, convinced they would switch the moment he made them an offer of fifteen minutes' fame. "You, I don't even get invited into your house." He turned and posed toward the street. "I'm beginning to feel like a tourist attraction sitting here on your front stoop posing for pictures every time that tourist bus goes by. Are you sure you're not getting a percentage from the bus company? Just kidding, although that's what I'd do in your place. What the hell? You have to be asking yourself, am I right, why does this guy Olds keep hanging on? I don't usually have to work this hard to get a date, you know. I hit on someone, I say something suave like 'What sign were you born under?' or 'Do you come here often?' and, zippo, I score. But you. This is like one-on-one with Moses Malone. I dribble, you take it away. I shoot, you stuff it back down my throat. I fake and you just wait for my drive. What's the score now, about eighteen to nothing, Kelly?"

Neil indicated the house with a look. "In there I work. In there I wait for Ben Jonson to show up and ask me my sign so that I can ask him, 'Do you plan to come here often?' I am at least as good at my profession as you are at yours, Olds, and since I obviously think mine superior to yours, simply worth more—do I make that clear?—I prefer to work at mine, not yours. If you would just go away and not come back. I'm certainly not keeping score so that I can brag back home that the great Billy O. hit on me—is that the expression? I don't get to singles bars much—twelve times or eighteen times without scoring." He was rather pleased with himself for that summary, even though he knew that Olds' importuning visits were his alibi for not getting any writing done.

Olds leaned against the low fence and watched his own forearms muscle up as he stretched against it. He vaulted it easily, then vaulted back, held the rail like a ballet barre and did three deep knee bends. Narcissus at play, wholly unselfconscious about checking his vitality in front of a witness. Was Neil supposed to applaud?

"Do you really think those clowns who watch TV eleven hours a night *want* literary quality in their programs? No, don't answer that," he said disgustedly, sitting down on the edge of the fence. "Let me rephrase that. Do you think they will even *tolerate*—tolerate?—quality? They're the problem, the nerd herd I'm trying to address. They resent quality; that's why it's up to people like you and I in our separate spheres. And ideally together." He smiled the blazing white

163

smile. "If we could do this thing just right . . . hit it right on the button . . . we could revolutionize the medium. You and I could do what Billy O'Shakespeare did to the schlock theater of his time. He took drama, which was just low-budget crapola no first-rate artist would touch, and transformed it, made the dumb shits *want* quality. And a terrible beauty was born, as another Irishman once said."

There was a half-minute of silence while both men stared off over the plum-red and purple moors. A single gull sailed overhead and disappeared.

"Chekhov." Olds eyed the sailing bird, shot him down with an imaginary gun. "Road-company symbolism." He appeared to be stuck in his improvised hymn to possibility. Churchill used to practice stuttering, Neil remembered, to enlist the sympathy of his listeners. "I'll tell you something. Even John Finn, my resident genie, hasn't figured it out yet. Something even Goldie, my woman, and I never discuss . . . "

Neil had learned long ago that when people who wanted something from you felt themselves getting desperate, they offered you something—what banks who want your new account call with nervous redundancy "a free gift."

Whatever Olds' "free gift" for Neil was, it was obviously sticking in his throat. He was closer than Neil had ever seen him to confronting his obsession, the obsession that drove him to keep coming back pleading with Neil. He left the fence and straddled the other skinny metal lawn chair, staring over the back with his blazing blue eyes just a yard from Neil's own.

"You're a father, am I right?" Olds began. Neil nodded; Olds knew that already. Still with the preliminaries. "Girls, right? Two, did the report say? Two girls?"

"Yes, two girls. Women now."

"Tell me their names. My R-and-D people missed that."

"Felicity and Hilary." Neil felt a wave of sadness; he

had not thought of the girls for so long . . . "The first, I'm afraid, has always lacked the gift for happiness, and if there's a less hilarious woman alive than the second . . . "

"You know my Pamela. Goldie calls her 'Tropical Storm Pamela.' We called her Pammy at first, then Pandabear, and that stuck. She even uses 'Panda' on her union card. She's a pretty good camerawoman . . . should be, she started young enough, had all my toys to play with . . . Milo taught her a lot, I taught her some things . . . she tried to do some courses at UCLA, but they told her she had to take Science, whatever, so she quit. One-track mind, like her Daddy."

Having launched himself into what was plainly his main topic, Olds suddenly ran out of words and looked around him glumly, leaned his square chin on his folded hands.

"I want this to be for her. For my Panda. When we started out, the two of us, I said, 'This is a collaboration, honey.' We kicked ideas around just the way two equals would. It really was going to be just an historical movie . . . you know, the way *Butch Cassidy* was . . . sweet and tight and very, very old-fashioned film values. By that I mean not afraid to make its dramatic points visually, silently, slowly . . . the way the great silent films were all made."

Neil saw that his face lit up when he talked about film-making as it had not about anything else, even his daughter.

"No slick camera angles, no jump cuts here, jump cuts there. God, how long has it been since you saw a film actor make a point with a glance or a gesture . . . since you saw *acting* in a film? We decided we'd make it that way." He crossed his heart in a corny, childish gesture. "I swear, this is all for Pandabear. To get her what she wants for her first big directing shot . . . for that I'd go on my knees to Yassir Arafat . . . Weelll . . . " He laughed. "Somewhere along the line the soap-opera thing crept in. Maybe from her, maybe from me . . . like I said, we were spitballing this thing equally.

165

I began to think to myself, Okay, Billy, this is going to be it. I-t spells it, the biggie . . . Remember Ed Sullivan? 'Rilly rilly big'? Nail this sucker and then walk away from the whole 'rilly big shew,' hand everything over to Panda, my sorcerer's apprentice, just go away with Goldie someplace— hell, someplace like Nantucket . . . Have you been out to our house up on Cliffside yet? No? God, that's not hard to take, Neil. I wish you'd come up . . . hell, I wish you'd *move* up! Plenty of rooms . . . "

"I ask not because I'm interested, but just out of curiosity," Neil said. "What happens to your dream if the show simply fails? One is always hearing of these immense TV projects being canceled in three weeks after millions are spent on them."

"You can tell by the smell, I swear. My nose has been my most valuable tool in this business. You can't know what it's like in Hollywood when something new that really smells bankable is brewing. Every shark in the ocean smells the blood and comes to the party. You've heard the expression 'jungle drums'? I swear I've laid awake at night in Beverly Hills and heard them passing the message. *Sam Greene's new series is dreck, cancel!*" He was drumming on an invisible drum with his hands. "*Oldsun Productions is mining diamonds, buy in, get a piece of the action!*

"Panda and I decided from the start that 'Nantucket' would be her first director's shot . . . what the hell, the United States was George Washington's first job as President, wasn't it? . . . and I'd stay on with her as producer just long enough to launch this baby . . . Hey, Neil, we are talking about—are you ready?—thirty million dollars in start-up costs—that's what it takes to launch something this big . . . read *Variety* . . . and then just slow fade to Nantucket, or Santa Barbara, or Majorca, or wherever the hell Goldie thinks she'll be happy."

166

Neil didn't say a word. Now that Olds was leveling—if that's what this was—he might as well be allowed to get it all out of his system at once.

It was the first week of October and the warm weather was just losing its grip on the surrounding water. The breeze off the Atlantic over the Commons was getting an edge to it. Olds hugged himself another inch deeper into his windbreaker and continued, looking down at the deck now.

"The thing about hiring you for the project was pure accident, coincidence, whatever you want to call it. Panda wanted to do her own casting. She does this thing with types . . . she calls them 'archetypes,' but I don't think she really knows what that means, she just likes the word . . . she used it in *Love Toys* . . . she was my assistant director on that . . . she just stops people in the street who look like what she wants in a given character and she gets them to take a five-minute screen test. Then she casts her actors from that *gestalt* . . . do you know that word? I think it's Yiddish . . . sort of an overall impression . . . she really did spot you once and tell me about you for the judge's part, then again in front of the bank there. Listen, this will kill you, the irony I'd guess you'd call it . . . the same day my R-and-D . . . research-and-development people . . . another Yiddish expression—" he laughed—"give me a complete print-out on past treatments of this bank-robbery story . . . and they have underlined your name . . . because of what Dan Buckle—you remember I mentioned him? my old boss who works for me now?—says, namely, you can write like a bastard." He sighed and rubbed his neck. "God, at times like this I wish I still drank. Just kidding, folks . . . Now Panda and I start a tug of war. She says, 'So go hire this Kelly and see if he's worth keeping around for writing continuity or research or whatever,' you know? That's how we started. Then you come on all hard-assed, the only guy in America, as far as I can tell, who doesn't want to make a movie or a TV series. Oh, no, you want to write a book about Ben Jonson that maybe five hundred other professors will read . . . Jesus . . . Well, let me give you a piece of advice gratis: If you think I'm an annoying sonofabitch when someone tells me I can't have something I want, don't ever tangle with Panda. She has made up her mind that you are some kind of whaddaya call it . . . a talisman . . . like a St. Christopher medal for Catholics, I guess you'd say . . . for this project. That girl . . . " He shook his head in admiring wonderment. "She will kill to get what she wants, I swear . . . my little Pandabear. So you can see—no, strike that—you can only *begin* to see why this one last time . . . my swan song, so to speak, Neil . . . why I want her to have it all. Have that . . . what'll I call it? . . . that reassurance you'd provide. Okay, call it superstition, call it West Coast lunacy, call it what you will, but . . . it means almost everything to me now, Neil, this goddam project . . . " He trailed off, then brightened, spoke toughly again. "Not to mention what will be thirty million rubles on the line by the time we open." He slumped back and put his face up to the weak sun, changed the subject before Neil could say anything.

"I took your advice, you bastard. Actually rowed an actual boat—dory, whatever they call it—out around the shore for an hour. I thought I'd die. Those goddam things are like an ark. I'll tell you, they aren't one bit like a rowing machine . . . Jesus . . . my back, my hands . . . I almost got washed out into the fucking Atlantic in that tide out there."

Pat on cue, the tourist bus went by the corner, slowed for the Quaker cemetery, and turned into New Lane. The driver was saying over his busy microphone, "Now, listen up, you folks . . . " but all the folks were pressed against the windows trying to catch a glimpse of William Olds rowing a lawn chair.

A logical mind becomes a matter of habit; Neil couldn't help noticing flaws. "I thought Goldie was going to be acting in your soap opera."

Olds shrugged carelessly. "So I lied. Panda won't hear of it, and she's the director. Hell, Goldie's the original good sport with the heart of gold . . . she'd pass up the female lead in the Second Coming to settle down with me, so . . . " Another father's sacrifice.

"Olds, I appreciate your motive in coming here, to save me from having to tangle with your frightful daughter, as you describe her. But it's still no soap. And no soap opera. Your project, your world, your ambitions are all alien to me. All I want is to get back on track writing my book on old Ben Jonson for those five hundred professors who are out there dying to read it."

The star simply walked over to his moped, looked at Neil once over his shoulder, kicked the machine into life, and putted off toward Cliffside yelling a final word into the wind. "These are the stupidest fucking machines ever built!"

The coppery aftertaste of resentment Neil had felt after Olds' first uninvited visit was not there this time. Instead he felt a wave of sadness, an indefinable but sure sense that, beneath all the glamorous trappings and optimistic chatter, William Olds and his precocious daughter Pamela were just two unloving, unhappy, trapped human beings.

11

Neil started for his neglected worktable and then shuddered at the thought of starting to beat again on the poor effigy of Ben Jonson. Instead he grabbed his heavy blue sweater from the basket on the deck, shrugged it on, and wheeled out the purple peril, his beat-up Ross Eurotour. A fast, hard ride along the bike path out toward Sconset might help to break the grip of the three tensions competing inside him—his agony about D over in England, his genuine concern that he had been unsuccessful in making any meaningful contact with Liam, and his weariness at being badgered by these movie people. He could not help wondering how the foster mother of that little girl at Faces was managing with the child in the hospital under such grim circumstances.

He angled away from the curious little village of Sconset and left his bike in a nearly empty rack above Pebble Beach. The mackerel sky hinted that he might end by riding back in the rain if he walked too far, but he decided to leave that to chance and set out along the shore.

A father and son were trying to launch a kite, but neither had the least idea how to do it, and despite their sprinting and hauling and yelling "Now, now!" at each other, the blue-and-white affair never did get airborne.

What they did know how to do was play together. They whooped and hollered and jumped in the air and hugged each other anyway.

Neil continued to walk slowly, aimlessly, along the beach. He stopped and skimmed three flat stones into the Atlantic. London 3612 miles. Did anyone but children believe that a message in a bottle would reach England by way of the Gulf Stream if you threw it into the ocean here? Phone would be quicker in any case. Even mail quicker than bottle. Coward, Kelly. Short hop by Gull Air to Boston, then long hop to London; that would be definitive. And then what? He kept strolling on the hard-packed tidal sand, arcing the occasional pebble out into the blue-green chop of the separating sea. He watched the sea. If there was a school of requiem sharks out there, he'd like to see their spinning ballet again.

The beach ran slightly east by north along here, and he could see above him the slow accumulation of a high edge of unstable clouds moving in on the coast. There had been a veil of icy cirrus all morning, aloof above the decks of true rainclouds following closely. Now the thin salt accent of stratus was starting to streak in just above the sea, below the middle mackerel sky building its darkness aloft, the real rain.

He had watched more than one fall storm barge clumsily in from the warm autumn sea here, its fury not fully apparent until the island was suddenly swallowed by its howl, wailing like Babel, making the place a great endangered ship, threatening to lift it and smash it.

He saw the body first as a dark clump on the beach fifty yards ahead of him. Closer to, Neil could discern the truth: it was a horribly butchered human form, weed-tangled and bloody, drained to a fishy white. The face was swollen and

171

hacked, but recognizable. It was Jake Jones. His bare feet were remarkably peaceful and clean-looking, sculptured feet. A gull pulled viciously with its yellow, hooked beak at a string of raw white gut and flew off screaming at Neil.

"Did you know him?"

"I knew his name." Neil was talking with a town cop who seemed too young to be a real policeman. These days they all did but for the inevitable old sergeant. "We met a couple of times, talked once. We weren't what you'd call friends."

"Where did you meet him?" They were standing on the first rise of hummocky dune grass about twenty yards above where the body still lay being studied by more cops.

"Where?" He wondered whether he should tell this youngster poised so earnestly with his ballpoint pen and notebook the whole complicated story Jake had told him or just give him a curt précis. Now that Jake was dead, Neil regretted his own impatience with the man's cynically fabulous tale. Jake, too, had tried to convince Neil that his life story would make a wonderful book. Now his death would make a small column in the week's newspaper. SHIPWRECK SURVIVOR DROWNS OFF NANTUCKET.

The cop cleared his throat. "Try to think. I mean, did you meet this Jones character in a bar? In the street? He ask you directions someplace? I mean, after all, you're a professor, you say, and this Jones was an ex-actor who skippered for Mr. Olds, right?"

"We met in a churchyard. Mr. Jones and I shared an interest in the Catholic liturgy, in a roundabout way." Neil wanted to sound credible and be accurate without appearing patronizing.

"Hold it, Professor, just a goddam minute. You are going to help me a lot if you simplify your language down

172

to plain words, okay? If you're going to talk about Catholic literature and that . . . "

Catholic literature indeed. Neil interrupted him. He knew perfectly well, police being what they are the world over, that as soon as he had finished making a statement to this lowest officer on the police totem pole, another one rank higher would come along and ask him to repeat it. And so on ad infinitum.

"Can we just ride back to the station in your patrol car and let me make my statement there for a tape recorder? Do we need to remain here? I could just put my bike in your trunk."

After solemn consultation with two other cops, Neil's escort and his charge started back up Milestone Road toward town.

When they had parked the cruiser and found a quiet corner in the station house down on East Chestnut, Neil told the tape recorder how he had met Jacob Jones.

Neil had attended the nine-o'clock mass the previous Sunday at St. Brendan's, the little Catholic chapel out by Hooper Farm Road. It was the usual dreary gray-shingled workingman's chapel built at the end of the last century when Catholics were just beginning to count on the island. Garish interior sanctuary, cheap statues brilliant with jeweled crowns and oozing blood, all evidence of Mediterranean influences.

The priest, a bearded boy who didn't have a clue, explained St. Matthew's gospel to them in terms so outrageous that he missed heresy only by detouring through invincible ignorance. There was to be what promised as a longish baptismal ceremony involving twin infants and a large clan of Portuguese fishermen after mass, so Neil quietly slipped out the side door after communion.

It was raining, and hard. Neil cursed himself for guess-

173

ing wrong and coming so far without his umbrella, but risked another guess that, given the rain's intensity, the squall would pass in twenty minutes.

To the south of the small church was the historic burial ground where the first Catholic captains were memorialized. A man in half-boots and dungarees, a Greek sailor's cap squashed by long use on the back of his head, and a short black pipe clutched in his teeth, was dashing from that direction to the little portico shelter where Neil stood. He was carrying a half-sized black iron chair from one of the graves but he didn't appear fazed to find someone already sheltering in the space.

He set the chair down and wiped it off with his sleeve. "Just started pissing down out of nowhere."

Neil wanted reassurance for his guesses as much as the next man. "Do you think it's just a squall?"

The man shrugged and sat down. "I never predicted the weather right in my life, even in southern California."

The tail end of a scattered hymn drifted from the chapel window into the silence around them and between them.

I give the glory to my God,
His all the mercy and the power.

As if he had been waiting for that final benediction, the fellow on the iron seat knocked his pipe out and put it away, then spoke to Neil.

"You're Kelly, aren't you? The one who's writing the book about some ancient poet? The one Billy's trying to hire? I was in the car that day."

"I don't know about 'ancient,' but I guess I'm the one you mean."

"Why don't anyone write good sea stories anymore? All poetry and pornography and politics. My boss, Bill O? You really piss him off." He laughed and shook both fists in the air gleefully.

174

Another nut, the one who had stayed in the car eating ice cream.

"I could tell you a few. Stories."

Here it comes, thought Neil. He had been through this before. Some thickhead hears that you write books. He gets you in a corner at a party—or a churchyard, it doesn't really matter to a truly determined bore—and proceeds to bend your ear with a massively dull account of his trip to Hawaii with two friends in a catamaran. Amateurs are convinced that they all have a story "worth a fortune" and that the "writing it down" part is just some gimmick they can turn over to a craftsman, the way a man might draw up plans for a dream house, then just hire a carpenter and end by owning a mansion. He realized wryly that, of course, this was just what filmmakers did—they had simply raised the rewards enormously.

"I'm strictly a biographer myself," Neil said. Rain, rain, go away.

"My story would be a biography, wouldn't it? I mean, if it's my life, it's a biography, right?"

"All my subjects are dead," Neil said pleasantly. "I never deal with anyone younger than three centuries old." It wasn't hard to tell that the man was a genuine sailor. Nantucket is full of costumed characters hanging around the wharves self-consciously waiting to be photographed, most of them from places like southern California. "You're not from Nantucket."

The man snorted. "Hell, no. Never even saw it before last month. I'm from Santa Barbara originally, if you can imagine that."

Neil didn't see the problem imagining that, but if it was the sort of remarkable detail that was to characterize Jones' biography, someone else could indeed write it.

"I was in movies for years. Actor. You see the remake

175

of *Mutiny on the Bounty* with Brando? I was a seaman in that. That's when I got interested in sailing. I could tell you some tales about Brando . . . Before that I wasn't ever on a ship in my life. Can you believe that? I was in *Heart of the City*, you see that? *Big Sky*? I was in six episodes of *Little House on the Prairie*, I was almost a regular, but it didn't work out . . . "

It was happening, Neil realized grimly. This idiot would stand here reeling off his screen credits till Doomsday if he let him.

" . . . so after we got back from Tahiti—two years we were out there?—I swore I'd learn to sail and get myself a little boat and just cruise, baby. You know, up to Oregon, down to San Pedro, nothing fancy." He jabbed Neil with a hard elbow in the ribs. "So how did I end up smuggling hashish and getting shipwrecked off the Lebanese coast six months later, you ask?" He chortled appreciatively at his own line.

Down came the rain with new intensity. Nothing for it but to stand and wait. They also serve, et cetera. Jones relit his smelly pipe almost as if from memory and kept chattering away excitedly.

A few worshippers edged past them out into the downpour, running for the parking lot.

"I got in with these guys in San Pedro, see. A pretty loose bunch of characters. Turk had a tryout with the Lakers once, big guy. They have this beautiful deal worked out to smuggle about four million dollars' worth of good Lebanese stuff they can get there. But—this is the problem, see?—they got to get it to Cadiz, up in Spain on the Atlantic side of Gibraltar, then they can transship it in a big boat to Panama, up the coast to Pedro, and we're home free. This guy's brother Charlie was going in with them, but his wife

176

wouldn't let him, so they offer me Charlie's piece, 'cause I'm an experienced crewman, see? When I see this goddam leaky fishing boat they got in Haifa later, I almost go find a good Jewish girl to marry so she can tell me, 'No, Jacob, you can't go.' "

Behind them, through the window, a baby's thin hiccupping wail could be heard.

"We were stoned about half the time. It's a wonder we didn't all end up in some Arab jail for life. Half of us got to Lebanon, half—the Jewish half—got to Haifa. There's this old-time cameraman from MGM working in the Israeli documents office, and he is our connection. We were actually both involved in *Mutiny on the Bounty*, isn't that amazing? All the Jews in *Mutiny* had this South Seas Seder one Passover out there and we made sacramental wine out of taro juice or some goddam thing and he tells everyone he's going to migrate to Israel. And he does!

"When we get to sea, we have a goddam oil-company road map for a sailing chart. I'm not kidding. Joe forgot to get charts, so we are just going to run this rotten old scow along the coast of North Africa there, taking sightings on buildings so we won't get lost. Laurel and Hardy got nothing on us, right? We measured the distance out with a piece of string and discovered we had to go farther than we thought. About eight, ten times farther."

He pulled up his collar. "This shit could keep up for an hour the way it looks. Christ, Kelly, do you have any idea how far it is across the Mediterranean? I go thinking a piece of cake—what do I know from the Mediterranean? Joe Belocas doesn't know either. He's a high-school language teacher, you'd think he'd know. Everyone is mellow, and when we were studying this map in the back of Joe's mother's dictionary in their house, it looked cool. The

177

Romans used to *row* it, for Chrissakes, so what can it be? It's over three thousand miles across, Kelly! That's from here to England, for example. Jesus.

"God shortened the trip for us. We hit this storm. Right in the middle of it, we are sailing around in fucking circles like a schizophrenic seagull with his head up his ass looking for the Rock of Gibraltar. And bam, right in the middle of it, people start letting go with searchlights at us and shooting the shit out of our bridge. We are all flat on the deck when I let go for a second and get my ass washed over the rail and I wake up half dead in a Catholic hospital in Lebanon. This nun is leaning over me telling me I have been out for three days.

"This fat little priest comes in and pulls the curtains around us and I think, Oh-oh, this bird wants to hear my confession. But he starts congratulating me for being a Jew. This Christian militia they have picked me up and they are very hot for Israel. I've been talking Yiddish in my sleep, singing hymns, giving everybody my blessing. Apparently we got caught in the crossfire between this Israeli gunboat and some PLO commandos who were trying to sneak into Israel to blow up a bus. This priest, who hates the fucking PLO, thinks I am an Israeli sailor, and it's illegal for them to keep me, but they think I'm a hero, so they make up some story and take care of me.

"They load me up with free samples of antibiotics, give me a good meal, hang this St. Christopher medal on me—" he fished the silver medal from the hair on his chest—"and they tell me how to get back over the border.

"I get to the American consulate and sign everything they put in front of me. I probably joined the Peace Corps or something, but I signed, and they stuck me on a plane and got me out of there.

"So now I go visit Catholic churches every once and a

178

while. For luck. I don't want to get involved in the actual religion, but I like the singing—you people have nice, soothing music—and, frankly, I've never had such good luck as now. I see what the guineas in the Mafia mean, the ones who cut a guy's throat Saturday night and go to Sunday mass. If it works, do it. For me your religion has been totally lucky."

Neil left the porch, rain or no rain. There are worse fates than being soaked through.

He finished his summary of the bizarre meeting for the police tape recorder and spread his hands. "That's it. Jones wanted to tell me his adventures, and because it was pouring, I stayed long enough to listen. That was the last time I saw him alive."

The young cop turned off the machine and looked at the old sergeant who had edged into the room to listen halfway through Neil's deposition. "They measured it with a piece of string?"

The old cop just shrugged. He had probably heard of dumber criminals.

"I was reading in the *Inquirer* the other day about this bank robbery they're making the movie of. Those guys broke in the vault with a *spoon*. A spoon," he repeated amusedly.

12

Jack Darling had a dilemma. A lifetime of solving all problems by hitting them wasn't going to help him this time. What he had to do was find someone, anyone, he could trust enough to explain it to so that they could help him figure it out. Danno wouldn't do. He was dumber than Jack himself and they both knew it. None of the people down at Cy's would do, bunch of drunks, more big mouths than you could trust. Nell was the one he wanted to tell. He lay in his bed and felt the damp creeping into his sheets through the gaps in his window frames and hugged himself and tried to think.

He wished he had Nell for his woman. He had never felt anything like the sweet pain in his chest that he got when he saw her. She seemed so tiny and beautiful, not like Lucy. He had lived with Lucy for almost a year, a big, rip-roaring, noisy woman who didn't mind the odd backhand from him and would throw anything she could find at him when she got mad. Lucy was fun, but Nell was like a flower. Damn fool Swede. Jack would sure take better care of C.J. than *he* ever did, if that's what she wanted. Maybe now C.J. was hurt, when she got cured Nell would like him better.

Jack had decided the day he first heard about C.J. being abused that he would kill Jake Jones. He had gone about it in the way he approached any idea, by having some drinks at

Cy's and finally hammering on the bar and telling Danno, "I'm gonna kill that goddam Jew rapist bastard."

He had gone down to Old South Wharf, where the *Lucky Oldsun III* was berthed, with a plan in mind no more complicated then to take Jake Jones for a ride in his own big-ass cruiser and drown the fucker, then sink the boat. Easy enough to steal a little boat on the way out to get back in.

When he got to Slip 110, where *Lucky Oldsun* was berthed, what he saw by the pier lights stopped him short. Someone else had got there ahead of him and was busily in the process of hunting Jack's quarry. The man with the scalded face took a long hit of Early Times and watched as his predecessor clumsily, messily, and with almost fatal results to himself assaulted Jake Jones.

The would-be killer obviously knew little about boats and piers. He had come near midnight, walking quietly on rubber-soled sneakers along the brick wharf, with a three-foot harpoon carried casually in his hand.

In gift shops and marine-supply stores all over Nantucket anyone can buy off a display rack or from a floor barrel real harpoons, ranging down in size from the eight-foot giant with the six-inch spearhead to the tourist's favorite, the three-foot boat harpoon. Even this compact, deadly tool is constructed with killing in mind, and heavy enough to withstand the strain of an expected enormous pull by its victim. A three-inch-thick wooden handle over twenty inches long has sunken into it a fourteen-inch iron shaft an inch thick with a four-inch, barbed head sharp as a razor at its tip, the whole secured to two yards of manila rope.

In a shop near the Whaling Museum that afternoon Jake's assailant had stood in a back room inspecting the barrel

181

of boat harpoons while the owner yelled at a stockboy down in the basement to get those trash barrels out back for the morning pickup before he left and don't forget it this time.

On the spur of instant opportunity he had lifted the weapon from the display barrel and dropped it casually into one of the trash barrels by the rear door. Retrieving it after dark was simple. Now he hefted it pleasurably as he walked toward his intended victim. He stepped cautiously along the wooden pier running from the wharf alongside the gleaming cruiser. His plan was as uncomplicated and functional as his weapon. He was going to attract Jones' attention, and when the man came to the rail to see who was banging on his handsome boat, he would harpoon the sonofabitch right through the heart and leave him there.

He had thrown the javelin once in high school; this couldn't be that different. The slips on either side of *Lucky Oldsun* were vacant and on her near, port side there were two empty slots, so he chose the lefthand pier.

He stepped softly back and forth along the pier the full length of the splendid machine, trying to look into every window to see where his quarry was sleeping. He was sure as hell not going to step onto that boat. He and boats were not acquainted, and he was positive that if he set foot on deck he would trip on a coil of rope or hit his head on a low doorway and screw the whole thing up.

In the dim light from the wharf he studied his problem, but saw no sign of Jake Jones. He balanced himself on the farthest end of the pier, one hand on the capped piling there, the hand gripping the harpoon against the boat, stretching full length to look over the forward rail to see if Jones was on deck there. He almost yelled with fright when he saw him less than two feet away, facing him, stretched out in a light sleeping bag.

If the *Lucky Oldsun* had not at that precise moment

182

played back a foot against her mooring ropes as the tide started its shift, the startled, open-mouthed stalker would not have lost his precarious balance and gone six feet into the water, roaring a curse and clutching his weapon.

And if Jake Jones, who had waited many years with an unfulfilled vow in his heart to someday save another man from the sea as he himself had been saved, hadn't woken to see some stupid drunk fallen off the end of the pier and floundering in the water below him yelling, "I can't swim, goddammit! I can't swim!" . . . but he did.

Jake yelled, "Hang on, dummy," touched his St. Christopher medal for luck, and dove cleanly into the harbor water to reach the thrashing figure in three easy strokes. That was when he felt an awful smash on the side of his neck and shoulder and then another across his face that broke his nose and blinded him temporarily. He was caught for a fraction of exploding consciousness between believing this was actually happening to him and thinking he was dreaming. He yelled, "Stop it, stop it!" at the drowning man, who was apparently holding an oar or something and waving it around his head. That was when the barbed iron point of the short spear caught him in the mouth and ripped out through his cheek, slicing away part of his jaw and leaving the shaft still secure in the hand of its user. Who then drove the ugly weapon upward from waist level deep into the gut of his would be rescuer.

Straining and gasping, the hunter hauled himself up the slimy metal ladder to the wooden pier and lay there a minute shaking with terror and exertion. He felt too weak to stand, let alone run, but he knew he was finished here and must get away before a watchman appeared. He looked around him once. No one. And not a sound now from the water. The whole episode had taken less than one minute, but he had no way of knowing it hadn't been half an hour. Shivering

183

in his soaked clothes, he ducked between two locked galleries and fell onto a path of crushed shells, puking salt water. He pushed himself to his hands and knees, then to his feet again, and started to run into the wide darkness away from town, trying to recall where he'd left the moped.

Jack Darling had laughed and taken a belt of Early Times. Sonofabitch, didn't know he had it in him. Then he heard the faint moans and words from the water below as Jake Jones, partly screened from his view by the pier, grabbed feebly onto the piling and, with the iron agony nailed into his body, mewed for help.

Shit—Jack shook his head—that tough old bastard! Well, sir, Jack said to himself, let's just give our friend a hand there, Jack. Maybe offer him a little drink. He untied a small outboard moored three piers down and rowed it to the bow of *Lucky Oldsun*.

"Christ sake, man," he said quietly to the tormented man in the water, "you got yourself in quite a fix there." He leaned over the moaning, paddling Jones, seized the end of the harpoon line and tied it with a swift, sure knot to the eyebolt on his starboard gunwale. Then, allowing for the drag, he started his motor slowly and steered his borrowed craft out into the channel. He had got an idea into his head and it made him grin to think about. The man he was so mercilessly towing stopped his complaining the second the water hit his mouth.

Jack's funny idea was simply to run the outboard out around North Wharf to where his own boat, *Darling Clemtine*, was moored and transfer his towline to the bigger fishing boat and let the damn outboard float free on the tide. Then, dragging his now dead burden that had been Jake Jones, the transfixing harpoon designed to withstand tremendous pull locking ever deeper into the flesh of the corpse, Jack steered clear around Great Point and down the coast past Sankaty Head Light. There, where everyone said a school of spinning sharks was hanging around, he untied the line and turned the murdering rapist Jew basterd over to them.

"Come and get it, it's all kosher," he bellowed to the dark.

Be funny, he thought, turning away back northwesterly, if some old shark went for a mouthful of Jew and got himself about forty inches of iron in his sandwich. Didn't seem hardly fair, really. He took a long, philosophical swallow of Early Times. Too bad he couldn't never tell Nell what he just done for her. He hoped she'd appreciate it, whoever done it.

Now Jack lay in his bunk and tried to figure it all out. What if the cops came after him? He was pretty sure they'd be around sooner or later, after he told everyone in Cy's that he was going to off that Jew. Shit, why didn't he ever keep his big mouth shut? He sure as hell wasn't about to tell any cops that he seen that other guy do it with the harpoon. Besides, the Jew movie guy was still a little alive when he towed him off. Did that make him an accessory? Damn lawyers have all these tricky terms to trick you up. Shit, he never told a cop anything on anyone in his life, he wasn't going to start now. But if he never did tell them what he saw, they were sure as God going to lay it on old Jack Darling. If someone's going to have to go to Walpole and have a bunch of big-ass niggers beat on them for the next twenty years, what about that? He could sure use some good advice.

When the police came for him, Jack was so docile they couldn't believe it. He greeted them by name; they had all arrested him before. "Hi, Walt. Billy. John, Lemmy. I didn't do it, Walt."

"Didn't do what, Jack?"

185

"Didn't do nothing, you know that."

The four who had agreed to go in and cuff him brought him out, all five of them smiling like it was a joke. The two who'd stayed outside braced with riot guns weren't quite sure what was going on, they were so surprised and disappointed.

13

William Olds sat in his study staring at the Oscar that always stood on his desk, his first. He was concentrating, fighting against the drive in his gut to take a drink. If he let himself, he could feel the rush it used to give him, the beginning of the feeling of invincibility that always preceded the blackout and the hangover.

His thoughts swam drunkenly. Maybe if he got actually drunk his thoughts would get organized. What the hell had happened last night? What was going on? He had kissed his daughter good night in the upstairs hall and seen her mount the private stair to her room. She called it "going up scuttle," an eighteenth-century Nantucket expression she had latched on to and used to secure her demands for absolute privacy from everyone else in the company during this planning period.

Hours later, unable to sleep and afraid to start on the tranqs, he had heard Milo stumble in, sounding obviously swacked. It made him furious, but he avoided confronting his camera chief to avoid compromising his own authority by witnessing the man's staggering progress to bed. He lay awake listening to the wind, asking himself if he was losing his grip, if the crew—his employees, goddammit, he had made every one of them—even respected him anymore. He was sure of Panda, but who else? He tried not to entertain the nagging idea that he was captain of the *Titanic* here, producing a project that could end up being the biggest bomb in TV history, a hopeless concept already up to its ass in petty feuds and inconclusive experimentation.

Damn it, he was usually a fit, sound sleeper. What the hell was bugging him? Being three thousand miles from his shrink was beginning to seem like a not so good idea. He resented it that he had to urinate. Like a goddam old man with a prostate, like his father. If he hadn't reluctantly swung himself out of bed and trudged out into the hall, he would have missed seeing Goldie leaving Panda's private "scuttle" stairway as he stood in the half-dark hall.

Goldie? And Panda? Just girl talk? Or were those two . . . what? Were they what? In Hollywood everyone said that two people cutting a deal were "getting into bed together." Were Panda and Goldie making some deal behind his back, cutting him out? Trying to screw *him*? God, were they really in the sack together? His stomach lurched and he had to do more than pee when he reached the bathroom. Afterward he washed his mouth out with Lavoris and took a hot shower, trying to calm down.

He started back into his own room, but the light under Goldie's door next to his was like a beacon. He walked in on her creaming her throat and grabbed her hard by the arm, then shoved her into the chair. "Get your fat ass over here, I want to talk to you."

She held her hands reversed in front of herself, like a scrubbed-up doctor, staring at him, white around the mouth with sudden anger and fear.

He started by berating her, throwing questions at her, and accusing her as soon as he had slammed her into the chair.

"What do you mean, you were just talking? Since when do you and Panda just talk?"

"Talking! You know? I go yah yah yah, then she goes yah yah yah. Talking, for Christ's sake." She pulled her red velour robe around her and pouted.

"All right, let's start over again from the beginning. You went up to Panda's room when?"

"I don't know." She flinched when he glared at her as if daring her to lie to him. "After she came in."

"To talk about what?"

"Just to talk, I swear. I was outa tampons and I was having these cramps, and I thought maybe she'd have some . . . We just gabbed."

"About the project? About what?"

"About the project. A little. Mostly just talking."

"You trying to screw me, Goldilocks?"

Her arm hurt where the bastard had grabbed her.

"Ah, Billy, you're nuts. I think this place is getting to you, honest to Christ."

"Don't talk like that to me, you little bitch. Do you know what you're hired to do or not?" He fixed her with the stare she hated. She had seen those eyes glaze with anger before and it was like being hurt to be the one he was looking at.

"Yeah, yeah."

"Don't yeah, yeah me. Do you?"

"Yeah, Bill." Now she was scared, the way she knew he wanted her to be. She had to pee real bad. She clutched hard. "I know what I was hired for."

"Then don't start getting ideas into your dumb head. I can tell Channel Three you are going to act in this show. I can tell Kelly or the *Boston Globe* or anyone else, but I don't want you to start believing it, because the day you do, you're out."

"Yeah, yeah." Her tough, weary answer was almost a whimper now.

189

"Did you and Panda talk about a part for you?"

Goldie watched him through slitted eyes, wishing to Christ he'd knock off the heavy-father bit and let her go make pee-pee. She had a minor tremor of inspiration, for her a rarity. "If you must know . . . gee, Billy, you make me feel like a real asshole sometimes . . . I asked her if she thought if maybe I laid Kelly, would he, you know, go along with working on the show . . . " She paused, then spoke up in her littlest-girl voice. "I wuz only trying to help."

Olds put his hands over his eyes. "Jesus H. Christ. What put that moronic idea into your head? You pinhead!" he yelled at her. "You dummy with a twat for a brain! If you want to fuck that old fart because he reminds you of your homeroom teacher in tenth grade or whatever, just go do it, but don't walk in there waving a flag saying Oldsun Productions presents Miss Barbara Gold and Her Inimitable Cunt! You hear me?"

"I hear you, Billy. Jeez, they can probably hear you in LA."

He slumped back in his chair, arms hanging down, head back, and started to laugh. "My God. What did Panda say?"

"She didn't think it was such a great idea."

"She didn't, huh? God, I wonder why. You were going to give that schoolteacher the incomparable gift of your well-used woman's body and he was going to become—what, your love slave? Then you were going to bring him to me on a leash, and I was supposed to reward you with a bonus, maybe even a part?" He roared with helpless laughter, waving the idea away. "I gotta get out of here before I die laughing."

She looked with cold hatred at his open mouth and red, swollen face, still laughing. She knew what she'd like to do.

14

"Urolagnia," Panda told her, laughing at the idea. "The word for wanting to piss on someone is urolagnia."

"Yeah? There's really a word for it? It makes it sound like lasagna."

"That's the big edge a Dana Hall education gives you, Goldie. You want to do it on my father and I know the word for it."

"I knew guys—you know, weirdos—who, like, will pay you extra to do it on them, but they just call it a golden shower. God, it's disgusting that there's a real word for it."

Panda shrugged cheerfully. "It would serve him right."

Goldie was massaging her as she lay naked on the flowered sheet. "You can say that again."

"It would serve him right."

That made them both start giggling. After Goldie had told her about getting chewed out by Billy O., Panda had made a shrewd guess about what had sparked the outburst. She and Goldie were getting careless.

She turned, excited by the danger of having Billy almost know, and pulled Goldie down on top of her. She was still damp from the shower, but it was easy to slip off the big towel and be skin to skin.

Goldie had never imagined before this new thing with Panda that making it with another girl could be so good.

She'd always thought those dykes were gross. With Panda it was special. And when you thought about it, like Panda said, every guy she ever made it with would slap her ass or just bang away at her without hardly waiting for her to get in the mood or just treated her like a fucking bag of garbage. Making love to Panda was like doing it to herself but that much better. Fuller. She liked the sound of that inside her when she thought of it: fuller. She loved to watch her come. She loved to lick her. Guys, phooey. Boy, if Billy O. ever knew me and Panda were making it, would he ever blow his stack . . . What Panda was doing felt good . . . she should do it . . .

Panda let herself be kissed and sucked and looked at the ceiling. Bloody hell. Suppose Billy did know now about Goldie and her. So what? A shudder passed through her that wasn't entirely a response to Goldie's attentions. The idea of standing up to her father once and for all, facing him down and breaking the last bonds of her childhood adoration, shook her. Hate and love and lust racked her body in spasms that were convulsive. She climaxed with a tearing groan that seemed to split her apart. She knew what she had to do.

Goldie wasn't surprised to be sent on another errand for Panda when all she wanted to do was sleep, but she wasn't sure this professor would give her the time of day. Some men—and she had an instinct for which ones—really wouldn't, and it was embarrassing.

15

The first story to break, in Boston's more sensational daily, and then promptly on the evening TV news, was some creative reporter's imagined scenario for Jake's death, just coherent enough to appear credible. It was on the wires, picked up because of Billy O.'s name being involved, and repeated five hundred times before anyone had actually checked the details or confirmed it beyond the fact of his body being discovered on the beach.

The account was a luridly detailed guess dressed up as hard fact. Jake Jones, well-known Hollywood character actor, ex–Israeli war hero, and skipper of Billy O.'s fabulous luxury boat, *Lucky Oldsun III*, had apparently stolen a small power boat during the night and gone out to shoot dawn photographs of the feeding frenzy of man-eating sharks known to be cruising off the Nantucket coast. He somehow fell or was pulled by the giant predators from his boat and was mauled by the killer creatures. His exsanguinated and mutilated corpse was then driven over the shoals by high winds and the incoming tide into waters too shallow for the monsters of the deep. The body was recovered where it finally beached, below the famous tourist attraction Sankaty Lighthouse. The presence of drugs in the body was suspected and the police were investigating. Jones had a history of drug trafficking, and had only recently been questioned by state and local police in a case involving the sexual abuse of a five-year-old Nantucket girl whom Billy O. had promised a role in his forthcoming Nantucket soap opera.

Olds was on the phone raging to his attorney before he had even finished reading the moronic story and adding up its inaccuracies and libels. "I don't care if you did just step off the damned plane, Roger. I wouldn't care if you were still on it. Turn your ass around and get back here now, goddammit! These fuckers are trying to crucify me!"

16

John Finn's prolonged absence from sentimentality was notorious among his colleagues, but when he heard that Jake was dead, he cursed and raged up and down the huge living room.

"Goddam waste!" he roared in his most resonant outdoor stage voice. The crystal chandelier tinkled like shaken ice. "I paid forty-nine ninety-five plus tax for this damn toy for his damned birthday. Are you telling me that's all money down the drain? Where the hell is that guarantee?" he yelled frantically, tossing papers and books off the tables and shelves of the room. "There was a thirty-day money-back guarantee."

He subsided into a muttering rage, still lifting odd books and dropping them, looked again at the elegant little yachtsman's knife and cursed it again. "Made by the fookin' people who make your Wilkinson swords, they claim. What the hell am I supposed to do with a yachtsman's knife, for Christ's sake? Look at that little beauty. It has a shackle tool on it, does anybody want to tool a shackle? Here you go, then. That's a lanyard holder there. Almighty God alone knows what a lanyard is, but if you want to hold one, there's no finer knife for it. A marlinspike. How often do you really need a marlinspike and there's none to hand within miles? What am I offered? Not only a pleasure to use, but a delight to hold in your hand, as the biship said to the actress." He tossed it on the mahogany table, making a gouge, and walked away, his mourning done.

"Whose idea was it to give him a surprise party anyway?" Goldie whimpered. "I'll bet he's surprised, all right. I was gonna buy him a shirt with his name painted on it."

Milo blew his nose. "I got him a light meter. Every picture that schlemiel ever took, the light was wrong, I swear."

They all drifted out of the room, off to any part of the vast house where each could be alone. The day was glorious, with enamel-blue skies and soft winds sweeping Nantucket Sound, but the discovery of Jake's savagely mutilated body on the beach had put them all in a fog of gloom.

Milo cursed the cold he felt coming on and tried hard not to think about the police descriptions of the corpse, battered and sliced and chewed by sharks. God, sharks. He had to get out of here, out of this project, go someplace . . .

Sitting on her bed, Goldie stared out over the sea and hugged herself, trying to imagine what it must be like to be eaten alive by those ripping teeth she had seen in that Jewelry place downtown.

Panda lay on her bed in the high room facing the sea and read the TV ratings sheet for the first three weeks of the new season, but even her mind kept drifting.

What the hell was she supposed to do about Bill and Goldie now . . . ? *Did* he know? The bruises on Goldie's arms were real enough . . . God, he was a jealous bastard, he'd kill her . . . The great Baby Billy and his fucking tantrums . . . His psychiatrist was too busy conning other celebrities to talk to him, his law firm sends down some junior-executive trainee who couldn't fix a parking ticket, his doctor is off in goddam Maine somewhere fishing . . . What Billy needed was one, just one, strong, calm professional whom he respected to talk to him . . . She grimaced . . . and that Kelly he had let himself become obsessed with was the only person on Nantucket answering that description. God, like it or not, she was going to have to drag Kelly into this to calm Bill down by some damn means . . . Where was Bill, anyway?

17

Neil sat at his wicker desk feeding the sheets into his typewriter and filling them and rolling them out without any fully conscious sense of what he was writing. He had begun with organizing some research notes for the book, but switched after two pages of lists to writing another letter to D. He wondered how he could even begin to explain Jake's death and the whole sorry mess involving the child.

He had received another letter too full of David Humbles and the theater and David Humbles and the Duchess of Kent's reception for the Irish minister. He seemed to be sitting on an empty beach feeling the tide recede from him, out and out. He ignored everything else and wrote about them.

. . . I try to think sometimes of all those Nantucket captains lost, shipwrecked, and you are my Nantucket, my faraway island . . . Being without you is not wholly unlike being adrift from some part of myself in an open boat on the sea's blue backside. I stare at the ocean some days until my eyes feel boiled. The beach lurches, the capsized boat our love that we were both the same in is bobbing somewhere mid-Atlantic on the sea bottom, anchor aloft, the whole world upside down. I swim and swim toward some mirage of sound that is your voice or some trick of memory that is your face, always, whatever it is, just out of reach . . .

He tried to recall the exact, not approximate, color of her eyes and could not. How she wore her hair, and could not. He tried to remember where the freckles were on her back and raged inwardly that he could not. Good God, was he in love or not? Was she even real, or had he created her out of imaginary incidents?

And in that confusion of emotional purposes love promotes in any man shipwrecked between two women, Neil remembered with bitter vividness the great mornings of his life with his wife, Georgia. How many years ago, yet how sharp the memories rushing up in him. Mornings when the act of waking beside her seemed sacred, their young children fed, grouching and laughing, and sent off to school, and the two of them back into bed like young lovers. Sweet Georgia Brown he had sung to her as she sashayed past the mirror with a pose over the shoulder and a toss of the bare bottom for his eyes only, *speculum mundi*, freckled and white, vanishing life-size to shower. And he, one second the dozing docent, next suddenly up for ablutions, checking the clock against a ten-o'clock class wherein metaphorically he would teach the young to witness Mrs. Donne undressing. Ah, research, portable and compendious. "*Lavabo inter innocentes*," he had chanted into the bathroom. "I shall wash between children and children . . . " the uses of orthodoxy . . .

Doxy. He was thinking of Dolly again. Doncella, bright fish. He remembered her swimming, burnt red on the rocks at Budleigh-Salterton, where they had both fallen asleep on the pebble beach and both got fried.

He left his desk and, in a rare gesture of absolute frustration, turned on the TV. The National League playoffs. The short, brutal stroke of Garvey's bat breaks the perfect arc of Eckersley's pitch, drives it whizzing—the verb "whiz" was imagined for the sizzling trip the ball takes off in. The outfielder has no claim on it, but, guessing, gauging, leaping,

199

he tries the impossible, cups it, hauls it down, a free thing stopped in flight, damn it, the split second it might have gone out. It still seemed possible on the replay.

The last person he expected to appear at his window that evening, tapping to get his attention, was Milo. The sagging face and castoff, outlandish outfit were unmistakable. Only a new terror in the man's eyes, a kind of horror, had not been there before.

Neil let him in through the garden door.

"This is nuts." He stood uncertainly. "You remember me? Milo?"

"What's nuts? Yes, your're Olds'—cameraman?"

"Please." He slumped into a chair. "Preserve what dignity I have left. Cinematographer." He flicked the distinction away with his fingers after he made it. "Retired cinematographer, I guess. Can I talk to you?"

"Did Olds send you?"

"Nah. Jeez, no." He ran his hand through his thin hair nervously, bit a piece a cuticle off and put it in his pocket.

"Jake was my friend. I mean, we weren't asshole buddies or anything, but we used to talk a lot, not just about shop, you know, about life, anything. I used to kid him about thinking he could operate a camera . . . " He took a deep breath and almost sobbed. "I tried to commit, you know, suicide last night, and right in the middle I got too scared. How's that for courage?" He looked up with a self-mocking grin on his face. "My old man used to say to me: If you start something, Sidney, go through with it. He'd of kicked my ass if he knew I couldn't even kill myself. I quit in the middle."

Neil sighed to himself and reached for the bottle of Jack Daniel's, held up two glasses with a questioning look.

"Jesus, yes."

They both took a good shot of the lovely whiskey. Neil

waited for him to continue, asking himself, Why tell me, why me?

"Do you know what a cinematographer does, Professor?"

"Tell me." Everybody has to get what's on his chest off in his own way.

"Light determines scene," Milo said. "If you know that, you know as much as anyone in the business; it's the one absolute law of making movies. But it's subliminal, see? Ask a hundred people why they love San Francisco, they'll tell you the cable cars, the Golden Gate, the fog, whatever. But if you press them, you'll find out what they remember is the light there. Fog is nothing but a certain condition of the light. San Francisco is the best-lit city in the world. The light in LA used to be great, that's one reason why movies started there. Now it's so polluted all film is shot indoors or at night. Boston has good light, Cambridge . . . light that makes you think, that's why education is so big there . . . You think I'm kidding? . . . You think I'm daffy, probably . . . Let me tell you, Honolulu . . . terrible light for thinking, that's why they're all stupid, those Kanakas. Places like that always end up amusement parks. London, gorgeous, better since they put a ban on smoke there . . . it's getting back to what it must have been in the eighteenth century, a very creative light . . . "

"You haven't mentioned Nantucket. How's the light here?"

"It's to laugh. Bill thinks it's special, he tells me to catch it. People get daring or demented or desperate or some goddammed crazy thing here. I'm supposed to catch it and can it and take it back to the studio and duplicate it . . . Bill thinks this soap opera will turn people on in a new way if we make them look as if we had this light here, this gray ocean light . . . I was standing there on the beach below the

201

house last night, no moon, those clouds rolling in, you could just see the edges of the water when it foamed up, just phosphorescent, and it seemed so simple just to walk into it . . . like a scene in one of those great old movies where David Niven walks through the ground fog up this long stairway to paradise . . . " He started to sing softly, moving his hands back and forth, " 'I'll climb a stairway to paradise, with a new step every day . . .' I should of taken an overdose of sleeping pills like everyone else . . . fadeout. I get out to my chest and I panic, I'm fighting this fucking cold ocean and yelling at it, 'Let me alone, you fucker!' and trying to turn around and get knocked on my ass by those waves . . . so I ended up on the beach crying like a little baby . . . I think it was that kid comedian we saw in that club . . . he got to me, that kid . . . "

"Shouldn't you be talking to a doctor, Milo? Why tell me?"

"I knew you'd ask me that. At least you listened before you did, you didn't just boot me out. You know why? Because, number one, I'm not sick—you know, doctor sick. And, number two, I have been trying to figure out how you can stand up to Billy like you do. You don't take *any* shit from him, and all the rest of us do, all the time. I guess I want you to tell me how come you can be like that and I can't. *I'm* a professional. I'm very good . . . it isn't as though I'd get blackballed or anything, but it's like once you work for Billy for a few years, he owns you and you stop thinking for yourself. Isn't that pathetic?" He held up his glass. "This is so fucking stupid I'm making myself sick. We can't drink around him because he's a dried-out alcoholic. Hitler wouldn't let his generals smoke around him. We're all well off because we work for him, because his pictures make so goddam much money, but we're all like his serfs. Do this,

202

do that." He groaned and emptied the glass in one swallow. "You're right, why the hell am I bothering you? I guess it's like these kids and their gurus. You lose faith in one, you need another one to tell you what to do. You don't know what I should do, do you?"

"I know you shouldn't kill yourself."

"Yeah? You think so? I'm not so sure. God, that water was cold. Now, course, there's Jake. I'm getting bent all out of shape about a cold bath, at the same time he's getting his ass chewed off by some goddam sharks. Jesus. He'd never molest any little kid, you know. Not Jake."

"This project of yours seems to have had more than its share of bad luck."

"I think there's some kind of a curse on it, I swear. If it was me, I'd quit tomorrow and go make another *Star Wars* screamer, but Bill has this obsession, like a monkey on his back about this thing . . . so of course *we* all have to have it, too."

"His daughter seems to have a lot of influence over him. Maybe she should be asked by you all to persuade him to give it up."

"Panda? She wants it as bad as him. Worse, probably. You want to talk about obsessed? She's like a fanatic. She's going to be the youngest director ever to win an Oscar, she's going to win an Emmy, she's going to be this and that . . . Besides, they aren't just exactly alike, they hate each other's guts if you ask me." He walked to the window and looked out at the flowers. "Pretty. Those purple ones."

"Statis."

"Yeah? Are we sicker than normal people, Kelly, or what?"

"Mr. Milano—"

"Please, Milo."

"Milo, you arrived here unannounced and uninvited, so perhaps you'll forgive me if I ask you a blunt question."

"Shoot."

"Did *you* hurt that child?"

It was obvious that the question shocked him, left him staring blankly. "The little kid?" he finally blurted. "Jesus, it never occurred to me anyone would think I . . . "

"Didn't it? The scandal? The little girl saying something about pornographic movies . . . ? You say you know that Jake Jones *didn't* do that . . . "

Milo looked at him. "You know something? I'm about as normal as anyone about sex. I was married for seven years to this makeup girl—she'd tell you 'cosmetician'—in LA. She screwed around a little, I screwed around a little, a very average California joke-shop marriage. We divorced. I lived with a woman three years older for a while, a greeting-card designer. I took a few other ones home, hit on a few broads in the bars . . . your absolutely average heterosexual male. I even answered an ad in the personals column once, got an anorexic college teacher who wanted to chew on my schwanz all night, she thought it was a great non-fattening protein source . . . Hey, you mean people will think if I tried to, you know, do the suicide bit, that it was because I . . . ?"

Neil knew the question was a genuine shock to him.

"Holy shit. So in a way it's lucky nobody knows. Except you." He looked at Neil anxiously. "Are you one of these people who make citizen's arrests? I mean, are you going to run to the cops and tell them . . . you know . . . ?"

"No. I believe you. I think you tried to kill yourself because it suddenly occurred to you that the world really didn't have much meaning for you, not for any other reason."

"Thanks. I guess." Milo sat back in his chair and looked

204

at the ceiling. "I had an eighth-grade teacher once. He was like you. Mr. Prince. He seemed about a hundred years old, and he taught us Geography and Social Studies. He used to talk about the First World War all the time, draw these freaky maps on the blackboard . . . this was in Secaucus, New Jersey . . . and go on and on . . . we used to wonder what the hell he was talking about . . . like he was way above all our heads, you know? I almost went back after school once to tell him when Ronnie Simmon told us all behind the school he was going to drink a bottle of iodine. But I didn't. Ronnie drank some Drano that night, out behind his garage, and I always wondered if I told Mr. Prince, would he have been able to stop him . . . "

"Do you believe that idiotic story that Jake Jones went out at midnight to photograph sharks?"

"I'll tell you something, no. Makes no sense. But what does?"

"Well, I won't claim I've helped you, Milo, any more than a bartender could have, but I really don't know what else we have to talk about."

"You've got like this wall around you, haven't you? No one can get through unless you let them."

"Milo, perhaps I wish sometimes that were true. But I'll tell you honestly, people get through my defenses all the time. When you walked in, I was trying to deal with one of them."

"Uh-oh, a woman, right?"

"Yes."

"Well, at least that proves you're human. She giving you a bad time?"

"She's in Europe. I don't know what she's giving me. Just to set your mind at ease, yes, I'm having a regular human bad time in my head. I think she's getting interested in another man. The book I'm trying to write just sits there like a stone. I waste too much time worrying and going in circles. See? Just like everyone else. But I'm not going to kill myself over it, I'm just going to keep hacking."

"Why?"

"Because nothing else makes as much sense."

"Lieutenant, you're gonna love this."

"You wanna bet? I don't want to hear it. What the hell is it now?"

Lieutenant Darrol had been on the phone half the afternoon trying to explain what was going on to Captain Schaum, who had taken off on vacation after they'd all covered base by talking to Olds Saturday morning. Now Schaum was calling every half-hour, it seemed like, from Las Vegas asking what the hell is this he hears from his sister in Boston about drugs and mutilated corpses and what the hell?

The drugs angle was the one all the papers were playing up, and Schaum wasn't any too thrilled to find out from his married sister that this Jake Jones had been busted or jailed or some goddam thing on a smuggling charge in Lebanon.

"The PLO?" Darrol had said with a sinking heart. "You mean we got those terrorist weirdos here now?"

He had just hung up from the captain's sarcasm and was cleaning out his ear with his little finger when Sergeant Miller broke into his cubbyhole with the latest flash.

"A shark washed up on the beach at Squam Head. Seven and a half foot long."

"Yeah? That's thrilling, Miller. You want to know what you can do with it, all seven and a half feet?"

"Wait, Loot. It gets better."

"It bit you on the ass."

"No, it was dead."

"Shit."

"It's got a harpoon in it." He paused for dramatic effect. "Right up through its mouth."

"So some nut tried to harpoon a shark. Are they an endangered species now? Give the guy a medal if you catch him, then arrest him."

Sergeant Miller was grinning like a kid telling his first dirty joke, rushing the punch line. "It goes right out through its brain, kills the big fucker." He stuck a thick finger up into the roof of his own mouth to illustrate. "An eh ah aw ommi."

"Sergeant, will you get your finger the Christ out of your mouth? Now, what did you say?"

"Guess what was on it."

"Oh what? The fucking harpoon? What is this, 'Family Feud'? I'm supposed to guess what's on the goddam harpoon that killed the goddam shark?"

"Right. Guess."

"You get one chance to finish this stupid story, Miller, then you're on late patrol for a month."

"Human guts." The sergeant beamed, stabbed himself in the belly with an invisible weapon, and hung his head to the side, tongue protruding.

"Say that again, without the dramatic interpretation."

"Franklin and his girlfriend, Jenny, found it. He wasn't even on duty, just showing his girl the beach in his new sand buggy, goes like a bastard in soft sand. They spot this shark's carcass above the tide line. Then they find this three-foot harpoon sticking out through his head. You know Frank, he's a crazy bastard, so he lays down on the sand next to this thing and tells Jenny to take his picture. He puts his

208

fucking hand right in this thing's mouth. Guess what he grabbed."

"Human guts."

"Right. A heart and a bunch of lungs and all kinds of slimy shit. You get it, Loot? They must be off this actor we found all chewed up."

Lieutenant Darrol closed his eyes and reached an unavoidable conclusion. "Are you saying that the harpoon was in that actor *before* it got into that fish?"

Miller nodded happily. "Fish must've bit and rammed that thing right up through his own skull, like a huge fucking fishhook."

Darrol put his head down, then picked it up again sharply. "Hold it. Why the Christ should I believe that idiot Franklin's assessment of what was in the fucking shark's mouth? The harpoon I'll believe, but what makes him so sure the slimy guts didn't belong to another fish, for Christ's sake?"

Miller almost busted a gut grinning. "They were wearing a St. Christopher medal. You know any Catholic sharks?"

Slowly, like a man in a dream, Lieutenant Darrol picked up the phone and dialed Las Vegas.

Captain Schaum had waited three years to keep his promise to take his wife back to Vegas. Milly saved up to play the slots and she had reminded him every week for three years that he had promised. She had dreamed the week after they returned in 1981 that she hit the jackpot; she was sure it was a sign. The captain said in a measured, strained voice, "Darrol, what are you talking about, human guts?"

The lieutenant explained very carefully, prepared to jerk the phone away from his ear at any instant.

"You know that means—if those things are human guts, Fred—that someone stuck the harpoon in the actor first, before the fish bit him," Schaum said.

Lieutenants learn to let captains make the crucial connections without interfering. "I think you must be right, Charlie. I think someone stuck the actor, then fed him to the goddam fish."

"Jesus. Wait till Milly hears this one. I better get back there before they find famed superstar William Olds with a smoking gun stuck up his ass. Fucking movie people, why didn't they stay in Hollywood where they belong?"

Lieutenant Darrol could hear the baritone voice of Mrs. Captain Schaum in the background warming up to a low scream. He was glad the captain hung up with a quickly murmured, "I'm coming back." Given a choice between a man-eating shark and Milly Schaum, he knew which one he'd take.

19

The congregation at the nine-thirty mass at St. Mary's sang the final hymn together with obvious thanksgiving for the brilliant day awaiting them outside.

> *Sea and islands, all are laughing,*
> *Earth is glad with joyful cry . . .*

It was not true, but poetry is often not true to its precise moment.

When Neil had picked up his *Times* at the Hub and walked through the warming lemon sun over the cobblestones and blood-red bricks to Madaket Road, he found Pamela Olds sitting in his living room.

He greeted her as politely as the circumstances permitted.

"Good morning, Miss Olds. You've broken into my house."

"Search me, I haven't stolen anything."

"I realize that local custom leaves things unlocked, and I realize that anyone barging in here uninvited will readily discover that I have nothing worth stealing, but it's considered bad form, you know, to barge in at all."

"I wanted to read your book on Ben Jonson and I couldn't wait for it to get to my neighborhood bookstore.

Besides, my neighborhood bookstore only sells fat paper-backs with undressed popsies on the covers."

"I very much doubt that," Neil said dryly.

"Okay, I lose. I bet myself you'd say, 'Good morning, Miss Olds. No, I have no interest in working on your TV project, Miss Olds. Please tell your famous and distinguished father to drop dead, Miss Olds . . . ' Something like that. You are really a one-track-mind kind of person, you know."

"Sorry. By the way, what you said is all true. I have no interest, and do tell your famous and et-cetera father . . . et cetera. And now if you'll excuse me, I fought my way through a solid wall of sullen Indian Summer tourists to buy this *Times*, I intend to read it. If you are going to keep sitting there despite the obvious fact that you're not wanted, you may take Section Three. I never read it."

He sat and read his paper, Book Review first.

"Do you even see me? I mean, you treat me like dirt. People I know think I'm really smart, you should know. I mean, people come to me for advice, professional and personal advice."

Neil did not look up. It could have been any wife bitching about being ignored to any husband.

"I'll bet you ten thousand dollars you can't tell me without looking up now what I'm wearing. Even come close."

Neil turned the page and saw that Dan Greenberg had a humorous piece this week. "You'd lose," he said. "I don't make ten-thousand-dollar bets, and I don't hustle my guests, even the uninvited ones, but since you ask, you're wearing an olive-brown lambsuede shirt, pleated pants tapered at the ankle in a purple-brown color, and a sleeveless coat sweater, ribbed, knit, about mid-thigh in length and brown boots. I'd say you dressed rather carefully this morning. Go to church, did you?"

"Hey, that's pretty good."

212

"Let's be accurate, Miss Olds," he said, looking up for the first time. "That's perfect."

"You'd make a great witness."

"Is that why you came?" He was reading Greenberg. "You need a witness? Very well, I shall swear you were here at—" he checked his watch—"eleven o'clock precisely."

"I came because I'm scared."

He glanced up wearily. "I doubt if I'm the person you should come to in that case."

"Boy, you're cold. Do people tell you that all the time? You are one cold bastard. Give me a break. Offer me one drink and let me sit here for ten minutes—ten minutes, I swear . . . God, I'm really shot . . . Tell me about the damn book you're writing, anything . . . then I'll go. Promise."

Neil sighed and reached for the Jack Daniel's. "You people ought to buy me a case of this stuff. Here, one drink."

"No ice, no water?"

"That's right. Just good old JD, neat."

"Look, will you just talk to me about something, anything . . . ? Tell me what you're writing about."

"Ben Jonson."

She snorted angrily. "Give me a break, will you? I know that. Tell me about him, what's he up to? Convince me old Ben wouldn't have written soaps if he'd been born the same time you were."

Neil smiled ruefully. It would be a hard case to make if he wanted to try. "I'll grant you, Ben was the type."

"He was out for the main chance, right? Am I right? I've read a few things, you know, in that goddam Survey of English Lit they made me take at UCLA. If there was a dollar—or a pound or whatever the hell they used then—in it, Ben was on the case, right?"

"Sometimes even if there was nothing in it, just for the fun of making trouble."

"He did time, right?"

"If you mean was he jailed, yes. Three times, as a matter of record. Once condemned to be hanged, but got out of it because he could read Latin—that was the law then. Killed his man in a swordfight at least twice, drunk and disorderly many more times than that . . . you name the trouble, our Ben was in the thick of it. Which is precisely why my publisher thinks we can make a lively book and an eventual TV series of his adventures."

She crowed triumphantly, held up her glass. "So you're writing your own soap opera, but set in the seventeenth century. You're a fraud, Kelly; you're doing just what we're doing."

"I've made no attempt to disguise my project. Nor have I any covert plan to use history as a springboard to take off into flights of melodramatic hokum to spin my story out for five or ten years in a repeated series of fake love triangles and hokey betrayals. No, Panda, I am not doing the same thing you are. I am trying to make a useful object out of my poor sow's ear of research data. You are trying to cook up a sow's-ear soup and sell it as diet soda."

Neil rather liked the sound of that as he said it and suffered only the mildest twinge of conscience when he spoke about a project he wasn't really working on at all.

But Panda, if she had heard his ringing denial of her charge, had stopped listening to him, seemed frozen at some place inside her own head.

"I think my father is going completely off the deep end, Kelly." She blurted it out.

"Then you, as his daughter, had better get help for him, Miss Olds. Some old-fashioned people might think you have a clear moral obligation to help him yourself."

"I called his shrink; he's too damn busy to come. I called his personal lawyer; they want their man in New York

214

to handle it, some jerk who hardly knows him. They all smell failure on him, it's like he was a leper. I even called his damn brother . . . his family . . . none of them will even speak to him . . . ten years since he spoke to his own family."

"Is he afraid this project is going to fail? Is that depressing him?"

"*I'm* scared!" she screamed at him. "Is that a crime? I'm twenty-four years old and the only father I've got is turning into some ranting weirdo in front of me, does that make me unnatural, that I'm shit scared?" She held up her hand. "See that? I'm shaking. I'm like a rock usually. I started to eat a damn egg this morning and I couldn't hold my fork, I'm shaking so badly. He's crazy, I think, not just depressed or something." She ran both hands into her hair and gripped her head. "He's boozing again . . . I won't even tell you what he's like then . . ."

Neil tried to keep talking calmly, even though it meant repeating the same assertions. There was nothing he could do for William Olds, who needed professional help, not vague reassurances from someone he'd just met. As he talked, watching Panda for any sign that she was calming, he thought sadly of the isolation and dependency of the rich and famous. A man was hostage to the adoration of his fans, who knew nothing real about him, and to his accountant, his psychiatrist, and his lawyer. If they were not there to make him possible, the star might self-destruct any time.

A random line from Blake ran through his mind: " . . . if the sun and moon should doubt, they'd immediately go out."

"You don't understand, you just don't understand what I'm telling you," she said bitterly. "Are you afraid to? Listen, you're the Good Samaritan in the Bible story. It's you or it's going to be no one. He doesn't trust any of us anymore . . . me, Milo, John . . . He's furious at Goldie . . . I think he's ready to kill her, I swear . . . He'll listen to you," she wailed. "Do you realize you're the only person who's said NO to his face for a long time? Even the bastards out to screw him are afraid of looking him in the eye, they sneak around making deals behind his back . . . Okay, he's my father, but I'll tell you something about Bill . . . there's an infantile streak in him a mile wide. He goes nuts if he wants something and he can't get it."

"That's not a complex psychological problem, Panda. That's a tantrum."

"Goddammit, that's what about half the psychosis in the world is, a goddam murderous tantrum. He beat Goldie up . . . I locked my door . . . I think he's going to kill someone, maybe himself . . . "

Neil knew that he had to get past the staring panic in her face. "Miss Olds—Panda, all this is worse than useless. If your father is having some kind of breakdown, he needs professional help, not a visit from me. If you think—if you really think that he may be unhinged enough to hurt you or Goldie, tell the police and get yourself a lawyer to counsel him. If you need physical protection, you're rich enough to hire someone to protect you. I can't help you."

Tears streamed down her face. "Just let me stay here for a while. He's looking for me, I know he is. He'll kill me if he gets hold of me, he really will." Her pupils were dilated. Adrenaline or drugs? They made her face seem shrunken, white and fragile, skull-like.

Neither of them had heard the Rolls stop out front. They did not know that Olds was there until he stood in the doorway, pointing to his daughter.

"You. Out to the car."

She screamed one long, shrill "No-o-o . . . " and grabbed for Neil's arm, sinking her nails into his wrist.

"Neil, I'm sorry about this," Olds said sadly. "We

216

always seem to be having family set-to's in front of you. My daughter is ill. I'm taking her back with me. Come on, Panda, there's no reason for drawing this ugly scene out any further. I've called Dr. Orlov and he's coming in on the next plane." He laughed shakily, a weak echo of the famous chuckle. "My psychiatrist can't come, but yours can, so you have to be the one who's sick. Let's go back to the house and get some rest, Baby."

Neil watched him. Olds' breathing was shallow. He was drawn and exhausted, but his voice was calm and even convincing.

"No!" Panda shrieked again. "He really wants to kill me. You beat up Goldie, you bastard. Get away from me. Make him," she hissed at Neil. "Make him get out of here. It's your house. If I go with him, he'll kill me."

"I didn't beat up Goldie, Panda," Olds said in a low, patient, urgent voice. "I grabbed her arm, that's all. Again Neil, I apologize for . . . this . . . Panny, you're overwrought and you're saying absurd things you'll be sorry for later . . . Neil will come with us if that's what you want, won't you, Neil . . . ? His eyes were nakedly pleading. "If that will make you feel safer . . . will you, Neil?"

"Don't go with him!" she yelled. "The last time he started drinking he almost killed three people by driving his car up on the sidewalk. Didn't you?" Her voice broke and spit flew from her mouth, her voice was a hoarse bark. "Didn't you almost kill three people and it took Jerry a year to hush it up and settle out of court?"

"You made that up, Panda. I might have talked about it, but I swear to you, I haven't started on the booze again." His color deepened to a thick red, the long white scar on his neck livid. He took a slow breath and spoke so that each word was deliberate, a man trying to be understood underwater. "What happened in California years ago has nothing

217

to do with this. I used to get drunk because for a while I stopped believing I could lick the world. I probably sounded drunk to you if you heard me yelling at Goldie . . . Hey, Jake was my old friend . . . I'm upset, Baby . . . You think I don't feel it like a knife in my gut? all that hideous, cheap-shot publicity linking Jake to that little girl? If that snow-balled, this whole big project could fall apart, Pammy." He held his hands out to her. "This has been all for you from the beginning. It means everything to me because you mean everything to me. Maybe I pushed too hard. Maybe I've rushed you because I was so eager for you to succeed bigger than I ever did . . . like one of those goddam Little League fathers who want their kids to pitch a no-hitter every time out . . . "

"Don't you 'Little League' me, you fake, you rotten prick. I'm big league, and *that's* what you're afraid of; that's what you can't face. You're past it, old man, and you just can't accept it." She turned on Neil in new fury. "And people like you piss me off. You stand around in judgment on people like me, and I'm worth ten of you. Even *he* was—" she gestured contemptuously at her father—"ten years ago. I'm *making* something, goddammit. Brand new. Have you ever made anything *new* in your whole stupid, middle-class life? And don't give me some warmed-over puke book you wrote about William Shakespeare or some other artist you're not good enough to kiss their ass."

"Alas, Panda, none of us is." Perhaps a touch of don-nish irony would help keep everyone in touch with reality.

She smacked her forehead with her palm and imitated Theda Bara emoting. "Alas! Jesus Christ, who was the last person in Western civilization to say 'alas,' Ben Jonson? You are some hot shit, Kelly . . . another constipated, para-sitic, frigid, intellectual crap artist. Even Goldie, poor, dumb Goldie, said you were like that character in a play we saw by what's his name, the Peter Pan guy . . . all Mister Cool in the drawing room, but put him on an island and the goddam butler would show him up for the wimp he is."

Neil knew that she was running out of the manic energy that had fueled her outburst. "If this is mourning for Jake, Panda, isn't it getting to be an exercise in self-indulgence?"

That sent her off into a new burst of anger. "Christ, you're like my shrink, that goddam Orlov he's bringing in to tranquilize me. If I say this, I mean that. If I don't say anything, that means I want to say something really bad. Clever pricks like you . . . both of you, you're just like . . . you're like the CIA, listening in on people's subconscious and filing it away somewhere to be used later when you want to turn the screws on them . . . " She stood almost tottering with fatigue, waved her hand weakly at the air. "Okay, okay, I'm a little paranoid . . . don't blame me, it runs in the family. Just get off my case. Daddy dearest and Panda will have to work out their problems in their own way . . . It's my problem, right? I can at least do as I goddam please with my own problem, am I right . . . ?"

Neil could see her brittle bravado crumbling into a muddled plea for understanding. Her moral resources didn't seem to include much honest courage or self-respect, how could they? If her rudeness and raging bitchery did not cow her victims, she had nothing to fall back on but childish whining and unattractive self-pity.

The sun, angling in suddenly through the hawthorn tree outside the west window, illuminated William Olds like a follow-spot and he flinched.

"Pammy—" he moved toward his daughter warily— "come home with Dad." He reached out a hand to take hers.

She whipped her hand across his face and gave a final animal scream. "You . . . you . . . No! She turned to Neil's desk, snatched up the scissors, and held them like a dagger.

"Panda," Olds said tiredly, "put those down. Come on, Baby, you'll hurt yourself. Give them to Daddy . . . " But he moved a step back, away from her, lit by the sun again.

"You hear him? 'Come on, Baby' . . . come to Daddy-kins . . . Let's have Truth Time, Daddy? We used to play a wonderful game called Truth Time, didn't we, Daddy?" She was hiccupping now, the tears and mascara smeared across her face, her nose running. She wiped her free hand across her mouth. "Daddy and Pammy are sweethearts." She looked triumphantly at her father, who paled in the harsh sunlight fixing him. Her tone became resonant with hate. "Aren't we, you lousy fucking pig? How about that for the lifestyle page of *People* magazine, huh, Kelly? You ever hear about what them hillbillies do to their little girls down in Cornpone, Tennessee? That's what the great Billy O. did to me . . . "

Olds shouted at her. "Stop this! Stop and put down those scissors! . . . Panda, don't do this to yourself . . . Don't do it to *me*, Pammy . . . "

"Do it to you?" she screamed at him, her eyes shining with hatred. "I did it to you enough times before, didn't I? Didn't I? Listen to this, Kelly . . . Don't you come near me, you scumbag, or I'll cut your eyes out . . . you'll have more than a scar on your goddam neck if you come near me . . . " She dropped her voice again, as if recounting a dream. "I went to Jimmy Vaccarro's birthday party when I was twelve years old. His father was my father's dealer, you like that? Daddy was very into coke in those days . . . I was scared to death when those kids started passing around some junk— angel dust, probably—and I ran out of Jimmy's house and took Ginny Morrisey's Fiat and drove like crazy back to our house. Boy—" she blubbered and hiccupped again—"was that the wrong move! Daddy was giving a pool party . . . a lot of grownup creeps in the nude . . . So Panda sat there in the car for fifteen minutes shaking and then Panda said to hell with it, and she took off her teeny yellow polka-dot bikini that Daddy gave her because he was so proud of her new cute little tits and walked in there bareass. I was a sensation, wasn't I, Daddy? A twelve-year-old sweetie with a thirty-two chest, just as cute as cotton candy. *They applauded me!* Alice in fucking wonderland, with my long golden hair and my adorable little butt . . . " She growled, a dirty laugh turned to a cat noise. "Daddy wouldn't let any of those greedy people get near me . . . enough of them tried . . . Daddy wanted me all to himself, didn't you? He gave his brave little girl a teeny spoonful of coke and a tiny, tiny glass of gin and tonic . . . and do you know how it came out in the third reel after all those boring old farts got their droopy dicks and saggy tits back into their designer outfits? They all went home. But Daddy and Panda went into the big bedroom holding hands. We lay side by side on the big waterbed, and my Daddy showed me how much he loved me. Didn't you, Daddy?" Her voice was husky and bawdy now, the obscene whisper of a dirty phone call.

She blinked as if trying to awake. Black tears streaked her face. "And when Daddy was finished telling me I was his best girl, and his holy of holies . . . "

Olds groaned and covered his face, the scar pulsing against his skin.

" . . . and his lazy river and his golden child . . . I rolled over on my cute little hip, because I knew it was then or never . . . and I told him that if I ever caught him screwing another woman, I'd cut his balls off . . . I read that in a dirty paperback Jeanie Shubkin brought to school . . . God, that made him horny . . . And we've been sweethearts ever since . . . " She swayed above the desk, supporting herself with one hand, emptied by her performance, stabbing the scissors dully into Neil's manuscript over and over. "Haven't we, Billy? . . . Haven't we?" she sobbed, her mouth a swollen smear, her face bleared with murderous pain.

Olds' voice was barely audible in the sunny room. "Panny, Panny, you don't have to do this. You and I are different, Baby . . . how many times have we talked about that? . . . Aren't we? Isn't that what makes us unbeatable?" He wasn't reaching for her now, but holding one hand in front of his chest, as though to ward off an attack.

"Different." She spoke the word from some depth in herself. "Tell me how, Billy. Let's talk about child abuse, Bill-lee." Her tone taunted him now. "Tell me how you're different from that creep who molested that kid in town. Or maybe that was you, too . . . " She giggled uncontrollably, her eyes gleaming with furious tears.

"Panda, I want to say just one thing. One thing. Tell you . . . just as part of your education." He wet his lips and touched his mouth absentmindedly. "I swear to you, Goldie came to me months ago, in Malibu . . . when we were first talking about the Nantucket project. She said she wanted a part, a real part, a continuing role. And she said that if I didn't give it to her, she'd take you away from me."

She watched him as if he were a snake, terrified.

"Don't you see, Baby? You're her revenge on me, that's all. She doesn't love you . . . or want you . . . not the way I do." His shoulders sagged. He extended both arms to her. "For this I have no shame, Baby. I love you and I'm begging you. Panny, Panny, when you came to me this morning . . . I thought . . . it was like the beginning for us again, holding you . . . "

Panda put the tip of her finger to the corner of her mouth, an unconscious echo of her father's gesture, then put the fingers of both hands over her lips and watched him, shivering.

"Don't let Barbara Gold use you, Baby. That's all she's doing, using you. I can understand that she fooled you. Hey, you're still a kid . . . you don't know women like her . . . I do. She's a blackmailing dike taking her last shot at a career, and you're her hostage." He grinned lopsidedly. "Gosh, I think I mixed another metaphor there, didn't I? Come back to your old Dad, Pan."

Panda would not answer him. She half crouched behind the old wicker worktable panting like an animal at bay, her eyes darting from Neil to her father, who stared at her with a devouring intensity.

Neil was suddenly furious with them both, and weary of their pain. All these people from the kingdom of falsity who carried their self-worship and their ache of lust everywhere with them like a contagious disease. There was no pity in the anger that made him speak, and he didn't care if it sounded literary.

"I want you both out. You should call your loathsome soap opera 'The *Essex*,' not 'Nantucket.' It was the poor captain of the *Essex* whom Melville saw on Main Street and who became Ahab. His ship had been rammed by a killer whale and the few crew members who escaped in a dory spent months drifting, and finally the strong ones killed and ate the weak. Those who survived lived in hell after that, not Nantucket . . . "

All three of them were empty of words then. Words had all been turned to weapons, and each felt mortally wounded.

"More shit literature from teacher," Panda said through clenched teeth. "What do you want, an A? I bet you were the kind of kid who always had his damn report ready and always got an A. We'll leave when we're ready. You don't own this dinky house, you rent it, so shut up. You don't even know what we're talking about, my Daddy and I . . . Do you want to know what Goldie means to him?"

"I don't want to hear anything . . . "

"Too damn bad . . . I'll tell you anyway, because then he can't hurt *her* . . . Goldie. She's his beard, goddammit. Does a schoolteacher even know what that means? She doesn't expect any part in this show, because she wasn't hired for that. She was hired to act, but not in the damn show . . . that's just his goddam cover story . . . A beard is someone you hire as a disguise . . . did you know that? Goldie is his thousand-dollar-a-week disguise . . . everybody is supposed to think he sleeps with her so they'll never find out he sleeps with *me* . . . only I turned him off when we came here . . . I was sick of him . . . I was sick of you, Billy . . . and now Goldie and I are lovers. Wow, that really freaked him . . . "

Olds groaned and appealed to Neil with a desperate gesture. "Neil, Neil, what can I say? You can see she's deeply upset . . . Pan, if I call the doctor from the Cottage Hospital right here on Nantucket, the one who patched up your leg after your little moped accident . . . the one you liked so much, remember? . . . if I call her, will you let her take you over to the hospital for a rest?"

A blue-and-white police Ford came slamming to a stop outside behind the white Rolls and two cops were at Neil's door before anyone could speak again.

"Is Mr. Olds here? Mr. Olds?" The dark-haired one was peering through the screen door. "We come in?"

Neil let them in. They took in the disheveled, weeping girl in a swift glance, then spoke to Olds. "There's a problem at your house, Mr. Olds. We been looking around town for your car. Frank suggested we look out here, seeing you come out here quite a bit. You better come back with us, sir. Your daughter, too." They both seemed embarrassed by what they had to say.

224

Olds spoke wearily. "What problem? Christ, what now?"

"Miss Gold, sir," the blond one said politely. "The maid found her dead up in her bedroom a little while ago."

"God. Goldie? Suicide?" He looked wildly at Panda.

"No, sir." The dark cop cleared his throat. "Someone killed her, it looks like."

20

Captain Schaum got off the plane at Nantucket Airport and practically ran over to Darrol, who sat waiting at the edge of the field in a blue-and-white.

"Where's the body? Who's doing the PM?"

Darrol smiled, waited a beat. "Hi, Captain. Which body?"

"Not the shark, schmuck, the human."

"Which human?"

"Oh, shit." Schaum threw his holdall into the back seat and rested his forehead on the doorframe. Now he wished he had not passed up that second scotch on the plane. "You're not going to tell me there's more than one, are you, Fred?"

Fred held up two fingers. "Two. *Dos. Duo.* One male Caucasian. One female, also Caucasian."

"Oh, Christ. Maybe I shoulda stayed in Vegas, retired or something *in absentia.* Gimme a cigarette." He climbed into the front seat heavily and held out his hand.

"You quit."

"Gimme a cigarette. I'll quit again tomorrow. Who's the woman?"

"The actress shacking up with Olds, the one with the great lungs. Christ, what a waste."

The captain inhaled half a cigarette and shuddered. "How?"

"You better take another drag. Stabbed. You ready for this one? A marlinspike in the brain."

Schaum started coughing so hard he had to lean out the window and hawk. "Drive this thing. Give me that again, real slow and easy."

"Barbara Gold was found in her bed about eleven this morning by the cleaning girl, John Keohane's girl Theresa from over on Silver. She works for them three days a week. Dead on the pillow, bleeding from the neck, under her left ear. Theresa ran and told this midget actor there, Finn, and he runs up and has a look and feels the pulse, but she's cold. He runs back down and tells this other guy, this Milo or Milano, and the two of them start running all over the house trying to find Olds, but they can't find him. He's out and the daughter's out.

"Someone finally got around to calling us. The Keohane girl, apparently. Mary was on switchboard, she'll have it. I went out there with Miller and Boriski.

"The murder weapon was in the bed with her, partially under her. A yachtsman's knife, one of these fancy jobs you can buy in the stores for fifty bucks, tourist's knife, got all kinds of crap on it. One end is a four-inch marlinspike like a needle. Someone—Christ, they hadda be in bed with her—drove it up into her brain from behind her left earlobe, right in up to the hilt.

"Dr. Jennaro was supposed to do the PM on the actor got stuck with the harpoon, so I guess he'll do her, too. But not till tomorrow, over at Sullivan's Funeral Home. Sully says business hasn't been so good since the sightseeing bus full of senior citizens hit the lighthouse. How's your wife taking it?"

"Milly? She hit the slots for seventeen hundred. You'd think it was seventeen million. I left her still standing there, trying to break the world's record for feeding it back in.

She's got this theory now, the kind the casino's get rich on people having."

"You, Milly, Sully—everybody hits the jackpot this time, huh?"

"Yeah. Oh, my."

21

John Finn found his employer up in the fishing tower of *Lucky Oldsun III*, thirty feet above the water, watching the lemon-and-gold sunset and drinking from a bottle of Courvoisier. Olds waved the bottle to him and beckoned him up.

John Finn and heights were not friends. Swallowing hard and taking each step levelly as it came, never looking down, he ascended to the deck, up the short teak stairway to the cabin roof, up the narrow aluminum ladder to the radar platform, and finally up the spiderwork metal ladder twelve careful steps to the tiny platform. Olds, absorbed in the view, merely lifted his eyebrows and glanced at him. He hung on and tried not to be dizzy.

"I thought you were afraid of heights, John."

"It's such a fine evening, William, that I could not forbear from joining you. Everyone thinks short men are afraid of heights; it's a form of prejudice, like saying that Jews never play football."

"Name one. Jew. That played football."

They had played this trivia game before. "The immortal Marshall Goldberg."

"Damn right. Drink?" He offered the actor the bottle of brandy he was holding by the neck. It was half empty.

"I won't say no." Finn took a long swallow of the

burning, silky drink. "Ah, as the poet said, 'a pint of plain is your only man.' "

"Did he?" Olds said absently. "She said I'm all through, John. 'Sat true? What do you think? You're a clever, perceptive, perceptible sonofabitch. Am I all through?"

Finn joined him at the rail, shoulder to shoulder in the little space. "Did she say that, William? Panda?"

"My golden child." He lifted the bottle to her and drank. "Am I, John?"

"Well, yes, William, I'd have to say you truly are."

Olds looked solemn. "Shit. Really? I'm fifty-one years old, John. Name a great man who was all through when he was fifty-one."

"Mozart."

"No musicians."

"Jesus of Nazareth. Alexander the Great. Freddie Bartholomew. And, of course, Marshall Goldberg. That's about it."

"Bet your ass. Bunch of child stars! Everyone else just reaching their prime at fifty-one, am I right?"

"It's prime time for some, William, there is no doubt of that. Do you know how old *I* am, William?"

"You? The fuck I care about you? You aren't any age, you're like a . . . a turtle, for Christ's sake, you were born whatever age you are now."

John looked out at the glowing sky thoughtfully. "There was a woman," he began, "in the great Irish book your man Kelly and I were discussing not long since, who gave birth not in the prescribed, biochemical way, but as authors do, aesthoautogenetically, you might say . . . all by herself, you understand—a pure act of will and imagination . . . no man involved on the starting-up end at all. She produced, as you might expect, a thirty-seven-year-old Spaniard, and had

230

hell's own time explaining what he was doing in bed with her when he appeared. He had no memory, of course," he added, "never having lived before."

"Of course." His employer nodded agreeably. It was always nice to talk with John, he kind of went on and on, like sweet canned music.

"That would be grand, wouldn't it, William?"

"What, John? I'm afraid I'm too drunk to follow you very closely."

"Life without sex. The total absence from experience of the expense of spirit in the waste of shame, as another Irish writer put it."

"God, yes."

"You didn't know I was in love with Goldie, William, did you?"

"No shit. No, I didn't, John. I'll be damned."

The little man sighed. "Yes, you will. I'll see to that, William."

"Wha's that suppose to mean, pal?" He grabbed the actor with rough affection by the scruff of the neck and shook him. "My loyal little sidekick."

"I loved her with all my small heart, William. Let the rivers of pity that well up in your greater one pour, it's pitiful, but it's true. For this year and more Goldie has shared your starry couch and taken your verbal abuse—and more latterly your physical abuse . . . "

"Hey, pally, tha's a lie. All *I* did . . . "

"I saw what you did, William," he said sadly. "I was at the other end of the hallway when you pushed into her room at three in the morning and grabbed her and started throwing her around. I heard her cry. Oh, how I wanted to rush in and save her. Like in the films, you know. And I know you killed her, William."

231

"Go away, John, get off my boat. You're beginning to bore me, and no one's allowed to bore *me*." He took a small drink. "Goldie doesn't even matter, that's the truth."

"Don't even say that, you great, dirty bugger," Finn hissed. "Aren't you already low enough? You killed her, you handsome prick." His voice rose. He stood up to Olds, conscious of the difference in their sizes. "I was willing to wait. I'm a good waiter. Men like you always get tired of a thing eventually, and our girl Goldie was going to find herself eventually out on her divine ass, just another unemployed ex-starlet dumped out of Billy O.'s starwagon. I was willing to wait for that. What else could I do?"

"You're breaking my heart."

"I'd have courted her then!" Finn shouted. "And I'd have had her, too," he said more calmly. "Alexander Pope, a poet and a dwarf, William, once said that if he could court any woman with his words for one hour, he could have her . . . "

Olds laughed. "I'll tell you the truth, John. Truth-telling time. You never could have got into Goldie's pants." He stabbed a finger into the other man's chest. "She thought you were ri-ridiculous."

"Have you ever been ridiculous, William?"

"Never." He belched sourly.

"Then I'm going to make you do something ridiculous, William, so that your rich personal history will include that . . . "

"You? I may be drunk, John, but I can still throw you off here with one goddam hand, never spill a drop."

"Ah, William," Finn said wistfully, "as you discovered with Goldie, a keen knife is a great redresser of inequalities." He lifted from the leather sheath in his waistband the thick-handled Finnish fileting knife he had bought for this occasion, its eight-inch narrow blade tapered to a pinpoint. "Do you see this wonderful instrument sent to us by the cruel Finns? Finns again awake, eh?" He pressed the tip hard against the groin of the man standing before him. It drove through the cloth and stung his belly.

Olds sucked in his gut and paled greenly in the half-light up from the cabin. "Hey, John, what the hell . . . "

"I thought you'd like to know," Finn said evenly. "What it was like for Goldie when you produced that knife I bought for Jake and you stuck into her brain. She must have known for at least a few seconds, don't you think, William, what was going on? Just as you do now."

Olds brushed at him. "Get out of here with that thing, you idiot." He wiped at him with the brandy bottle and tried to move aside, but in the cramped rectangle of the fishing tower he could only thump the bottle against Finn's arm and move a few inches. The bottle went out of his hand over the rail and splintered somewhere below. A pair of harbor swans glided over to investigate.

Finn, breathing hard, leaned forward and drove the knife into him an agonizing slow inch. Olds bellowed with pain, his back pressed against the tower strut.

"Climb up, William."

"What do you mean? What?" Both Olds' hands were clutching around Finn's wrist, trying to ease the long knife slicing into his bowels. He was screaming, but he didn't know it, locked in the obscene dance. "For Christ's sake, John . . . what . . . ?"

"Up, you miserable excuse for a human being. Up, Captain Vere. I always wanted to play Billy Budd, one of my many unfulfilled ambitions . . . but at least I can mutiny, eh? . . . Up on the rail, climb, you bastard!" he roared and twisted the thin blade to emphasize his command. Olds shrieked with the outrage of new pain and tried to scramble up onto the rail, but slipped and fell against it to the tiny tower deck at Finn's feet. He crouched on all fours, gathering himself, but the point of the knife—oh, God, with his blood on it—a sickening wave of realization . . . the point was now under his left eye. He jerked his head back and rose awkwardly.

"Up. Climb it."

Shakily, crying and whimpering, realizing that he had just messed himself. Full of shame, Olds put his knees up on the hard thin rail, wrapped both arms around the stanchion supporting the sunroof, and scrambled onto the rail. He felt the edge of the knife, then the awful steel point again, this time directly between the cheeks of his ass, penetrating him.

"Up, you smelly bastard. Stand up!" Finn bellowed.

With a gasping, bulky heave he got both feet beneath him on the aluminum rail and crouched half upright, hanging on to the support and swaying, trying to speak, gasping . . . wanted to explain to John that the canvas sunroof was in the way . . . couldn't . . .

"Stop gibbering, William, and stand like a man. You look like a ridiculous monkey, William. Stand up, I said!" he screamed furiously, jabbing the knife viciously upward.

Olds used his last strength to kick out at his tormentor and missed as the little actor simply leaned away, then slashed hard with the knife against the shinbone in front of him, making a long streak of blood and fiery pain.

Olds howled and pulled himself upward, incoherent now with fear and pain, with the knowledge of his own insides emptying themselves, the terrible slicing to the bone . . .

"Now," announced Finn in an echoing voice that could be heard across the whole basin, "everyone can see the wonderful world of William Olds in a handsome nutshell. Look at him! You could write all his graces and gifts on the

234

point of a pin and legions of angels could dance in the space left over. Nothing! William the Conqueror is a big nothing!"

Across the basin on the north side several boats had lit up and figures had appeared on their decks. Behind the *Lucky Oldsun* on South Wharf a couple who slept in one of the gallery spaces peered out their window at the macabre dance on the tower. Close by suddenly a fire siren and a police blinker were blatting and swiveling.

"You're ridiculous, William, do you admit it? Not me, you!"

Olds hung on, tried to nod his head weakly. Anything to gain time. John was completely insane. Where the hell was everybody? There was even still some light left in the sky . . . Was that a siren? . . . God, please, the cops . . .

"Admit it, goddammit!" Finn roared at him, hacking the frightful knife across the other shinbone.

"I admit it," Olds screamed. "I . . . " He lost his frantic grip on the slippery metal pipe, flailed, screamed again, swung out with the grip of one hand in an arc over the port side of the tower, felt his weight wrench his fingers loose, angled off the tower in a spastic, impossible lunge for the rail, and slammed into the jutting edge of the radar deck below, then spun, breaking an elbow against the port structure of the cabin, smashing off the angled housing just enough to project his crumpled body into a scraping, splintered wreck on the wooden pier below his tormentor, who watched with maniacal satisfaction, shouting, "Yes, you ridiculous bastard, yes . . . "

With his last resources of consciousness Olds could hear that booming voice coming after him. The knife . . . he couldn't take the knife again . . . where the hell was everyone? . . . he crawled and dragged himself, not knowing he was crying with pain, one arm wouldn't work at all . . .

235

crabbing with one hand and one fiery leg along the pier . . . which way was he going . . . suddenly reached the end of the pier and put his hand into empty darkness and fell, plunged into the cold water, cracked his head against the piling, tried to swim . . . drowning . . . heard the voices . . . saw a hand. He wanted desperately to beg Finn not to cut him again . . . wouldn't hurt Goldie . . . screamed, swallowed salt and oil and everything was black. The pair of swans shook their wings and hissed and glided out of sight.

William Olds was unconscious for two days before he died. The doctors wanted to fly him off-island for immediate surgery on his neck, which appeared to be refractured, but the additional risk of movement was too great. A team of specialists including the man who had operated on him when he had been torn apart in the car crash were flown to Nantucket to operate there.

The cerebral hemorrhage from a tiny aneurism like a blister at the top of his brain came swiftly at four in the morning while a special nurse monitored the life-support equipment. The graph suddenly exploded in an electronic convulsion of jagged lines, the signature of death.

22

TV and newspaper reporters took over the island for a month, extending the expired tourist season, to the universal approval of the Chamber of Commerce. America saw more of Nantucket on the evening news than had been seen in the previous two centuries. The entire national population stood on Main Street behind the NBC, CBS, and ABC cameras and counted the cobblestones and tracked the murderers from the far beaches to the tiny courtroom facing Broad Street, its fifty seats always full. Four books about the murders and the trials and the charges and the incest and the bloody Hollywood feuds were in the bookstores—and two of them on the best-seller list—before Christmas.

Jack Darling's young and inexperienced Legal Services attorney started the series of moves that eventually escalated into three trials, three separate high-court appeals, and four drawn-out suits for damages. She was a shaky, sallow woman still amazed at herself for daring to practice law one year out of Suffolk Law School. After hearing her client's story, she heard herself saying calmly that there was no problem. The person inside her who said things like that astonished her.

She astonished Jack, too. "No problem!" He squinted at this nut they'd sent him for a lawyer. "Hey, girlie, it's my ruby-red ass for Murder One. That's a problem. Unless I tell the cops on this other guy . . . but I ain't, so . . . you went to law school . . . hey, you did go to law school, didn't you? . . . you figure an angle. But don't tell me no problem. And don't tell me plead guilty and throw myself on their mercy or whatever . . . Zippo, Walpole for fifteen to life . . . "

Marilyn Greenblatt hugged the person inside her who was not fazed by this. That person, and Marilyn Greenblatt along with her, as always, was going to be the Attorney General of Massachusetts when she was forty-one, but now, at twenty-six, no one would have bet on her chances. Except perhaps her Trials teacher at Suffolk Law, who secretly thought she might become Chief Justice someday if she could find a cure for her halitosis.

It took her two weeks of argument to convince Jack that he should even tell her the name of this Mr. X he said he had seen attack Jake Jones with the harpoon.

He looked at her disgustedly for the fortieth time. Ugly broad. Did she know how bad her breath was? Fucking blast furnace. What was that going to do to a jury? He wasn't sure he wanted her leaning over the jury box and wiping out the front row when she started to defend him. But neither did he have any choice. He sighed. Boy, he was so tired of being stupid, not being able to think of things, ideas. He finally told her the name, going against the grain of a lifetime of refusing to help the cops.

She went to see Jonathan that afternoon. The musician, as Jack Darling described him with final obvious relief.

She drove out to the house in Quidnet that the Faces people shared, but the woman with the little girl there told her that Jon was probably at the store.

C.J. pressed close to Nell's side while she talked with the lady. Since she had come back from the hospital, she had held Nell's hand a lot and walked very close to her wherever they went. Two other children who had been abused by Eddie had told their parents about him after they saw a film at school where doctors and nurses with puppets had showed everyone about how some bad men touched children.

Everybody knew now who had hurt C.J. Except possibly C.J. herself. She still remembered that Eddie had loved her and taught her to sail. If Cynthia Johanson hadn't told the police about those porno movies on that boat, she'd be almost sure it was Eddie who did the other stuff to her, but it was all mixed up. Her whole world had dissolved and reformed, like a dream, and she was afraid. She still liked Wendy, but she hated that old Guy for taking Wendy away to marry her just because they were in some junky business in Boston now. She hated Boston, all hospitals. She wished Liam would come back, but he said he'd visit her on TV and when he was famous and told jokes on the Johnny Carson show, he'd give their signal, which was very secret and was touching the tip of his little finger with the tip of his tongue.

She would see a comedian in a National Lampoon movie years later perform precisely that gesture and it made her shudder without knowing who the actor was or why she shook. The boy who was holding her hand said, "You scared?" and slipped his arm around her suavely and she forgot about the actor. Fifteen is the right age for letting go of the hangups of childhood.

Jon had never really believed that he would live out the rest of his natural life without having someone knock on the door and say, "We know you killed Jake Jones."

When Marilyn Greenblatt found him, he was putting a new reed on a clarinet for a kid in the high-school band. He looked up at her as he finished the job; he knew this was it and he was almost relieved. He gave the clarinet back to the waiting boy and told him no charge.

It wasn't that he wanted to confess; he felt no guilt. What he did feel strongly in the center of himself was a tremendous urge to explain the whole thing to someone.

In his own mind it was all so simple and clear. He had been doing his job in that McDonald's in San Ysidro when the man came in with the brown paper sack full of ammunition and started spraying machine-gun bullets everywhere. He had just finished serving that Mexican family, and the little girl had lifted the plastic cup of Coke and then suddenly her face was a scream of blood. Jon had opened his mouth to yell and had been paralyzed with the insane, immediate fear that if he yelled the man would see him and aim at him. He had stood there frozen for a full second, the slicing knife in his hand half raised, and watched the others die, then he dove to the floor, fear and shame flooding him, but fear overcoming everything else. He had crawled away with his ignoble wound and swore that if he ever had the chance again, he'd be a man, never again dive for cover while someone injured a little girl. Killing Jake had been his atonement.

Marilyn Greenblatt's arguments to Jon were simple and persuasive. As he listened to her, an enormous weight of waiting and fear lifted from his chest.

Jack Darling was willing to swear that he saw Jon stab Jake Jones with the harpoon, but that it was apparently an accident . . .

"It doesn't take much brains for a jury to figure out I went there with that thing to kill him, does it?"

"Irrelevant. You didn't kill him. You didn't even attack him. Maybe you went to spear a halibut. How are they going to prove intent? Did you tell anyone you were going to kill Jones?"

Jon laughed for the first time. "I told the guy who subbed for me on piano that night I was going shark-hunting."

Jack Darling was further willing to swear that when he came up to Jake in the boat, Jake was still alive and conscious, moaning and trying to call for help. Jack was drunk as an owl. He knew Jones was hurt, but not how bad, so he towed him along behind his boat for a joke. The only way Jack could have murdered him was either by drowning him or by making his original wounds worse to the point where he bled to death. But he cut him loose in the water, then lost him when he tried to grab the rope and pull him into the boat . . .

"Yeah?" Jon eyed her cynically.

She looked right back at him. "Put yourself on the jury. Prove he didn't." She argued calmly. No way the medical examiner had been able to fix the cause of death. They couldn't talk about water in his lungs after the shark bit his goddam lungs and heart out, or mortal wounds from the weapon or anything else. They could convict the shark if they wanted to. Jon should walk with malicious mischief resulting in personal injury. Jack would get three to five years suspended for some version of the same. She was positive she could unstick anything any district attorney could paste together out of this mess. And she was right. Jon got off with an assault conviction and his two-year sentence was suspended. The cause of Jake's death could have been heart failure as well as any of the obvious choices, the medical examiner admitted it. Jack Darling did actually serve a year, but that was so much better than what he had expected at first that he did it smiling. He met a couple of pretty good old white boys in there and made good friends with them. Wrote some poetry, which he sent to Marilyn Greenblatt.

John Finn's legal fees were paid by Oldsun Productions, at Panda's insistence. There were seven witnesses, including two cops, to the final sequence of events on *Lucky Oldsun III*'s fishing tower. Although there were differences about what each thought he had seen, they all agreed that they had heard every word Finn had said, and that he had never threatened Olds with death. He had, they agreed, simply tried, for whatever reason, to make him climb up on the tower railing and then had ridiculed him. He was convicted for assault with a deadly weapon, the fish knife, but given a suspended sentence in light of Olds' apparent involvement in the death of Barbara Gold. John Finn's dignified recital of his love for Goldie was splendid theater, and he gave the performance of his life, except, he thought, for those grand moments on the boat tower when he had played opposite the great Billy O. for an audience of seven.

The case against William Olds for the murder of Barbara Gold had been circumstantially established from the beginning. He had been known, on the basis of his daughter's admission of incest with her father, to have a strong motive in his jealousy over the alleged love affair between Panda and the victim. He had been given the opportunity by the easy access he had to Goldie's bedroom, which was, by his arrangement, just one door down from his own. The means had been readily at hand—the yachtsman's knife tossed on the living-room table by John Finn the previous day, on which Olds' fingerprints were found.

Olds' original statement, through his lawyer, that he had simply picked up the knife to examine it, then put it back on the table in the presence of his daughter, Panda, was not supported by the daughter's statement. It was clearly established that Olds had dragged or pushed Goldie into her room in the early morning of Saturday, and that after he left she had shown fresh bruises on her arm to Pamela Olds and said that Olds had hit her.

The most damaging fact revealed by forensic examination of the body of Barbara Gold was that she had traces of male semen on her body and in her vaginal orifice and that the blood type they revealed was identical with that of William Olds and with no other male in the household.

Panda would inherit everything, become the new head of Oldsun Productions. A group of prominent women campaigning for a federal law to protect sexually abused children asked her to become their national chairwoman. A publisher advanced her $1.4 million for a book about her relationship with her father. An editor went to see Neil about Panda's suggestion that Neil collaborate with her on the book, do the actual writing, for twenty-five percent of the profits. The editor was astonished at the vehemence of the refusal he received. He thought to himself as he beat a retreat from Madaket Road: *Now, there's a really violent person . . .*

23

In the taproom of the Ocean House, which had become in the way those things happen the unofficial press headquarters for the media swarms scouring the island, the eddies and tides of gossip had lessened gradually after the first incredible week, but they still stirred.

Each new arrival was examined with professional suspicion by the early birds who had staked out early claims to the best, juiciest story they had ever reported. With the official tourist season past, all new arrivals in the bar were assumed to be potential rivals, perhaps with a new angle.

"You just arrive?"

"Leave her alone, Nick."

"The hell I will. Hi, I'm Nick Duran, the *Post*, who're you?"

Good heavens, the local newspaper had sent someone to interview her. To her surprise on arriving, the island, which she had expected to be quite deserted in October, seemed caught up in some bustling event, people dashing everywhere, even TV cameras . . . Ah, she had it. Neil had mentioned that some group was making a movie here. When he had failed to mention it further after the first reference, she had assumed the thing had fizzled as such things often do.

"Just a late-flying tourist, I'm afraid."

"Yeah? English? That an English accent?"

"You can see he's quick. Hi, I'm Sandy Mosse. Don't tell me Murdoch sent you over on this one. God, we'll all have to move into high gear just to cover your lies. Why do you people lie so much? I mean, the *National Enquirer*'s one thing . . . "

"Honestly, I'm not the press or the TV. Why on earth should I lie? I'm simply visiting Nantucket."

"If you say so. What's your name again?"

"Dorothy Allen."

The man was obviously not fully convinced. He did what reporters always do, he asked another question. "You know people here on the island, Dotty?"

"Dorothy. If you absolutely insist on being chums, I should tell you that my friends at home call me Dolly . . . "

"Sandy doesn't, but I do. Beer?"

"No, thank you, this will do. Yes, I do know someone here, a teacher . . . "

"Well, have a nice visit, Dotty. Nick, you want a ride out to that beach? Lorraine is going to shoot some background footage; she says the surf is dramatic today."

Dolly had sworn to herself that she would not once, no matter what the provocation on this journey, say "rude Americans." But she said it anyway. She savored her Beefeaters and tonic and tried not to think about the value of the pound against the dollar with drinks at two dollars and fifty cents. She tried instead to imagine, now that she was imprudently here, how she was going to reveal that fact to Neil Kelly.

She ordered another ruinously expensive gin and tonic to help her sort it all out.

She had become annoyed at first when Neil's letters

245

had taken on their Ancient Mariner tone, as if he were a shipwrecked soul cast up on a coral strand somewhere, thrusting hopeless notes into a series of bottles which he then entrusted to the fickle sea. Then she had become actively indignant because the letters, even those gloomy, ambiguous epistles from the other side of the world, had stopped.

She drank and tried not to let her bitterness spoil her expensive drink. There she had been, acting out the impossibly demanding role of best friend to Sybil, who couldn't be seen dating David Humbles until her divorce was final, trudging along with that impossible man to every rendezvous with Sybil. There would be Sybil, who, Dolly was now convinced, friend or no, deserved the insufferable David, simpering and coy as a debutante, gushing her surprise at meeting them some place it had taken a solid week of boring phone calls to arrange.

And whilst she was performing both corporal and spiritual works of mercy meriting beatification, and never breathing a word of her duplicitous role to a soul, even Neil . . .

She sipped her drink speculatively. One could hardly suppose that a man as intelligent as Neil Kelly had imagined that her casual references to David Humbles—she was sure in her heart, having edited dozens of memoirs and collections of letters, that even her letters should not hint at Sybil's subterfuge . . . Did Neil think she and David . . . ? Oh, God, that was too truly ghastly. But just barely possible, men being what they were.

The gin reached that stage in its involvement in her metabolic processes where, given her jet lag, and given her dismay and lack of lunch, it entered her bloodstream calmly and found itself racing to the centers of action.

246

She paid her check and left the taproom to look for a bus or a cab or some damned contrivance to get her to this Madaket Road place. With her luck, it was on another island or, failing that, over a rutted dirt road ten miles off. That would be like Neil and his martyr's complex, to stick himself out of reach of civilization except to professional explorers.

Dolly saw the large yellow bus standing ready just down Federal Street, with the driver collecting tickets. She tripped only slightly on the uneven sidewalk and asked him if he knew where Madaket Road was. He assured her that he did. She nodded wisely. How clever of her to have asked the right question. If she was getting a little tipsy from her two gins and tonic—her three gin and tonics?—she must be especially careful to double check everything.

She said offhandedly, "I don't suppose you know where the American scholar Neil Kelly lives. By any chance." She could tell he was enchanted, as so many Americans were, by the way the British said "chawnce."

"Oh, yeah," he said. "We stop right on the corner there, everybody asks about it."

"Do they really?" Did she say that aloud or just think it. "How much is the fare?"

She was shocked. Drinks was—were—was one thing, but seven-fifty for a bus ride? She did the arithmetic of the pound at one dollar and twenty-three cents in her head and got a bit muddled. It was apparently going to cost her close to three hundred pounds to take a bus! Thank God she hadn't simply climbed into a cab. This was what Weimar Germany must have been like. She tried to think of other historical examples of runaway inflation. Poor Neil. What must bread cost? She asked the driver gravely if he would inform her when they were at the place she had requested.

"Oh, yeah," he said cheerfully, "you'll hear my announcement."

With that reassurance Dolly entered the bus, nodded to each of the dozen other passengers, dropped like a stone into the seat behind the driver's, and fell fast asleep for the ensuing twenty-four miles of her trip around the island.

24

While Dolly Allen was circumnavigating Nantucket Island in her sleep, Neil Kelly was arriving back at his house from his last—please, God, his last—trip to the police station.

He had done what had to be done with abhorrence. All he had wanted at the end of the killings and the endlessly repeated depositions was to return to his work and forget forever the monstrous clan, Olds' people, and their malign influences everywhere on the island. He wanted to get back to his mutilated book, he wanted to write again to Dolly and sum up these weeks so that she would understand his morbid letters . . .

But first he knew that he had an obligation to talk to Sergeant Miller, the policeman who had visited him and taken his statement about Olds' visits before the final, awful one.

He had spelled out in plain detail the attempts made by Olds to inveigle him into working on the soap-opera project. He had hoped that once the statement was recorded and filed by the police, he could wipe them all out of his mind and get on with his shattered work. But one unanswered question remained, would not let his conscience rest. He had told Miller everything he could remember of any importance, but at three in the morning a week later he was still poking at the fragment of memory as if it were a cavity, a place needing completion. One part of his inhibited recall, he suspected, was blocked by an old-fashioned resentment and suspicion that Panda had tried to use him as her alibi. He was slightly ashamed of himself, admitted to himself that his sheer dislike of the girl could be making him vindictive. But he knew also that letting the whole thing drop would be a sin of omission, a clear act of moral cowardice.

He rode his beat-up purple bike down Gardner and India, which they were starting to rip up again to find the original cobblestones, coasted down to the police station on East Chestnut, left the bike unlocked on the narrow walk, and went in and asked for Sergeant Miller.

It took a young cop with a Styrofoam cup of coffee balanced on a notebook five minutes to dig him out of the back. When he arrived, he eyed Neil warily and took him back to a small, bare room.

"You remember something you forgot?" Miller produced two folding chairs and jerked them open with one hand.

"Yes, I'm afraid so. Is that pretty common?"

"Commonest thing in the world. Sometimes it helps, sometimes it's a pain in the ass. Which is yours going to be?"

"Before I even begin," Neil said hesitantly, "perhaps I'd better ask if all the physical evidence from the various crime scenes is still intact."

"Intact? You mean do we still have it? You name it, we got it. The evidence room upstairs got full, we cleared out a section of the garage. That got full. We got stuff under lock and key down the wharf, out that house . . . "

"Perhaps what I'm thinking of isn't properly described as evidence," Neil said, feeling more and more like a civilian fool as the sergeant scratched his neck wearily and waited for him to get it out. "From the room where Miss Gold was killed. The bed linens . . . that sort of thing."

"God, I think so, yeah, sure. We took every damn sheet and towel and nighties and whatnot . . . you name it. We could start a store. Captain said last Monday his wife said that's no way to treat stuff of that quality . . . maybe we can hold a Winter White Sale when we get through with it. Hey, no, not really, don't quote me saying that. I hafta be careful, I found out. The guy who owns that house is apeshit, he can't even get back in there yet . . . "

"I keep recalling," Neil started, still unsure what he was recalling, "something Olds said to his daughter that last morning they were at my house."

"Shoot." Miller flipped his book open and looked semi-interested. "I oughta tell you, this one is just about a lock. I mean, he's dead, Olds, and so what are we gonna charge him with? There was enough circumstantial to make a case, but, hey, with the guy dead himself now . . . "

"I don't think Olds killed Goldie—Miss Gold."

"Is that right." It wasn't a question so much as a bored challenge. "Do you have a theory about who did?"

"Yes, I believe that Pamela Olds did."

"Hold it, hold it, for Christ's sakes, hold it. You think you got some evidence she did? I'm not talking about reasonable doubts concerning the assumed perpetrator, William Olds, I mean any hard evidence?"

"No. I scarcely believe that my memory of a passing remark would constitute hard evidence in even the most liberal interpretation of the law."

"Then is this worth the bother? Listen, Professor, I respect your coming down and all. I'm glad you took it to heart when I told you if you remembered anything else, even the most seemingly trivial thing, and all that, and now you come down with whatever it is. I'll put it in the file and then

251

it'll be off your mind and on mine, or at least in my file cabinet."

"If Pamela Olds—"

"We all call her Panda now, so you can, too."

"If Panda did kill Miss—Goldie, then you certainly want to know, though, am I correct?"

"Oh, you are so right you're correct."

Neil settled back a bit. He had spent a lifetime thinking clearly and paying attention to detail and studying logic, and so the existence in his mind of a single illogical detail rankled him. And if William Olds, whatever his crimes against his daughter, had not killed Goldie, then he shouldn't have his memory burdened with the universal assumption that he had.

"When William Olds and his daughter, Panda, were arguing in my living room, just moments before the two policemen arrived to inform us of Goldie's death, Olds said something peculiar."

"I've heard those tapes of what you recalled of their argument, Professor, and I will have to agree with you, they were a peculiar couple of people. Goddam weirdos is what they were."

Neil was not deflected by his interruption. "Olds started to beg his daughter to come back to him, to love him again. He was trying to tell her, true or false, that Goldie had told him she would seduce Panda as revenge if he didn't give her, Goldie, a big part in the show. The man was stripped naked, emotionally. He said something like 'For you I have no shame,' and then he said, almost as if he were realizing it himself for the first time, 'When you came to me this morning and I held you in my arms . . . it was like we were back in the beginning, and I thought . . . ' Approximately that."

"So?"

"Panda shuddered just then, said nothing. I think she had gone to him that morning."

"So?"

"He said 'when I held you in my arms' and 'it was like in the beginning.' I think they made love."

"You mean sex. They did it, right? Intercourse."

"Yes."

"So are you saying Olds was past it for getting it up again later when he was with Goldie? Some guys, you know, three, four times is nothing, even at his age."

"I think he was never even in Goldie's room. He loathed her, physically and every other way. She was a chattel to him, a thing he employed, not even a whore."

Miller sighed. "Professor, the PM showed clear traces of male semen in her vagina and on her thighs. I mean—"

"As it would have if someone else had transmitted it from William Olds to Barbara Gold."

Miller sat up straighter. "Say that again."

"If Panda Olds had sex with her father that morning, then deliberately went into Barbara Gold's bed and manually or otherwise transferred his semen to her new partner, and while doing so killed her, the evidence would be exactly the same."

"That's true. It would also be a really rotten thing to do."

"There is really no other possible explanation if William Olds never went into that room. Would the hand towels from Panda's bathroom still show any traces of semen she might have left on them?"

"Probably."

"And would the sheets from Barbara Gold's bed show pubic hairs from Panda if she was there, sexually active?"

"Definitely."

"And the sheets in Olds' bed the same?"

"Professor, you are either about to get me my promotion to lieutenant or a kick in the ass from Captain Schaum

253

on TV. Come with me. Everything you just said to me I want you to say to Lieutenant Darrol and the captain. Holy cow. I made the Fall River paper before, this oughta get me into *People* magazine at least."

The District Attorney was even more interested than the police. The cases of Darling and Van Veler first, then John Finn second, had shaped up from the beginning as good, minor political leverage for a future senatorial candidate. When he realized that he was going to try Panda Olds for the murder of her lover, a murder she had tried to pin on her father, and he thought of the publicity, he almost wept for pleasure.

He was right about the publicity. Before the entire circus had concluded, it made the celebrated Von Bulow trial in a neighboring state seem like a decorous civil suit among friends.

Almost everyone on Nantucket had an opinion, or a fragment of remembered conversation, an observation about Panda Olds that they wanted on record. One selectman recalled that when William Olds discovered that the cobblestoned streets in the center of town had not, in historical fact, been there when the famous robbery took place, he had said cheerfully to the Board, "Well, then, gents, we'll just have to fake it. They're too photogenic to leave out." But that his daughter, right there at the meeting, had cursed him for being unwilling to make the film right and proposed that the town let them dump several thousand tons of dirt on Main Street to create the original road. He said he was a lot less offended by her suggestion than by her terrible language to her father. Others at the same meeting remembered it just the opposite, Panda Olds cheerful and smiling, her father brutal and insulting.

It would last for months. More women's groups took sides. Several lesbian groups saw her attack on Goldie when she should have struck back at her father as a tactical error, but exactly the sort of self-defeating gesture women have been driven to for centuries, hurting other women because they themselves have been hurt by men.

A rival feminist organization blamed Panda for consciously choosing a traditional male model of action in killing her lover, for aping a man rather than acting without guile. They saw her surrender of her woman's right to act violently and her imitation of the violent male as the serious, personal issue.

Panda would eventually be convicted and sentenced to life in prison. It was clear that she had been in William Olds' bed and that she had been in Goldie's bed. Further, it was evident that Goldie had indeed been in Panda's bed within the previous two days, when the sheets were changed. Her attorney had tried, in his summation to the jury, to suggest that it was at least as likely that William Olds had changed sheets or taken his daughter's pubic hairs with him into Goldie's room in order to leave them, but no one was persuaded of that. Panda never did go to prison. On appeal, the Superior Court threw out her conviction for the manner in which the evidence had been stored while awaiting trial. It was found that the police captain's wife had been allowed to take the bed linens from the cardboard boxes into which they had been piled and fold them neatly onto the shelves of the evidence room.

25

Neil jerked awake from a fitful nap on his deck in the late afternoon sun, disturbed by some sudden racket. He looked through the hawthorn trees, but it was only the damned yellow tourist bus making its monotonous rounds. He closed his eyes and automatically listened to the driver utter his predictable "Now, listen up, you people . . . " but was shocked awake again not only not to hear it, but to hear his own name instead. The man was distinctly saying " . . . where Neil Kelly, the famous Shakespeare scholar and close intimate friend of William Olds, is living. It was here that police . . . "

Neil rushed over to his fence enraged, yelling at the driver, who droned on, oblivious to anything, already making his transition into pointing out the Quaker graveyard. The ten or twelve passengers on the bus, bored to stunned silence by the relentless river of information pouring over them, were delighted with this sudden diversion out the windows. An excited man in a blue sweatshirt was shaking his fist at them and howling inaudibly. And aboard the bus, suddenly more drama. The woman sitting behind the driver, who had been sound asleep for the whole trip, suddenly awoke and began telling the driver loudly that she wanted to get off. She started beating on her window, but the driver kept shaking his head, saying no one could get off till the end of the tour.

The woman protested in some foreign accent that she didn't care about the tour, she wanted to get off. She finally jerked her stubborn window up and began screaming like a madwoman out of it, "Neil, it's me. Save me! Save me!"

"Hey, lady," the bus driver said. "Hey, lady."

The howling man outside was left standing as they drove off, frozen in a posture of idiocy. Then suddenly he could be seen far behind on a purple bicycle, pedaling like mad across the Quaker graveyard, shouting more inaudible lunacies, trying to catch them.

The woman was encouraging the lunatic by more waving and shouting. "Save me, El Duro, save me!"

"Lady, for Pete's sake . . ."

The lunatic reached the side of the wheezing, jouncing bus and called out, "Dolly, what the hell are you doing on that bus?"

"This man is kidnapping me!" she yelled back.

"Hey, lady . . ."

"Shut up," she snapped at the driver. "I'm having a conversation with the gentleman on the bicycle."

"Shut up!" all the people in the bus shouted in chorus. Who cared about some old jail? This was interesting.

"I thought this was a, you know, bus. But it never stops," the madwoman cried out the window. "I'm doomed to ride it until I die." She grabbed her hat as it flew off and clutched it to her chest melodramatically.

Some of the passengers decided she was loonier than the one on the bicycle.

"I'll follow you to the ends of the earth on my passionate purple bicycle, my darling," the nut cried, weaving dangerously all over Main Street as he pretended to whirl a laria over his head. "I weel lassoo thee bus!"

257

The driver surrendered with a groan at the Civil War monument and stopped the bus. "Hey, lady," he said dejectedly, "you win. Get off and get on that guy's bike if you think he knows more about historic Nantucket than I do. No refund, though."

"I knew you were a gentleman," Dolly said grandly.

"Just get off, that's all I ask."

She adjusted her hat askew and turned to her fellow passengers. "I want to thank those of you who cheered for my side when we were in the thick of it back there. I don't think I've ever traveled with a nicer bunch of sports." She waved queenly, pausing to let a woman from Knoxville, Tennessee, snap a flash picture of her leaving.

They all bid her goodbye delightedly and watched her join the bicycle lunatic. When they kissed, all the passengers applauded. The driver sheepishly tooted the horn, anxious to be thought a good sport, too.

Dolly enjoyed the kiss tremendously, but needed to understand.

"What is going on? Has there been a murder or something?"

Neil almost smiled at the innocence of the question.

"Your letters said nothing of any trouble. Yet I find Nantucket swarming with reporters, your name on everyone's lips."

"It didn't seem as important as—"

Good heavens, as what? World War III?

"As David Humbles," he said weakly.

"Oh, David Humbles be damned," she said crisply. "My allergy returned and that silly twit finally was persuaded by our combined wiles to marry Sybil Carmichael. That *was* the point, you know. I did mention that, did I not? Perhaps not."

Neil, ashamed of forgetting, tried to remember seeing the name. He hmmed noncommittally.

"David Humbles has been disposed of very nicely, thank you. It's you I'm concerned about. Your letters sounded positively funereal. Now tell me, what has been going on here on this lovely little island of yours?"

Neil sighed and let some long-held tension in himself go. It *was* a lovely little island. The air seemed particularly soft, the moors especially subtle and wild today. "Well," he began, "call me Ishmael . . . "

S. F. X. Dean lives and writes in Amherst, Massachusetts. He has written six previous novels, five of them featuring Professor Neil Kelly.

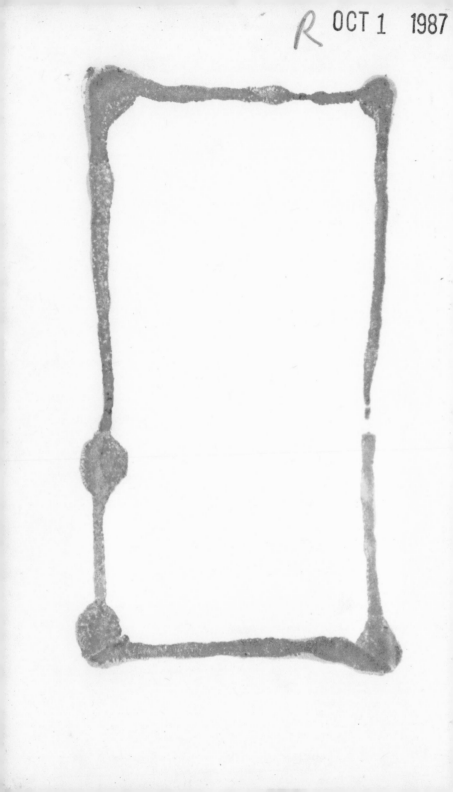